DANGEROUS AGES

ROSE MACAULAY

BRITISH LIBRARY

First published in 1921

This edition published in 2020 by
The British Library
96 Euston Road
London NW1 2DB

Cataloguing in Publication Data
A catalogue record for this publication is available from the British Library

ISBN 978 0 7123 5387 8
e-ISBN 978 0 7123 6786 8

Text design and typesetting by JCS Publishing Services Ltd
Printed in England by CPI Group (UK), Croydon, CR0 4YY

CONTENTS

►•◄

►•◄ ►•◄ ►•◄

THE 1920s

►•◄

►•◄ **1919 (April):** The Amritsar massacre, where Brigadier-General Reginald Dyer ordered British Indian Army troops to fire into a crowd of unarmed Punjabi civilians, killing at least 400 people. The debate about his actions continues in 1920, as Neville reads in *The Observer*.

Sigmund Freud's writings on psychoanalysis had begun to be translated into English from around the 1910s, but the 20s sees a greater number of authorised translations and unauthorised versions for the layman.

►•◄ **1920 (June):** The Femina-Vie Heureuse Prize is set up as an English literary award, equivalent to the French Prix Femina (1904–present). Macaulay won with *Dangerous Ages* in 1922.

►•◄ **1920 (July):** The Supreme War Council and the government of the Weimar Republic meet in Spa, Belgium, to discuss German disarmament and World War reparations.

►•◄ **1920 (October):** Oxford University admits women as full members of the university, with the right to receive degrees. Previously they had been allowed to study and take exams but were not awarded degrees.

►•◄ **1921:** *Dangerous Ages* is published.

In 1921, the average life expectancy for women in England and Wales was 59.6 years (and 55.6 for men).

By 1921, there are 2,100 female doctors on the Medical Register in Britain, up from approximately 1,000 before the First World War (and 25 in 1891).

▶•◀ ▶•◀ ▶•◀

▶•◀ **1924 (January):** Ramsay MacDonald becomes the first Labour Prime Minister – the culmination of what Mrs Hilary calls 'this Labour nonsense that is so fashionable now'.

▶•◀ **1929:** *Marriage and Morals* by Bertrand Russell is one of the most prominent publications in the debate about free love and marriage, prompting protests and criticisms.

ROSE MACAULAY (1881–1958)

►•◄

Collated lists of famous opening lines to novels often include: '"Take my camel, dear," said my Aunt Dot, as she climbed down from this animal on her return from High Mass.' These are the first words of *The Towers of Trebizond*, the final and perhaps most famous novel of Rose Macaulay's prolific output. Published in 1956, it won the James Tait Black Memorial Prize that year.

Its author was born Emilie Rose Macaulay in 1881, the second oldest of seven brothers and sisters. Mrs Hilary in *Dangerous Ages* is probably partly a portrait of her mother, Grace. Macaulay grew up in England and Italy, and later read Modern History at Somerville College, Oxford University – though as a woman, attending from 1900, she was two decades too early to be permitted a degree. Her first novel, *Abbots Verney*, was published in 1906. She would publish a novel every year or two until the end of the 1930s, including seven in the 1920s. *Dangerous Ages* won the 1922 Femina-Vie Heureuse Prize, a short-lived English equivalent to France's Prix Femina.

Macaulay had many literary friends and acquaintances, including Dorothy L. Sayers, Rosamond Lehmann, Ivy Compton-Burnett, and Rupert Brooke. She was on the periphery of the Bloomsbury Group, writing a book on the works of E.M. Forster – one of a handful of her books published by Virginia and Leonard Woolf's Hogarth Press. In private, Virginia was occasionally disparaging of Macaulay, calling her 'a ravaged sensitive old hack' in her diaries, but they had a friendship nonetheless and Macaulay wrote to Leonard after Virginia died, saying, 'She is the one person who *should* not have died, who could not be spared. No one like her ever was nor could be.'

►•◄   ►•◄   ►•◄

Macaulay never married nor had children but had a long and secret relationship with a married ex-priest, Gerald O'Donovan. The affair ended only when he died in 1942. Macaulay herself died, suddenly, less than a year after being given a DBE in the 1958 New Year's Honours and thus becoming Dame Rose Macaulay.

▶•◀   ▶•◀   ▶•◀

PREFACE

▶•◀

How do women find their place in the world at every stage of life?
What do women want from love, or marriage or work as they get older?
How can they find recognition and fulfilment when the place in which
they find themselves is not the one they imagined it would be? This
addition to the British Library Women Writers series is about searching
for meaning and the disappointments and triumphs which can follow a
yearning for a different kind of life.

In this eleventh novel by the English novelist Rose Macaulay, the
author writes as a middle-aged woman in the period between the World
Wars. She seeks to address the concerns that women of all ages were
facing by looking at the relationships, hopes and regrets of a family of
women aged from their twenties to their eighties. Once described as
'the most prominent spinster in England', Macaulay wrote her novels
from the fringes of the Bloomsbury Group and addressed issues which
held resonance in her own life. These included the difficulties of the
mother and daughter relationship, which has such an important place
in *Dangerous Ages*, and how to navigate unconventional romantic
connections.

The female characters in the novel have reached 'dangerous
ages', where they are forced to look at how they can reconcile both
their ideals and the reality of their lives. They search for a magical
middle ground between personal and professional fulfilment and
look for recognition through love, marriage, a career and even
psychoanalysis.

Dangerous Ages ends on a strangely melancholic and ambiguous note.
Perhaps it is meant to encourage the reader to examine their own place

▶•◀　▶•◀　▶•◀

in the world, and what is worth striving for. Reading the novel almost 100 years after it was published allows us to consider how women have always struggled with these questions.

Lucy Evans
Curator, Printed Heritage Collections

DANGEROUS AGES

►•◄

CHAPTER I

NEVILLE'S BIRTHDAY

▶•◀

I

Neville, at five o'clock (nature's time, not man's) on the morning of her birthday, woke from the dream-broken sleep of summer dawns, hot with the burden of two sheets and a blanket, roused by the multitudinous silver calling of a world full of birds. They chattered and bickered about the creepered house, shrill and sweet, like a hundred brooks running together down steep rocky places after snow. And, not like brooks, and strangely unlike birds, like, in fact, nothing in the world except a cuckoo clock, a cuckoo shouted foolishly in the lowest boughs of the great elm across the silver lawn.

Neville turned on her face, cupped her small, pale, tanned face in her sunburnt hands, and looked out with sleepy violet eyes. The sharp joy of the young day struck into her as she breathed it through the wide window. She shivered ecstatically as it blew coldly on to her bare throat and chest, and forgot the restless birthday bitterness of the night—forgot how she had lain and thought, "Another year gone, and nothing done yet. Soon all the years will be gone, and nothing ever will be done." Done by her, she of course meant, as all who are familiar with birthdays will know. But what was something and what was nothing, neither she nor others with birthdays could satisfactorily define. They have lived, they have eaten, drunk, loved, bathed, suffered, talked, danced in the night and rejoiced in the dawn, warmed, in fact, both hands before the fire of life, but still they are not ready to depart, for they are behindhand with time, obsessed with so many worlds, so much to do, the petty done, the undone vast. It depressed Milton when he turned twenty-three; it depresses all those with vain and ambitious temperaments at least once a year. Some call it remorse for wasted days, and are proud of it, others call it vanity, discontent, or greed, and are ashamed of it. It makes no difference, either way.

Neville, flinging it off lightly with her bedclothes, sprang out of bed, thrust her brown feet into sand shoes, her slight, straight, pyjama-clad body into a big coat, quietly slipped into the passage, where, behind three shut doors, slept Rodney, Gerda, and Kay, and stole down the backstairs to the kitchen, which was dim and blinded, blue with china and pale with dawn, and had a gas-stove. It will be obvious to any reader, but not interesting, that Neville now made herself some tea. She also got some bread and marmalade out of the larder, spread two thick chunks, and slipped, munching one of them, out of the sleeping house into the dissipated and riotous garden.

Looking up at the honeysuckle-buried window of the bedroom of Gerda, Neville nearly whistled the call to which Gerda was wont to reply. Nearly, but not quite. On the whole it was a morning to be out alone in. Besides, Neville wanted to forget, for the moment, about birthdays, and Gerda would have reminded her.

Going round by the yard, she fetched instead Esau, who wouldn't remind her, and whose hysterical joy she hushed with a warning hand.

Across the wet and silver lawn she sauntered, between the monstrous shadows of the elms, her feet in the old sand shoes leaving dark prints in the dew, her mouth full of bread and marmalade, her two black plaits bobbing on her shoulders, and Esau tumbling round her. Across the lawn to the wood, cool and dim still, but not quiet, for it rang with music and rustled with life. Through the boughs of beeches and elms and firs the young day flickered gold, so that the bluebell patches were half lit, like blue water in the sun, half grey, like water at twilight. Between two great waves of them a brown path ran steeply down to a deep little stream. Neville and Esau, scrambling a little way up stream, stopped at a broad, swirling pool it made between rocks. Here Neville removed coat, shoes and pyjamas, and sat poised for a moment on the jutting rock, a slight and naked body, long in the leg, finely and supply knit, with light, flexible muscles—a body built for swiftness, grace, and wiry strength. She sat there while she twisted her plaits round her head, then she slipped into the cold, clear swirling pool, which was just, in one part, out of her depth, and called to Esau to come in too, and Esau, as usual, didn't, but only barked.

One swim round is enough, if not too much, as everyone who knows sunrise bathing will agree. Neville scrambled out, discovered that she had forgotten the towel, dried herself on her coat, resumed her pyjamas, and sat down to eat her second slice of bread and marmalade. When she had finished it she climbed a beech-tree, swarming neatly up the smooth trunk, in order to get into the sunshine, and sat on a broad branch astride, whistling shrilly, trying to catch the tune now from one bird, now from another.

These, of course, were the moments when it was enough to be alive. Swimming, bread and marmalade, sitting high in a beech tree in the golden eye of the morning sun—that was life. One flew then, like a gay ship with the wind in its sails, over the cold, black, bottomless waters of misgiving. Many such a June morning Neville remembered in the past. ... She wondered if Gerda and if Kay thus sailed over sorrow too. Rodney, she knew, did. But she knew Rodney better, in some ways, than she knew Gerda and Kay.

To think suddenly of Rodney, of Gerda and of Kay, sleeping in the still house beyond the singing wood and the silver garden, was to founder swiftly in the cold, dark seas, to be hurt again with the stabbing envy of the night. Not jealousy, for she loved them all too well for that. But envy of their chances, of their contacts with life. Having her own contacts, she wanted all kinds of others too. Not only Rodney's, Gerda's and Kay's, but those of all her family and friends. Conscious, as one is on birthdays, of intense life hurrying swiftly to annihilation, she strove desperately to dam it. It went too fast. She looked at the wet strands of hair now spread over her shoulders to dry in the sun, at her strong, supple, active limbs, and thought of the days to come, when the black hair should be grey and the supple limbs refuse to carry her up beech-trees, and when, if she bathed in the sunrise, she would get rheumatism. In those days, what did one do to keep from sinking in the black seas of regret? One sat by the fire, or in the sunlit garden, old and grey and full of sleep—yes, one went to sleep, when one could. When one couldn't, one read. But one's eyes got tired soon—Neville thought of her grandmother—and one had to be read aloud to, by someone who couldn't read aloud. That wouldn't be enough to stifle vain regrets; only rejoicing actively in the body did that. So, before that time came, one must have slain regret, crushed that serpent's head for good and all.

But did any one ever succeed in doing this? Rodney, who had his full, successful, useful, interesting life, Rodney, who had made his mark and was making it, Rodney, the envy of many others, and particularly the envy of Neville, with the jagged ends of her long-since-broken career stabbing her, Rodney from time to time burned inwardly with scorching ambitions, with jealousies of other men, with all the heats, rancours, and troubles of the race that is set before us. He had done, was doing, something, but it wasn't enough. He had got, was getting, far, but it wasn't far enough. He couldn't achieve what he wanted; there were obstacles everywhere. Fools hindered his work; men less capable than he got jobs he should have had. Immersed in politics, he would have liked more time for writing; he would have liked a hundred other careers besides his own, and could have but the one. (Gerda and Kay, poised on the threshold of life, still believed that they could indeed have a hundred.) No, Rodney was not immune from sorrow, but at least he had more with which to keep it at bay than Neville. Neville had no personal achievements; she had only her love for Rodney, Gerda, and Kay, her interest in the queer, enchanting pageant of life, her physical vigours (she could beat any of the rest of them at swimming, walking, tennis or squash), and her active but wasted brain. A good brain, too; she had easily and with brilliance passed her medical examinations long ago—those of them for which she had had time before she had been interrupted. But now a wasted brain; squandered, atrophied, gone soft with disuse. Could she begin and use it now? Or was she for ever held captive, in deep woods, between the two twilights?

> I am in deep woods,
> Between the two twilights.
> Over valley and hill
> I hear the woodland wave
> Like the voice of Time, as slow.
> The voice of Life, as grave.
> The voice of Death, as still. ...

►•◄

II

The voices, the young, loud clear voices of Gerda and of Kay, shrilled down from the garden, and Esau yapped in answer. They were calling her. They had probably been to wake her and had found her gone.

Neville smiled (when she smiled a dimple came in one pale brown cheek) and swung herself down from the beech. Kay and Gerda were of enormous importance; the most important things in life, except Rodney; only not everything, because nothing is ever everything, in this so complex world.

When she came out of the wood into the garden, now all golden with morning, they flung themselves upon her and called her a sneak for not having woken them to bathe.

"You'll be late for breakfast," they chanted. "Late on your forty-third birthday."

They each had an arm round her; they propelled her towards the house. They were lithe, supple creatures of twenty and twenty-one. Between them, Neville, with her small, pointed, elfish face, that was sensitive to every breath of thought and emotion like smooth water wind-stirred, and her great violet eyes brooding in it under thin black brows, and her wet hair hanging in loose strands, looked like an ageless wood-dryad between two slim young saplings. Kay was a little like her in the face, only his violet eyes were short-sighted and he wore glasses. Gerda was smaller, fragile and straight as a wand, with a white, little face and wavy hair of pure gold bobbed round her thin, white neck, and far-set blue eyes and a delicate, cleft chin and thin, straight lips. For all she looked so frail, she could dance all night and return in the morning cool, composed and exquisite, like a lily bud. There was a look of immaculate sexless purity about Gerda; she might have stood for the angel Gabriel, wide-eyed and young and grave. With this wide, innocent look she would talk unabashed of things which Neville (herself the product of a fastidious generation and class, and one as nearly sexless as may be in this besexed world, which, however, is not, and can never be, saying much), felt revolting. So would Kay. They would read and discuss Freud, whom Neville, unfairly prejudiced, found both an obscene maniac and a liar. They might laugh at Freud with her when he expanded on that complex on account of which mothers and daughters hate each other, and fathers and sons—but they both, all the same, took seriously things which seemed to Neville merely loathsome imbecilities. Gerda and Kay didn't, in point of fact, find so many things either funny or disgusting as Neville did; throwing her mind back twenty years, Neville tried to remember whether she had found the world as funny and as frightful when she was a medical student as she did now; on the whole she thought not. Boys and girls are, for all their high spirits, creatures of infinite solemnities and pomposities. They laugh; but the twinkling irony, mocking at itself and everything else, of the thirties and forties, they have not yet learnt. They cannot be gentle cynics; they are so full of faith and hope, and when these are hurt they turn savage. About Kay and Gerda there was a certain splendid earnestness with regard to life. Admirable creatures, thought Neville, watching them with whimsical tenderness. They had nothing to do with the pre-war dilettante past, with the sophisticated gaiety of the young century. Their childhood had been lived during the Great War, and they had emerged from it hot with elemental things, discussing life, lust, love, politics and social reform, with cool candour, intelligent thoroughness and Elizabethan directness. They wouldn't mind having passions and giving them rein; they wouldn't think it vulgar, or even tedious, to lead loose lives. Probably, in fact, it wasn't; probably it was Neville, and the people who had grown up with her, who were over-civilised, too far from the crude stuff of life, the monotonies and emotionalisms of nature. And now nature was taking her rather startling revenge on the next generation.

▶•◀

III

Neville ran upstairs, and came down to breakfast dressed in blue cotton, with her damp hair smoothly taken back from her broad forehead that jutted broodingly over her short, pointed face. She had the look of a dryad at odds with the world, a whimsical and elfish intellectual.

Rodney and Kay and Gerda had been putting parcels in her plate, and a pile of letters lay among them. There is, anyhow, that about birthdays, however old they make you. Kay had given her a splendid pocket-knife and a book he wanted to read, and Gerda an oak box she had carved, and Rodney a new bicycle (by the front door), and a Brangwyn drawing (on the table). Since the moment to introduce Rodney has arrived (though there will not be much of him in this book), it should be mentioned that he was the husband of Neville, the father of Gerda and Kay, a clever and distinguished-looking person of forty-five, and member, in the Labour interest, for a division of Surrey (though this sounds for every reason improbable, and, indeed, he looked more like a literary man). If Neville envied Kay and Gerda their future careers, she envied Rodney his present sphere. How to be useful though married: in Rodney's case the problem was so simple, in hers so complicated. She had envied Rodney, a little, twenty years ago; then she had stopped, because the bringing up of Kay and Gerda had been a work in itself; now she had begun again. Rodney and she were more like each other than they were like their children; they had some of the same vanities, fastidiousnesses, humours and withdrawals, and in some respects the same outlook on life, only Rodney's had been solidified and developed by the contacts and exigencies of his career, and Neville's disembodied, devitalised and driven inwards by her more dilettante life. She 'helped Rodney with the constituency,' of course, but it was Rodney's constituency, not hers; she entertained his friends and hers when they were in town, but she knew herself a light woman, not a dealer in affairs. Yet her nature was stronger than Rodney's, larger and more mature: it was only his experience she lacked.

Rodney was, and had always been, charming; there were no two words about that, whatever else you might come to think about him. Able, too, but living on his nerves, and wincing like a highly-strung horse from the annoyances and disappointments of life, such as quaker oats because the grape-nuts had come to an end, and the political and industrial news of the morning, which was as bad as usual, and four times repeated in four quite different tones by the four daily papers which lay on the table. They took four papers, not so much that there might be one for each of them, as that they might have the entertainment of seeing how different the same news can be made to appear. One bond of union this family had which few families possess; they were (roughly speaking) united politically, so believed the same news to be good or bad. The chief difference in their political attitude was that Kay and Gerda joined societies and leagues, being still young enough to hold that this helped causes.

"What about to-day?" Rodney asked Neville. "What are you going to do?"

She answered, "Tennis. River. Lying about in the sun." (It should be explained that it was one of the nine days of the summer of 1920 when this was a possible occupation.) "Anything any one likes. ... I've already had a good deal of day and a bathe. ... Oh, Nan's coming down this afternoon."

She got that out of a letter, and Nan was her youngest sister. They all proceeded to get and impart other things out of letters, in the way of families who are fairly, as families go, united.

Gerda opened her lips to impart something, but remembered her father's distastes and refrained. Rodney, civilised, sensitive and progressive, had no patience with his children's unsophisticated leaning to a primitive crudeness. He told them they were young savages. So Gerda kept her news till later, when she and Neville and Kay were lying on rugs on the lawn, after Neville had beaten Kay in a set of singles (Neville had once been a county player).

They lay and smoked and cooled, and Gerda, a cigarette stuck in one side of her mouth, a buttercup in the other, mumbled, "Penelope's baby's come, by the way. A girl. Another surplus woman."

Neville's brows lazily went up.

"Penelope Jessop? What's *she* doing with a baby? I didn't know she'd got married."

"Oh, she hasn't, of course. ... Didn't I tell you about Penelope? She lives with Martin Annesley now."

"Oh, I see. Marriage in the sight of Heaven. That sort of thing."

Neville was of those who find marriages in the sight of Heaven uncivilised and socially reactionary, a reversion, in fact, to Nature, which bored her. Gerda and Kay rightly believed such marriages to have some advantages over those more visible to the human eye (as being more readily dissoluble when fatiguing) and many advantages over no marriages at all, which do not increase the population, so depleted by the Great War. When they spoke in this admirably civic sense, Neville was apt to say, "It doesn't want increasing. I waited twenty minutes before I could board my bus at Trafalgar Square the other day. It wants more depleting, I should say—a Great Plague or something," which Kay and Gerda truly thought egotistical.

"I do hope," said Neville, her thoughts having led her to this, "I do hope very much that neither of you will ever perpetrate that sort of marriage. It would be so dreadfully common of you."

"Impossible to say," Kay said vaguely.

"Considering," said Gerda, "that there are a million more women than men in this country, it stands to reason that some system of polygamy must become the usual thing in the future."

"It's always been the usual thing, darling. Dreadfully usual. It's so much more amusing to be unusual in these ways."

Neville's voice trailed drowsily away. Polygamy. Sex. Free Love. Love in chains. The children seemed so often to be discussing these. Just as, twenty years ago, she and her friends had seemed always to be discussing the Limitations of Personality, the Ethics of Friendship and the Nature, if any, of God. (This last was to Kay and Gerda too hypothetical to be a stimulating theme. It would have sent them to sleep, as sex did Neville.)

Neville, brooding cynically over her private vision, to which Free Love had led her, of tribesmen dancing round a wood-pile in primeval forests, engaged in what missionaries, journalists, and writers of fiction about our coloured brothers call "nameless orgies" (as if you would expect most orgies to answer to their names, like the stars), saw the steep roads of the round world running back and back and back—on or back, it made no difference, since the world was round—to this. Saw, too, a thousand stuffy homes wherein sat couples linked by a legal formula so rigid, so lasting, so indelible, that not all their tears could wash out a word of it, unless they took to themselves some other mate, and then their second state might be worse than their first. Free love—love in chains. How absurd it all was, and how tragic too. One might react back to the remaining choice—no love at all—and that was absurder and more tragic still, since man was made (among other ends) to love. Looking under her heavy lashes at her pretty young (incredibly youthful, absurdly theoretical, fiercely clean of mind and frank of speech, their clearness as yet unblurred by the expediences, compromises and experimental contacts of life), Neville was stabbed by a sharp pang of fear and hope for them; fear lest on some fleeting impulse they might founder into the sentimental triviality of short-lived contacts, or into the tedium of bonds which must outlive desire: hope that, by some fortunate chance, they might each achieve, as she had achieved, some relation which should be both durable and enduring. As to the third path—no love at all—she did not believe that either Kay or Gerda would tread that. They were emotional, in their cool and youthful way, and also believed that they ought to increase the population. What a wonderful, noble thing to believe, at twenty, thought Neville, remembering the levity of her own irresponsible youth, when her only interest in the population had been a nightmare fear lest they should at last become so numerous that they would be driven out of the towns into the country and would be scuttling over the moors, downs, and woods like blackbeetles in kitchens in the night. They were better than she had been, these children; more public-spirited and in earnest about life.

►•◄

IV

Across the garden came Nan Hilary, having come down from town to see Neville on her forty-third birthday. Nan herself was not so incredibly old as Neville. Nan was thirty-three and a half. She represented the thirties; she was a bridge, in Neville's mind, between the remote twenties and the fantastic forties, through which men and women, it is said, move with blank misgivings, as in worlds not realised. The fifties are still more fantastic a dream. By the sixties one should have settled down a little, caught oneself up, brought to terms the enemies life and time. But it seems, and surely is, normal to be in the thirties; the right, ordinary age, that most people are. Nan, who wrote, and lived in rooms in Chelsea, was rather like a wild animal—a leopard or something. Long and lissom, with a small, round, sallow face and withdrawn, brooding yellow eyes under sulky black brows that slanted up to the outer corners. Nan had a good time, socially and intellectually. She was clever and lazy; she would fritter away days and weeks in idle explorations into the humanities, or curled up in the sun in the country like a cat. Her worst fault was a cynical unkindness, against which she did not strive because investigating the less admirable traits of human beings amused her. She was infinitely amused by her nephew and niece, but often spiteful to them, merely because they were young. To sum up, she was a cynic, a rake, an excellent literary critic, a sardonic and brilliant novelist, and had a passionate, adoring and protecting affection for Neville, who was the only person who had always been told what she called the darker secrets of her life.

She sat down on the grass, her thin brown hands clasped round her ankles, and said to Neville, "You're looking very sweet, aged one. Forty-three seems to suit you."

"And you," Neville returned, "look as if you'd jazzed all night and written unkind reviews from dawn till breakfast time."

"That's just about right," Nan owned, and flung herself full length on her back, shutting her eyes against the sun. "That's why I've come down here to cool my jaded nerves. And also because Rosalind wanted to lunch with me."

"Have you read my poems yet?" inquired Gerda, who never showed the customary abashed hesitation in dealing with these matters. She and Kay sent their literary efforts to Nan to criticise, because they believed" (*a*) in her powers as a critic; (*b*) in her influence in the literary world. Nan used in their behalf the former but seldom the latter, because, though with queer spasms of generosity, she was jealous of Gerda and Kay. Why should they want to write? Why shouldn't they do anything else in the world but trespass on her preserves? Not that verse was what she ever wrote, or would write, herself. And, of course, every one wrote now, and especially the very young; but in a niece and nephew it was a tiresome trick. They didn't write well, because no one of their age ever does, but they might some day. They already came out in weekly papers and anthologies of contemporary verse. Very soon they would come out in little volumes. They'd much better, thought Nan, marry, and get out of the way.

"Read them—yes," Nan returned laconically to Gerda's question.

"What," inquired Gerda perseveringly, "did you think of them?"

"I said I'd *read* them," Nan replied. "I didn't say I'd thought of them."

Gerda looked at her with her wide, candid gaze, with the unrancorous placidity of the young, who are still used to being snubbed. Nan, she knew, would tease and baffle, withhold and gibe, but would always say what she thought in the end, and what she thought was always worth knowing, even though she was middle-aged.

Nan, turning her lithe body over on the grass, caught the patient child's look, and laughed. Generous impulses alternated in her with malicious moods where these absurd, solemn, egotistic, pretty children of Neville's were concerned.

"All right, Blue Eyes. I'll write it all down for you and send it you with the MS., if you really want it. You won't like it, you know, but I suppose you're used to that by now."

Neville listened to them. Regret turned in her, cold and tired and envious. They all wrote except her. To write: it wasn't much of a thing to do, unless one did it really well, and it had never attracted her personally, but it was, nevertheless, something—a little piece of individual output thrown into the flying river. (It will have been gathered by now that Neville was an egoist.) She had never written, even when she was Gerda's age. Writing poetry hadn't, twenty years ago, been a necessary part of youth's accomplishment, like tennis, French or dancing, as it is to-day. Besides, Neville could never have written poetry with pleasure, because for her the gulf between good verse and bad was too wide to be bridged by her own achievements. Nor novels, because she disliked nearly all novels, finding them tedious, vulgar, conventional and out of all relation both to life as lived and to the world of imagination. What she had written in early youth had been queer, imaginative stuff, woven out of her childhood's explorations into fairyland and her youth's into those still stranger tropical lands beyond seas where she had travelled with her father. But she hadn't written or wanted to write much; scientific studies had always attracted her more than literary achievements. Then she had married Rodney, and that was the end of all studies and achievements for her, though not the end of anything for Rodney, but only beginnings.

V

Rodney came out of the house, his pipe in his mouth. He still had the lounging walk, shoulders high and hands in pockets of the undergraduate; the walk also of Kay. He sat down among his family. Kay and Gerda looked at him with approval; though they knew his weaknesses he was just the father they would have chosen, and of how few parents can this be said! They were proud to take him about with them to political meetings and so forth, and prouder still to sit under him while he addressed audiences. Few men of his great age were (on the whole) so right in the head and sound in the heart, and fewer still so delightful to the eye. When people talked about the Wicked Old Men, who, being still unfortunately unrestrained and unmurdered by the Young, make this wicked world what it is, Kay and Gerda always stipulated that there were a few exceptions.

Nan gave Rodney her small, fleeting smile. She had a critical friendliness for him, but had never believed him nearly good enough for Neville.

Gerda and Kay began to play a single, and Nan said, "I'm in a hole."

"Broke, darling?" Neville asked her, for that was usually it, though sometimes it was human entanglements.

Nan nodded. "If I could have ten pounds … I'd let you have it in a fortnight."

"That's easy," said Rodney, in his kind, offhand way.

"Of course," Neville said. "You old spendthrift."

"Thank you, dears. Now I can get a birthday present for mother."

For Mrs. Hilary's birthday was next week, and to celebrate it her children habitually assembled at The Gulls, St. Mary's Bay, where she lived. Nan always gave her a more expensive present than she could afford, in a spasm of remorse for the irritation her mother roused in her.

"Oh, poor mother," Neville exclaimed, suddenly remembering that Mrs. Hilary would in a week be sixty-three, and that this must be worse by twenty years than to be forty-three.

The hurrying stream of life clattered loudly in her ears. How quickly it was sweeping them all along—the young bodies of Gerda and of Kay leaping on the tennis court, the clear, analysing minds of Nan and Rodney and herself musing in the sun, the feverish heart of her mother, loving, hating, feeding restlessly on itself by the seaside, the age-calmed soul of her grandmother, who was eighty-four and drove out in a donkey-chair by the same sea.

The lazy talking of Rodney and Nan, the cryings and strikings of Gerda and Kay, the noontide chirrupings of birds, the cluckings of distant hens, pretending that they had laid eggs, all merged into the rushing of the inexorable river, along and along and along. Time, like an ever rolling stream bearing all its sons away. Clatter, chatter, clatter, does it matter, matter, matter? They fly forgotten, as a dream dies at the opening day. ... No, it probably didn't matter at all what one did, how much one got into one's life, since there was to be, anyhow, so soon an end.

The garden became strange and far and flat, like tapestry, or a dream. ...

The lunch gong boomed. Nan, who had fallen asleep with the suddenness of a lower animal, her cheek pillowed on her hand, woke and stretched. Gerda and Kay, not to be distracted from their purpose, finished the set.

"Thank God," said Nan, "that I am not lunching with Rosalind."

CHAPTER II

MRS. HILARY'S BIRTHDAY

▶•◀

I

They all turned up at The Gulls, St. Mary's Bay, in time for lunch on Mrs. Hilary's birthday. It was her special wish that all those of her children who could should do this each year. Jim, whom she preferred, couldn't come this time; he was a surgeon, an uncertain profession. The others all came: Neville and Pamela and Gilbert and Nan, and with Gilbert his wife Rosalind, who had no right there because she was only an in-law, but if Rosalind thought it would amuse her to do anything you could not prevent her. She and Mrs. Hilary disliked one another a good deal, though Rosalind would say to the others, "Your darling mother! She's priceless, and I adore her!" She would say that when she had caught out Mrs. Hilary in a mistake. She would draw her on to say she had read a book she hadn't read (it was a point of honour with Mrs. Hilary never to admit ignorance of any book mentioned by others), and then she would say, "I do love you, mother! It's not out yet; I've only seen Gilbert's review copy," and Mrs. Hilary would say, "In that case I suppose I am thinking of another book," and Rosalind would say to Neville or Pamela or Gilbert or Nan, "Your darling mother. I adore her!" and Nan, contemptuous of her mother for thinking such trivial pretence worth while, and with Rosalind for thinking malicious exposure worth while, would shrug her shoulders and turn away.

►•◄

II

All but Neville arrived by the same train from town, the one getting in at 12.11. Neville had come from Surrey the day before and spent the night, because Mrs. Hilary liked to have her all to herself for a little time before the others came. After Jim, Neville was the child Mrs. Hilary preferred. She had always been a mother with marked preferences. There were various barriers between her and her various children; Gilbert, who was thirty-eight, had annoyed her long ago by taking up literature as a profession on leaving Cambridge, instead of doing what she described as 'a man's job,' and later on by marrying Rosalind, who was fast, and, in Mrs. Hilary's opinion, immoral. Pamela, who was thirty-nine and working in a settlement in Hoxton, annoyed her by her devotion to Frances Carr, the friend with whom she lived. Mrs. Hilary thought them very silly, these close friendships between women. They prevented marriage, and led to foolish fussing about one another's health and happiness. Nan annoyed her by 'getting talked about' with men, by writing books which Mrs. Hilary found both dull and not very nice in tone, and by her own irritated reactions to her mother's personality. Nan was, in fact, often rude and curt to her.

But Jim, who was a man and a doctor, a strong, good-humoured person and her eldest son, annoyed her not at all. Nor did Neville, who was her eldest daughter and had given her grandchildren and infinite sympathy.

Neville, knowing all these things and more, always arrived on the evenings before her mother's birthdays, and they talked all the morning. Mrs. Hilary was at her best with Neville. She was neither irritable nor nervous nor showing off. She looked much less than sixty-three. She was a tall, slight, trailing woman, with the remains of beauty, and her dark, untidy hair was only streaked with grey. Since her husband had died, ten years ago, she had lived at St. Mary's Bay with her mother. It had been her old home; not The Gulls, but the Vicarage, in the days when St. Mary's Bay had been a little fishing village without an esplanade. To old Mrs. Lennox it was the same fishing village still, and the people, even the summer visitors, were to her the flock of her late husband, who had died twenty years ago.

"A good many changes lately," she would say to them. "Some people think the place is improving. But I can't say I like the esplanade."

But the visitors didn't, unless they were very old, know anything about the changes. To them St. Mary's Bay was not a fishing village, but a seaside resort. To Mrs. Hilary it was her old home, and had healthy air and plenty of people for her mother to gossip with, and was as good a place as any other for her to consume away like a withered flower now that the work of her life was done. The work of her life had been making a home for her husband and children; she had never had either the desire or the faculties for any other work, and now that was over and she was rather badly left, as she cared neither for cards, knitting, gardening, nor intellectual pursuits. Once, seven years ago, at Neville's instigation, she had tried London life for a time, but it had been no use. The people she met there were too unlike her, too intelligent and up-to-date; they went to meetings and concerts and picture exhibitions and read books and talked about public affairs, not emotionally but coolly and dryly; they were mildly surprised at Mrs. Hilary's vehemence of feeling on all points, and she was strained beyond endurance by their knowledge of facts and catholicity of interests. So she returned to St. Mary's Bay, where she passed muster as an intelligent woman, gossiped with her mother, the servants, and their neighbours, read novels, brooded over the happier past, walked for miles alone along the coast, and slipped every now and then, as she had slipped even in youth, over the edge of emotionalism into hysterical passion or grief. Her mother was no use at such times; she only made her worse, sitting there in the calm of old age, looking tranquilly at the end, for her so near that nothing mattered. Only Jim or Neville was of any use then.

Neville, on the eve of this, her sixty-third, birthday, soothed one such outburst. The tedium of life, with no more to do in it—why couldn't it end? The lights were out, the flowers were dead—and yet the unhappy actors had to stay and stay and stay, idling on the empty, darkened stage. (That was how Mrs. Hilary, with her gift for picturesque language, put it.) *Must* it be empty, *must* it be dark? Neville uselessly asked, knowing quite well that for one of her mother's temperament it must. Mrs. Hilary had lived in and by her emotions; nothing else had counted. Life for her had burnt itself out, and its remnant was like the fag end of a cigarette, stale and old.

"Shall I feel like that in twenty years?" Neville speculated aloud.

"I hope," said Mrs. Hilary, "that you won't have lost Rodney. So long as you have him …"

"But I haven't …"

Neville looked down the years; saw herself without Rodney, perhaps looking after her mother, who would then have become (strange, incredible thought, but who could say?) calm with the calm of age; Kay and Gerda married or working or both. … What then? Only she was better equipped than her mother for the fag-end of life; she had a serviceable brain and a sound education. She wouldn't pass empty days at a seaside resort. She would work at something, and be interested. Interesting work and interesting friends—her mother, by her very nature, could have neither, but was just clever enough to feel the want of them. The thing was to start some definite work *now*, before it was too late.

"Did Grandmamma go through it?" Neville asked her mother.

"Oh, I expect so. I was selfish; I was wrapped up in home and all of you; I didn't notice. But I think she had it badly, for a time, when first she left the Vicarage. … She's contented now."

They both looked at Grandmamma, who was playing patience on the sofa and could not hear their talking for the sound of the sea. Yes, Grandmamma was (apparently) contented now.

"There's work," mused Neville, thinking of the various links with life, the rafts, rather, which should carry age over the cold seas of tedious regret. "And there's natural gaiety. And intellectual interests. And contacts with other people—permanent contacts and temporary ones. And beauty. All those things. For some people, too, there's religion."

"And for all of us food and drink," said Mrs. Hilary sharply. "Oh, I suppose you think I've no right to complain, as I've got all those things, except work."

But Neville shook her head, knowing that this was a delusion of her mother's, and that she had, in point of fact, none of them, except the contacts with people, which mostly either overstrained, irritated or bored her, and that aspect of religion which made her cry. For she was a Unitarian, and thought the Gospels infinitely sad and the souls of the departed most probably so merged in God as to be deprived of all individuality.

"It's better to be High Church or Roman Catholic and have services, or an Evangelical and have the Voice of God," Neville decided. And, indeed, it is probable that Mrs. Hilary would have been one or other of these things if it had not been for her late husband, who had disapproved of superstition and had instructed her in the Higher Thought and the Larger Hope.

III

Though heaviness endured for the night, joy came in the morning, as is apt to happen where there is sea air. Mrs. Hilary on her birthday had a revulsion to gaiety, owing to a fine day, her unstable temperament, letters, presents and being made a fuss of. Also Grandmamma said, when she went up to see her after breakfast, "This new dress suits you particularly, my dear child. It brings out the colour in your eyes," and every one likes to hear that when they are sixty-three or any other age.

So, when the rest of her children arrived, Mrs. Hilary was ready for them.

They embraced her in turn; Pamela, capable, humorous and intelligent, the very type of the professional woman at her best, but all the time preferring Frances Carr, anxious about her because she was overworking and run down; Nan, her extravagant present in her hands, on fire to protect her mother against old age, depression and Rosalind, yet knowing too how soon she herself would be smouldering with irritation; Gilbert, spare and cynical, writer of plays and literary editor of the *Weekly Critic*, and with him his wife Rosalind, whom Mrs. Hilary had long since judged as a voluptuous rake who led men on and made up unseemly stories and her lovely face, but who insisted on coming to The Gulls with Gilbert to see his adorable mother. Rosalind, who was always taking up things—art, or religion, or spiritualism, or young men—and dropping them when they bored her, had lately taken up psycho-analysis. She was studying what she called her mother-in-law's 'case,' looking for and finding complexes in her past which should account for her somewhat unbalanced present.

"I've never had complexes," Mrs. Hilary would declare indignantly, as if they had been fleas or worse, and indeed when Rosalind handled them they *were* worse, much. From Rosalind Mrs. Hilary got the most unpleasant impression possible (which is to say a good deal) of psycho-analysts. "They have only one idea, and that is a disgusting one," she would assert, for she could only rarely and with difficulty see more than one idea in anything, particularly when it was a disgusting one. Her mind was of that sort—tenacious, intolerant and not many-sided. That was where (partly where) she fell foul of her children, who saw sharply and clearly all round things and gave to each side its value. They knew Mrs. Hilary to be a muddled bigot, whose mind was stuffed with concrete instances and insusceptible of abstract reason. If anyone had asked her what she knew of psycho-analysis, she would have replied, in effect, that she knew Rosalind, and that was enough, more than enough, of psycho-analysis for her. She had also looked into Freud, and been rightly disgusted.

"A man who spits deliberately on to his friend's stairs, on purpose to annoy the servants ... that is enough, the rest follows. The man is obviously a loathsome and indecent vulgarian. It comes from being a German, no doubt." Which settled that. Mrs. Hilary, like Grandmamma, settled people and things very quickly and satisfactorily; and if anyone murmured "An Austrian," she would say, "It comes to the same thing, in questions of breeding."

They all sat in the front garden after lunch and looked out over the wonderful shining sea. Grandmamma sat in her wheeled chair, Tchekov's letters on her knees. She had made Mrs. Hilary get this book from Mudie's because she had read favourable reviews of it by Gilbert and Nan. Grandmamma was a cleverish old lady, cleverer than her daughter.

"Jolly, isn't it?" said Gilbert, seeing the book.

"Very entertaining," said Grandmamma, and Mrs. Hilary echoed, "Most," at which Grandmamma eyed her with a twinkle, knowing that it bored her, like all the Russians. Mrs. Hilary cared nothing for style; she liked nice life-like books about people as she believed them to be, and, though she was quite prepared to believe that real Russians were like Russians in books, she felt that she did not care to meet either of them. But Mrs. Hilary had learnt that intelligent persons seldom liked the books which seemed to her to be about real, natural people, any more than they admired the pictures which struck her as being like things as they were. Though she thought those who differed from her profoundly wrong, she never admitted ignorance of the books they admired. For she was in a better position to differ from them about a book if she had nominally read it—and really it didn't matter if she had actually done so or not, for she knew beforehand what she would think of it if she had. So well she knew this, indeed, that the line between the books she had and hadn't read was, even in her own mind, smudgy and vague, not hard and clear as with most people. Often when she had seen reviews which quoted extracts she thought she had read the book, just as some people, when they have seen publishers' advertisements, think they have seen reviews, and maintain firmly in libraries that a book is out when it lacks a month of publication.

Mrs. Hilary, having thus asserted her acquaintance with Tchekov's letters, left Gilbert, Grandmamma, and Neville to talk about them together, and herself began telling the others how disappointed Jim had been that he could not come for her birthday.

"He was passionately anxious to come," she said in her clear, vibrating voice, that struck a different note when she mentioned each one of her children, so that you always knew which she meant. "He never misses to-day if he can possibly help it. But he simply couldn't get away. … One of these tremendously difficult new operations, that hardly anyone can do. His work must come first, of course. He wouldn't be Jim if it didn't."

"Fancy knifing people in town a day like this," said Rosalind, stretching her large, lazy limbs in the sun. Rosalind was big and fair, and sensuously alive.

Music blared out from the parade. Gilbert, adjusting his glasses, observed its circumstances, with his air of detached, fastidious interest.

"The Army," he remarked. "The Army calling for strayed sheep."

"Oh," exclaimed Rosalind, raising herself, "wouldn't I love to go out and be saved! I *was* saved once, when I was eleven. It was one of my first thrills. I felt I was blacker in guilt than all creatures before me, and I came forward and found the Lord. Afraid I had a relapse rather soon, though."

"Horrible vulgarians," Mrs. Hilary commented, really meaning Rosalind at the age of eleven. "They have meetings on the parade every morning now. The police ought to stop it."

Grandmamma was beating time with her hand on the arm of her chair to the merry music-hall tune and the ogreish words:

> "Blood! Blood!
> Rivers of blood for you!
> Oceans of blood for me!
> All that the sinner has got to do
> Is to plunge into the Red Sea.
> Clean! Clean!
> Wash and be clean!
> Though filthy and black as a sweep you've been.
> The waves of that sea shall make you clean. …"

"That," Mrs. Hilary asserted with disgust, "is a *most* disagreeable way of worshipping God." She was addicted to these undeniable statements, taking nothing for granted.

"But a very racy tune, my dear," said Grandmamma, "though the words are foolish and unpleasing."

Gilbert said, "A stimulating performance. If we don't restrain her, Rosalind will be getting saved again."

He was proud of Rosalind's vitality, whimsies and exuberances.

Rosalind, who had a fine rolling voice, began reciting "General Booth enters into Heaven," by Mr. Vachell Lindsay, which Mrs. Hilary found disgusting.

"A wonderful man," said Grandmamma, who had been reading the General's life in two large volumes. "Though mistaken about many things. And his Life would have been more interesting if it had been written by Mr. Lytton Strachey instead of Mr. Begbie; he has a better touch on our great religious leaders. Your grandfather," added Grandmamma, "always got on well with the Army people. He encouraged them. The present vicar does not. He says their methods are deplorable and their goal a delusion."

Rosalind said, "Their methods are entrancing and their goal the Lord. What more does he want? Clergymen are so narrow. That's why I had to give up being a church woman."

Rosalind had been a churchwoman (high) for nine months some six years ago, just after planchette and just before flag days. She had decided, after this brief trial, that incense and confessions, though immensely stimulating, did not weigh down the balance against early Mass, Lent and being thrown with other churchwomen.

▶●◀

IV

"What about a bathe?" Neville suggested to all of them. "Mother?"

Mrs. Hilary, a keen bather, agreed. They all agreed except Grand-mamma, who was going out in her donkey-chair instead, as one does at eighty-four.

They all went down to the beach, where the Army still sang of the Red Sea, and where the blue, high tide clapped white hands on brown sand.

One by one they emerged from tents and sprang through the white leaping edge into the rocking blue, as other bathers were doing all round the bay. When Mrs. Hilary came out of her tent, Neville was waiting for her, poised like a slim girl, knee-deep in tumbling waves, shaking the water from her eyes.

"Come, mother. I'll race you out."

Mrs. Hilary waded in, a figure not without grace and dignity. Looking back, they saw Rosalind coming down the beach, large-limbed and splendid, like Juno. Mrs. Hilary shrugged her shoulders.

"Disgusting," she remarked to Neville.

So much more, she meant, of Rosalind than of Rosalind's costume. Mrs. Hilary preferred it to be the other way about, for, though she did not really like either of them, she disliked the costume less than she disliked Rosalind.

"It's quite in the fashion," Neville assured her, and Mrs. Hilary, remarking that she was sure of that, splashed her head and face and pushed off, mainly to escape from Rosalind, who always sat in the foam, not being, like the Hilary family, an active swimmer.

Already Pamela and Gilbert were far out, swimming steadily against each other, and Nan was tumbling and turning like an eel close behind them.

Neville and Mrs. Hilary swam out a little way.

"I shall now float on my back," said Mrs. Hilary. "You swim on and catch up the rest."

"You'll be all right?" Neville asked, lingering.

"Why shouldn't I be all right? I bathe nearly every day, you know, even if I am sixty-three." This was not accurate; she only bathed as a rule when it was warm, and this seldom occurs on our island coasts.

Neville, saying "Don't stop in long, will you?" left her and swam out into the blue, with her swift, overhand stroke. Neville was the best swimmer in a swimming family. She clove the water like a torpedo destroyer, swift and untiring between the hot summer sun and the cool summer sea. She shouted to the others, caught them up, raced them and won, and then they began to duck each other. When the Hilary brothers and sisters were swimming or playing together, they were even as they had been twenty years ago.

Mrs. Hilary watched them, swimming slowly round, a few feet out of her depth. They seemed to have forgotten her and her birthday. The only one who was within speaking distance was Rosalind, wallowing with her big white limbs in tumbling waves on the shore; Rosalind, whom she disliked; Rosalind, who was more than her costume, which, however, was not saying much; Rosalind, before whom she had to keep up an appearance of immense enjoyment because Rosalind was so malicious.

"You wonderful woman! I can't think how you *do* it," Rosalind was crying to her in her rich, ripe voice out of the splashing waves. "But fancy their all swimming out and leaving you to yourself! Why, you might get cramp and sink! *I'm* no use, you know; I'm hopeless; I can only just save myself—others I cannot save."

"I shan't trouble you, thank you," Mrs. Hilary called back, and her voice shook a little because she was getting chilled.

"Why, you're shivering," Rosalind cried. "Why don't you come out? You *are* wonderful, I do admire you. ... It's no use waiting for the others, they'll be ages. ... I say, look at Neville; fancy her being forty-three. I never knew such a family. … Come and sit in the waves with me, it's lovely and warm."

"I prefer swimming," said Mrs. Hilary, and she was shivering more now. She never stayed in so long as this; she usually only plunged in and came out.

Grandmamma, stopping on the esplanade in her donkey-chair, was waving and beckoning to her. Grandmamma knew she had been in too long, and that her rheumatism would be bad.

"*Come out, dear,*" Grandmamma called, in her old, thin voice. "*Come out. You've been in far too long.*"

Mrs. Hilary only waved her hand to Grandmamma. She was not going to come out, like an old woman, before the others did, the others, who had swum out and left her alone on her birthday bathe.

They were swimming back now, first all in a row, then one behind the other; Neville leading, with her arrowy drive, Gilbert and Pamela behind, so alike, with their pale, finely cut, intellectual faces, and their sharp chins cutting through the sea, and their quick, short, vigorous strokes, and Nan, still far out, swimming lazily on her back, the sun in her eyes.

Mrs. Hilary's heart stirred to see her swimming brood so graceful and strong and swift and young. They possessed, surely, everything that was in the heaven above or on the earth beneath or in the water under the earth. And she, who was sixty-three, possessed nothing. She could not even swim with her children. They might have thought of that, and stayed with her … Neville, anyhow. Jim would have, said Mrs. Hilary to herself, half knowing and half not knowing that she was lying.

"*Come out, dear!*" called Grandmamma from the esplanade. "*You'll be ill.*"

Back they came, Neville first. Neville, seeing from far her mother's blue face, called, "Mother, dear, how cold you are! You shouldn't have stayed in so long!"

"I was waiting," Mrs. Hilary said, "for you."

"Oh, why, dear?"

"Don't know. I thought I would. … It's pretty poor fun," Mrs. Hilary added, having tried not to and failed, "bathing all alone on one's birthday."

Neville gave a little sigh, and gently propelled her mother to the shore.

– 29 –

She hadn't felt like this on *her* birthday, when Kay and Gerda had gone off to some avocation of their own and left her in the garden. Many things she had felt on her birthday, but not this. It is an undoubted truth that people react quite differently to birthdays.

Rosalind rose out of the foam like Aphrodite, grandly beautiful, though all the paint was washed off her face and lips.

"Wonderful people," she apostrophised the shore-coming family. "Any one would think you were all nineteen. *I* was the only comfy one."

Rosalind was always talking about age, emphasising it, as if it was very important.

They hurried up to the tents, and last of all came Nan, riding in to shore on a swelling wave and lying full length where it flung her, for the joy of feeling the wet sand sucking away beneath her.

V

Grandmamma, waiting for them on the esplanade, was angry with Mrs. Hilary.

"My dear child, didn't you hear me call? You're perfectly blue. You *know* you never stay in more than five minutes. Neville, you should have seen that she didn't. Now you'll get your rheumatism back, child, and only yourself to thank. It's too silly. People of sixty-three carrying on as if they were fifty; I've no patience with it."

"They all swam out," said Mrs. Hilary, who, once having succumbed to the impulse to adopt this attitude, could not check it. "I waited for them."

Grandmamma, who was cross, said, "Very silly of you, and very selfish of the children. Now you'd better go to bed with hot bottles and a posset."

But Mrs. Hilary, though she felt the red-hot stabbings of an attack of rheumatism already beginning, stayed up. She was happier now, because the children were making a fuss of her, suggesting remedies and so on. She would stay up, and show them she could be plucky and cheerful even with rheumatism. A definite thing, like illness or pain, always put her on her mettle; it was so easy to be brave when people knew you had something to be brave about, and so hard when they didn't.

They had an early tea, and then Gilbert and Rosalind, who were going out to dinner, caught the 5.15 back to town. Rosalind's departure made Mrs. Hilary more cheerful still. She soared into her gayest mood, and told them amusing stories of the natives, and how much she and Grandmamma shocked some of them.

"All the same, dear," said Grandmamma presently, "you know you often enjoy a chat with your neighbours very much. You'd be bored to death with no-one to gossip with."

But Neville's, hand, slipping into her mother's, meant, "You shall adopt what pose you like on your birthday, darling. If you like to be too clever for anyone else in the bay so that they bore you to tears and you shock them to fits—well, you shall, and we'll believe you."

Nan, listening sulkily to what she called to herself 'mother's swank,' for a moment almost preferred Rosalind, who was as frank and unposturing as an animal; Rosalind, with her malicious thrusts and her corrupt mind and her frank feminine greediness. For Rosalind, anyhow, didn't pretend to herself, though she did undoubtedly, when for any reason it suited her, lie to other people. Mrs. Hilary's lying went all through, deep down; it sprang out of the roots of her being, so that all the time she was making up, not only for others but for herself, a sham person who did not exist. That Nan found infinitely oppressive. So did Pamela, but Pamela was more tolerant and sympathetic and less ill-tempered than Nan, and observed the ways of others with quiet, ironic humour, saying nothing unkind. Pamela, when she didn't like a way of talking—when Rosalind, for instance, was being malicious or indecent or both—would skilfully carry the talk somewhere else. She could be a rapid and good talker, and could tell story after story, lightly and coolly, till danger points were past. Pamela was beautifully bred; she had *savoir faire* as well as kindness, and never lost control of

- 31 -

herself. These family gatherings really a little bored her, because her work and interests lay elsewhere, but she would never admit or show it. She was kind even to Rosalind, though cool. She had always been kind and cool to Rosalind, because Gilbert was her special brother, and when he had married this fast, painted and unHilaryish young woman, she had seen the necessity for taking firm hold of an attitude in the matter and retaining it. No one, not even Neville, not even Frances Carr, had ever seen behind Pamela's guard where Rosalind was concerned. When Nan abused Rosalind, Pamela would say, "Don't be a spitfire, child. What's the use?" and change the subject. For Rosalind was, in Pamela's view, one of the things which were a pity but didn't really matter, so long as she didn't make Gilbert unhappy. And Gilbert, so far, was absurdly pleased and proud about her, in spite of occasional disapprovals of her excessive intimacies with others.

But, whatever they all felt about Rosalind, there was no doubt that the family party was happier for her departure. The departure of in-laws, even when they are quite nice in-laws, often has this effect on family parties. Mrs. Hilary had her three daughters to herself—the girls, as she still called them. She felt cosy and comforted, though in pain, lying on the sofa by the bay window in the warm afternoon sunshine, while Grandmamma looked at the *London Mercury*, which had just come by the post, and the girls talked.

VI

Their voices rose and fell against the soft splashing of the sea; Neville's, sweet and light, with pretty cadences, Pamela's, crisp, quick and decided; Nan's, trailing a little, almost drawling sometimes. The Hilary voices were all thin, not rich and full-bodied, like Rosalind's. Mrs. Hilary's was thin, and Grandmamma's.

"Nice voices," thought Mrs. Hilary, languidly listening. "Nice children. But what nonsense they often talk."

They were talking now about the Minority Report of some committee, which had been drafted by Rodney. Rodney and the Minority and Neville and Pamela and Nan were all interested in what Mrs. Hilary called "this Labour nonsense which is so fashionable now." Mrs. Hilary herself, being unfashionable, was anti-Labour, since it was apparent to her that the working classes had already more power, money and education than was good for them, sons of Belial, flown with insolence and strikes. Grandmamma, being so nearly out of it all, was used only to say, in reply to these sentiments, "It will make no difference in the end. We shall all be the same in the grave, and in the life beyond. All these movements are very interesting, but the world goes round just the same." It was all very well for Grandmamma to be philosophical; *she* wouldn't have to live for years ruled and triumphed over by her own gardener, which was the way Mrs. Hilary saw it.

Mrs. Hilary began to get angry, hearing the girls talking in this silly way. Of course it was natural that Neville should agree with Rodney; but Pamela had picked up foolish ideas from working among the poor and living with Frances Carr, and Nan was, as usual, merely wrong-headed, childish and perverse.

Suddenly she broke out, losing her temper, as she often did when she disagreed with people's politics, for she did not take a calm and tolerant view of these things.

"I never heard such stuff in my life. I disagree with every word you've all said."

She always disagreed in bulk, like that. It seemed simpler than arguing separate points, and took less time and knowledge. She saw Neville wrinkling her broad forehead, doubtfully, as if wondering how the subject could most easily be changed, and that annoyed her.

Nan said, "You mean you disagree with the Report. Which clauses of it?" and there was that soft viciousness in her voice which showed that she knew Mrs. Hilary had not even read the Minority Report, or the Majority Report either. Nan was spiteful; always trying to prove that her mother didn't know what she was talking about; always trying to pin her down on points of detail, like the people with whom Mrs. Hilary bad failed to get on during her brief sojourn in London; they, too, had always shunned general disputes about opinion and sentiment, such as were carried on with profit in St. Mary's Bay, and pinned the discussion down to hard facts, about which the Bay's information was inaccurate and incomplete. As if you didn't know, when you disagreed with a thing's whole drift, whether you had read it or not. ... Mrs. Hilary had never had any head for facts.

"It's the whole idea," she said hotly. "And I detest all those Labour people. Vile creatures. ... Of course I don't mean people like Rodney—the University men. They're merely amateurs. But these dreadful trades union men, with their walrus moustaches. ... Why can't they shave, like other people, if they want to be taken for gentlemen?"

Neville told her, chaffingly, that she was a mass of prejudice.

Grandmamma, who had fallen asleep and dropped the *London Mercury* on to the floor, diverted the conversation by waking up and remarking that it seemed a less interesting number than usual on the whole, though some of the pieces of poetry were pretty, and that Mrs. Hilary ought not to lie under the open window.

Mrs. Hilary, who was getting worse, admitted that she had better be in bed.

"I hope," said Grandmamma, "that it will be a lesson to you, dear, not to stay in the water so long again, even if you do want to show off before your daughter-in-law." Grandmamma, who disliked Rosalind, usually called her to Mrs. Hilary "your daughter-in-law," saddling her, so to speak, with the responsibility for Gilbert's ill-advised marriage. To her grandchildren she would refer to Rosalind as "your sister-in-law," or "poor Gilbert's wife."

"The bathe was worth it," said Mrs. Hilary, swinging up to high spirits again. "It was a glorious bathe. But I *have* got rheumatics."

So Neville stayed on at The Gulls that night, to massage her mother's joints, and Pamela and Nan went back to Hoxton and Chelsea by the evening train. Pamela had supper, as usual, with Frances Carr, and Nan with Barry Briscoe, and they both talked and talked, about all the things you don't talk of in families but only to friends.

►•◄

VII

Neville meanwhile was saying to Grandmamma in the drawing-room at The Gulls, after Mrs. Hilary had gone to bed, "I wish mother could get some regular interest or occupation. She would be much happier. Are there no jobs for elderly ladies in the Bay?"

"As many in the Bay," said Grandmamma, up in arms for the Bay, "as anywhere else. Sick-visiting, care committees, boys' and girls' classes, and so on. I still keep as busy as I am able, as you know."

Neville did know. "If mother could do the same. ..."

"Mother can't. She's never been a rector's wife, as I have, and she doesn't care for such jobs. Mother never did care for any kind of work really, even as a girl. She married when she was nineteen and found the only work she was fitted for and interested in. That's over, and there's no other she can turn to. It's common enough, child, with women. They just have to make the best of it, and muddle through somehow till the end."

"You were different, Grandmamma, weren't you? I mean, you were never at a loss for things to do."

Grandmamma's thin, delicate face hardened for a moment into grim lines.

"At a loss—yes, I was what you call at a loss twenty years ago, when your grandfather died. The meaning was gone out of life, you see. ... I was sixty-four. For two years I was cut adrift from everything, and did nothing but brood and find trivial occupations to pass the time somehow. I lived on memories and emotions; I was hysterical and peevish and bored. Then I realised it wouldn't do; that I might have twenty years and more of life before me, and that I must do something with it. So I took up again all of my old work that I could. It was the hardest thing I ever did. I hated it at first. Then I got interested again, and it has kept me going all these years, though I've had to drop most of it now, of course. But now I'm so near the end that it doesn't matter. You can drop work at eighty and keep calm and interested in life. You can't at sixty; it's too young. … Mother knows that too, but there seems no work she can do. She doesn't care for parish work as I do; she never learnt any art or craft or handiwork, and doesn't want to; she was never much good at intellectual work of any kind, and what mind she had as a girl—and her father and I did try to train her to use it—ran all to seed during her married life, so it's pretty nearly useless now. She spent herself on your father and all you children, and now she's bankrupt."

"Poor darling mother," Neville murmured.

Grandmamma nodded. "Just so. She's left to read novels, gossip with stupid neighbours, look after me, write to you children, go walks and brood over the past. She would have been quite happy like that forty years ago. The young have high spirits, and can amuse themselves without work. She never wanted work when she was eighteen. It's the old who need work. They've lost their spring and their zest for life, and need something to hold on to. It's all wrong, the way we arrange it—making the young work and the old sit idle. It should be the other way about. Girls and boys don't get bored with perpetual holidays; they live each moment of them hard; they would welcome the eternal Sabbath; and indeed I trust we shall all do that, as our youth is to be renewed like eagles. But old age on this earth is far too sad to do nothing in. Remember that, child, when your time comes."

"Why, yes. But when one's married, you know, it's not so easy, keeping up with a job. I only wish I could. … I don't *like* being merely a married woman. Rodney isn't merely a married man, after all. … But anyhow I'll find something to amuse my old age, even if I can't work. I'll play patience or croquet or the piano, or all three, and I'll go to theatres and picture shows and concerts and meetings in the Albert Hall. Mother doesn't do any of those things. And she *is* so unhappy so often."

"Oh, very. Very unhappy. Very often. ... She should come to church more. This Unitarianism is depressing. No substance in it. I'd rather be a Papist and keep God in a box. Or belong to the Army and sing about rivers of blood. I dare say both are satisfying. All this sermon-on-the-mount-but-no-miracle business is most saddening. Because it's about impossibilities. You can receive a sacrament, and you can find salvation, but you can't live the sermon on the mount. So of course it makes people discontented."

Grandmamma, who often in the evenings became a fluent though drowsy talker, might have wandered on like this till her bed-time, had not Mrs. Hilary here appeared in her dressing-gown. She sat down, and said, trying to sound natural and not annoyed and failing, "I heard so much talk, I thought I would come down and be in it. I thought you were coming up to me again directly, Neville. I hadn't realised you meant to stay down and talk to Grandmamma instead."

She hated Neville or any of them, but especially Neville, to talk intimately to Grandmamma; it made her jealous. She tried and tried not to feel this, but it was never any use her fighting against jealousy, it was too strong for her.

Grandmamma said placidly, "Neville and I were discussing different forms of religion."

"Is Neville thinking of adopting one of them?" Mrs. Hilary inquired, her jealousy making her sound sarcastic and scornful.

"No, mother. Not at present. ... Come back to bed, and I'll sit with you, and we'll talk. I don't believe you should be up."

"Oh, I see I've interrupted. It was the last thing I meant. No, Neville, I'll go back to my room alone. You go on with your talk with Grandmamma. I hate interrupting like this. I hoped you would have let me join. I don't get much of you in these days, after all. But stay and talk to Grandmamma."

That was the point at which Nan would have sworn to herself and gone down to the beach. Neville did neither. She was gentle and soothing, and Grandmamma was infinitely untroubled, and Mrs. Hilary presently picked up her spirits and went back to bed, and Neville spent the evening with her. These little scenes had occurred so often that they left only a slight impression on those concerned, and slightest of all on Mrs. Hilary.

▶•◀

VIII

When Mrs. Hilary and Grandmamma were both settled for the night (for this is what happens to old and elderly people when they go to bed), Neville went down to the seashore and lay on the sand, watching the moon rise over the sea.

Beauty was there. But in elderly people was such pathos, such tragedy, such pity, that they lay like a heavy weight on one's soul. If one could do anything to help. …

To be aimless: to live on emotions and be by them consumed: that was pitiful. To have done one's work for life, and to be in return cast aside by life like a broken tool: that was tragic.

The thing was to defy life; to fly in the face of the fool nature, break her absurd rules, and wrest out of the breakage something for oneself by which to live at the last.

Neville flung her challenge to the black sea that slowly brightened under the moon's rising eye.

CHAPTER III

FAMILY LIFE

►•◄

I

If you have broken off your medical studies at London University at the age of twenty-one and resume then at forty-three, you will find them (one is told) a considerably tougher job than you found them twenty-two years before. Youth is the time to read for examinations; youth is used to such foolishness, and takes it lightly in its stride. At thirty you may be and probably are much cleverer than you were at twenty; you will have more ideas and better ones, and infinitely more power of original and creative thought; but you will not, probably, find it so easy to grip and retain knowledge out of books and reproduce it to order. So the world has ordained that youth shall spend laborious days in doing this, and that middle age shall, in the main, put away these childish things, and act and work on or in spite of the information thus acquired.

However, Neville Bendish entered her name once more at the London University School of Medicine, and plunged forthwith into her interrupted studies. Her aim was to spend this summer in reacquiring such knowledge as should prepare her for the October session. And it was difficult beyond her imaginings. It had not been difficult twenty-two years ago; she had worked then with pleasure and interest, and taken examinations with easy triumph. As Kay did now at Cambridge, only more so, because she had been cleverer than Kay. She was a vain creature, and had believed that cleverness of hers to be unimpaired by life, until she came to try. She supposed that if she had spent her married life in head-work, her head would never have lost the trick of it. But she hadn't. She had spent it on Rodney and Gerda and Kay, and the interesting, amusing life led by the wife of a man in Rodney's position, which had brought her always into contact with people and ideas. Much more amusing than grinding at intellectual work of her own, but it apparently caused the brain to atrophy. And she was, anyhow, tired of doing nothing in particular. After forty you must have your job, you must be independent of other people's jobs, of human and social contacts, however amusing and instructive.

Rodney wasn't altogether pleased, though he understood. He wanted her constant companionship and interest in his own work.

"You have had twenty-two years of it, darling," Neville said. "Now I must Live my own Life, as the Victorians used to put it. I must be a doctor; quite seriously I must. I want it. It's my job. The only one I could ever really have been much good at. The sight of human bones or a rabbit's brain thrills me, as the sight of a platform and a listening audience thrills you, or as pen and paper (I suppose) thrill the children. You ought to be glad I don't want to write. Our family seems to run to that as a rule."

"But," Rodney said, "you don't mean ever to *practise*, surely? You won't have time for it, with all the other things you do."

"It's the other things I shan't have time for, old man. Sorry, but there it is. … It's all along of mother, you see. She's such an object-lesson in how not to grow old. If she'd been a doctor, now …"

"She couldn't have been a doctor, possibly. She hasn't the head. On the other hand, you've got enough head to keep going without the slavery of a job like this, even when you're old."

"I'm not so sure. My brain isn't what it was; it may soften altogether unless I do something with it before it's too late. Then there I shall be, a burden to myself and everyone else. … After all, Rodney, you've your job. Can't I have mine? Aren't you a modernist, an intellectual, and a feminist?"

Rodney, who believed with truth that he was all these things, gave in.

Kay and Gerda, with the large-minded tolerance of their years, thought mother's scheme was all right and rather sporting, if she really liked the sort of thing, which they, for their part, didn't.

So Neville recommenced medical student, and, as has been said, found it difficult beyond belief. It made her head ache.

▶•◀

II

She envied Kay and Gerda, as they all three lay and worked in the garden, with chocolates, cigarettes and Esau grouped comfortably round them. Kay was reading economics for his Tripos, Gerda was drawing pictures for her poems; neither, apparently, found any difficulty in concentrating on their work when they happened to want to.

What, Neville speculated, her thoughts, as usual, wandering from her book, would become of Gerda? She was a clever child at her own things, though with great gaps in her equipment of knowledge, which came from ignoring at school those of her studies which had not seemed to her to be of importance. She had firmly declined a University education; she had decided that it was not a fruitful start in life, and was also afraid of getting an academic mind. But at economic and social subjects, at drawing and at writing she worked without indolence, taking them earnestly, still young enough to believe it important that she should attain proficiency.

Neville, on the other hand, was indolent. For twenty-two years she had pleased herself, done what she wanted when she wanted to, played the flirt with life. And now she had become soft-willed. Now, sitting in the garden with her books, like Gerda and Kay, she would find that they had slipped from her knee and that she was listening to the birds in the elms. Or she would fling them aside and get up and stretch herself and stroll into the little wood beyond the garden, or down to the river, or she would propose tennis, or go up to town for some meeting or concert or to see someone, though she didn't really want to, having quite enough of London during that part of the year when they lived there. She only went up now because otherwise she would be working. At this rate she would never be ready to resume her medical course in the autumn.

"I will attend: I will: I will," she whispered to herself, a hand pressed to each temple to constrain her mind. And for five minutes she would attend, and then she would drift away on a sea of pleasant indolence, and time fluttered away from her like an escaping bird, and she knew herself for a light woman who would never excel. And Kay's brown head was bent over his book, and raised sometimes to chaff or talk, and bent over his books again, the thread of his attention unbroken by his easy interruptions. And Gerda's golden head lay pillowed in her two clasped hands, and she stared up at the blue through the green and did nothing at all, for that was often Gerda's unashamed way.

Often Rodney sat in the garden too and worked. And his work Neville felt that she, too, could have done; it was work needing initiative and creative thought, work suitable to his forty-five years, not cramming in knowledge from books. Neville at times thought that she, too, would stand for Parliament one day. A foolish, easy game it was, and probably really, therefore, more in her line than solid work.

III

Nan came down in July to stay with them. While she was there, Barry Briscoe, who was helping with a W.E.A. summer school at Haslemere, would come over on Sundays and spend the day with them. Not even the rains of July, 1920, made Barry weary or depressed. His eyes were bright behind his glasses; his hands were usually full of papers, committee reports, agenda, and the other foods he fed on, unsatiated and unashamed. Barry was splendid. What ardour, what enthusiasm, burning like beacons in a wrecked world! So wrecked a world that all but the very best and the very worst had given it up as a bad job; the best because they hoped on, hoped ever, the worst because of the pickings that fall to such as they out of the collapsing ruins. But Barry, from the very heart of the ruin, would cry, "Here is what we must do," and his eyes would gleam with faith and resolution, and he would form a committee and do it. And when he saw how the committee failed, as committees will, and how little good it all was, he would laugh ruefully and try something else. Barry, as he would tell you frankly if you inquired and not otherwise, believed in God. He was the son of a famous Quaker philanthropist, and had been brought up to see good works done and even garden cities built. I am aware that this must prejudice many people against Barry; and indeed many people were annoyed by certain aspects of him. But, as he was intellectually brilliant and personally attractive, these people were, as a rule, ready to overlook what they called the Quaker oats. Nan, who overlooked nothing, was frankly at war with him on some points, and he with her. Nan, cynical, clear-eyed, selfish, and *blasée*, cared nothing for the salvaging of what remained of the world out of the wreck, nothing for the I.L.P., less than nothing for garden cities, philanthropy, the W.E.A. and God. And committees she detested. Take them all away, and there remained Barry Briscoe, and for him she did not care nothing.

It was the oddest friendship, thought Neville, observing how, when Barry was there, all Nan's perversities and moods fell away, leaving her as agreeable as he. Her keen and ironic intelligence met his, and they so understood each other that they finished each other's sentences, and others present could only with difficulty keep up with them. Neville believed them to be in love, but did not know whether they had ever informed one another of the fact. They might still be pretending to one another that their friendship was merely one of those affectionate intellectual intimacies of which some of us have so many and which are so often misunderstood. Or they might not. It was entirely their business, either way.

Barry was a chatterbox. He lay on the lawn and rooted up daisies and made them into ridiculous chains, and talked and talked and talked. Rodney and Neville and Nan talked too, and Kay would lunge in with the crude and charming dogmatics of his years. But Gerda, chewing a blade of grass, lay idle and withdrawn, her fair brows unpuckered by the afternoon sun (because it was July, 1920), her blue eyes on Barry, who was so different; or else she would be withdrawn but not idle, for she would be drawing houses tumbling down, or men on stilts, fantastic and proud, or goblins, or geese running with outstretched necks round a green. Or she would be writing something like this:

> I
> Float on the tide,
> In the rain.
> I am the starfish vomited up by the retching cod.
> He thinks
> That I am he.
> But I know
> That he is I.
> For the creature is far greater than its god.

(Gerda was of those who think it is rather chic to have one rhyme in your poem, just to show that you can do it.)

"That child over there makes one feel so cheap and ridiculous, jabbering away."

That was Barry, breaking off to look at Gerda, where she lay on her elbows on a rug, idle and still. "And it's not," he went on, "that she doesn't know about the subject, either. I've heard her on it."

He threw the daisy chain he had just made at her, so that it alighted on her head, hanging askew over one eye.

"Just like a daisy bud herself, isn't she?" he commented, and raced on, forgetting her.

Neat in her person and ways, Gerda adjusted the daisy chain so that it ringed her golden head in an orderly circle. Like a daisy bud herself, Rodney agreed in his mind, his eyes smiling at her, his affection, momentarily turned that way, groping for the wild, remote little soul in her that he only vaguely and paternally knew. The little pretty. And clever, too, in her own queer, uneven way. But what *was* she, with it all? He knew Kay, the long, sweet-tempered boy, better. For Kay represented highly civilised, passably educated, keen-minded youth. Gerda wasn't highly civilised, was hardly passably educated, and keen would be an inapt word for that queer, remote, woodland mind of hers. ... Rodney returned to more soluble problems.

▶•◀

IV

Mrs. Hilary and Grandmamma came to Windover. Mrs. Hilary would rather have come without Grandmamma, but Grandmamma enjoyed the jaunt, as she called it. For eighty-four, Grandmamma was wonderfully sporting. They arrived on Saturday afternoon, and rested after the journey, which is usually done by people of Grandmamma's age, and often by people of Mrs. Hilary's. Sunday was full of such delicate clashings as occur when new people have joined a party. Grandmamma was for morning church, and Neville drove her to it in the pony carriage. So Mrs. Hilary, not being able to endure that they should go off alone together, had to go too, though she did not like church, morning or other.

She sighed over it at lunch.

"So stuffy. So long. And the *hymns.* ..."

But Grandmamma said, "My dear, we had David and Goliath. What more do you want?"

During David and Goliath Grandmamma's head had nodded approvingly, and her thin old lips had half smiled at the valiant child with his swaggering lies about bears and lions, at the gallant child and the giant.

Mrs. Hilary, herself romantically sensible, as middle-aged ladies are, of valour and high adventure, granted Grandmamma David and Goliath, but still repined at the hymns and the sermon.

"Good words, my dear, good words," Grandmamma said to that. For Grandmamma had been brought up not to criticise sermons, but had failed to bring up Mrs. Hilary to the same self-abnegation. The trouble with Mrs. Hilary was, and had always been, that she expected (even now) too much of life. Grandmamma only expected what she got. And Neville, wisest of all, had not listened, for she too expected what she would get if she did. She was really rather like Grandmamma, in her cynically patient acquiescence, only brought up in a different generation, and not to hear sermons. In the gulf of years between these two, Mrs. Hilary's restless, questing passion fretted like unquiet waves.

►•◄

V

"This Barry Briscoe," said Mrs. Hilary to Neville after lunch, as she watched him and Nan start off for a walk together. "I suppose he's in love with her?"

"I suppose so. Something of the kind, anyhow."

Mrs. Hilary said discontentedly, "Another of Nan's married men, no doubt. She *collects* them."

"No, Barry's not married."

Mrs. Hilary looked more interested. "Not? Oh, then it may come to something. ... I wish Nan *would* marry. It's quite time."

"Nan isn't exactly keen to, you know. She's got so much else to do."

"Fiddlesticks! You don't encourage her in such nonsense, I hope, Neville."

"I? It's not for me to encourage Nan in anything. She doesn't need it. But as to marriage—yes, I think I wish she would do it, sometime, whenever she's ready. It would give her something she hasn't got; emotional steadiness, perhaps, I mean. She squanders a bit now. On the other hand, her writing would rather go to the wall; if she went on with it it would be against odds all the time."

"What's writing?" inquired Mrs. Hilary, with a snap of her finger and thumb. "*Writing!*"

As this seemed too vague or too large a question for Neville to answer, she did not try to do so, and Mrs. Hilary replied to it herself.

"Mere showing off," she explained it. "Throwing your paltry ideas at a world which doesn't want them. Writing like Nan's, I mean. It's not as if she wrote really good books."

"Oh, well. Who does that, after all? And what *is* a good book?"

Here were two questions which Mrs. Hilary, in her turn, could not answer. Because most of the books which seemed good to her did not, as she well knew, seem good to Neville, or to any of her children, and she wasn't going to give herself away. She murmured something about Thackeray and Dickens, which Neville let pass.

"Writing's just a thing to do, as I see it," Neville went on. "A job, like another. One must *have* a job, you know. Not for the money, but for the job's sake. And Nan enjoys it. But I dare say she'd enjoy marriage too."

"Does she love this man?"

"I don't know. I shouldn't be surprised. She hasn't told me so."

"Probably she doesn't, as he's single. Nan's so perverse. She will love the wrong men, always."

"You shouldn't believe all Rosalind tells you, mother. Rosalind has a too vivid fancy and a scandalous tongue."

Mrs. Hilary coloured a little. She did not like Neville to think that she had been letting Rosalind gossip to her about Nan.

"You know perfectly well, Neville, that I never trust a word Rosalind says. I suppose I needn't rely on my daughter-in-law for news about my own daughter's affairs. I can see things for myself. You can't deny that Nan *has* had compromising affairs with married men."

"Compromising." Neville turned over the word, thoughtfully and fastidiously. "Funny word, mother. I'm not sure I know what it means. But I don't think anything ever compromises Nan; she's too free for that. ... Well, let's marry her off to Barry Briscoe. It will be a quaint *ménage*, but I dare say they'd pull it off. Barry's delightful. I should think even Nan could live with him."

"He writes books about education, doesn't he? Education and democracy."

"Well, he does. But there's always something, after all, against all of us. And it might be worse. It might be poetry or fiction or psycho-analysis."

Neville said psycho-analysis in order to start another hare and take her mother's attention off Nan's marriage before the marriage became crystallised out of all being. But Mrs. Hilary, for the first time (for usually she was reliable), did not rise. She looked thoughtful, even a shade embarrassed, and said vaguely, "Oh, people must write, of course. If it isn't one thing it will be another." After a moment she added, "This psycho-analysis, Neville," saying the word with distaste indeed, but so much more calmly than usual that Neville looked at her in surprise. "This psycho-analysis. I suppose it does make wonderful cures, doesn't it, when all is said?"

"Cures—oh, yes; wonderful cures. Shell-shock, insomnia, nervous depression, lumbago, suicidal mania, family life—anything." Neville's attention was straying to Grandmamma, who was coming slowly towards them down the path, leaning on her stick, so she did not see Mrs. Hilary's curious, lit eagerness.

"But how *can* they cure all those things just by talking indecently about sex?"

"Oh, mother, they don't. You're so crude, darling. You've got hold of only one tiny part of it—the part practised by Austrian professors on Viennese degenerates. Many of the doctors are really sane and brilliant. I know of cases ..."

"Well," said Mrs. Hilary, quickly and rather crossly, "I can't talk about it before Grandmamma."

Neville got up to meet Grandmamma, put a hand under her arm, and conducted her to her special chair beneath the cedar. You had to help and conduct someone so old, so frail, so delightful, as Grandmamma, even if Mrs. Hilary did wish it were being done by any hand than yours. Mrs. Hilary, in fact, made a movement to get to Grandmamma first, but sixty-three does not rise from low deck-chairs so swiftly as forty-three. So she had to watch her daughter leading her mother, and to note once more with a familiar pang the queer unmistakable likeness between the smooth, clear, oval face, and the old wrinkled one, the heavily-lashed deep blue eyes and the old faded ones, the elfish, close-lipped, dimpling smile and the old, elfish, thin-lipped, sweet one. Neville, her Neville, flower of her flock, her loveliest first and best, her dearest but for Jim, her pride, and nearer than Jim, because of sex, which set Jim on a platform to be worshipped, but kept Neville on a level to be loved, to be stormed at when storms rose, to be clung to when all God's waters went over one's head. Oh, Neville, that you should smile at Grandmamma like that, that Grandmamma should, as she always had, steal your confidence that should have been all your mother's! That you should, perhaps, even talk over your mother with Grandmamma (as if she were something farther from each of you than each from the other), pushing her out of the close circle of your intimacy into the region of problems to be solved. … Oh, God, how bitter a thing to bear!

The garden, the summer border of bright flowers, swam in tears. … Mrs. Hilary turned away her face, pretending to be pulling up daisies from the grass. But she was not really like an ostrich, for well she knew that they always saw. To the children, as to Grandmamma, they were an old story, those hot, facile, stinging tears of Mrs. Hilary's, that made Neville weary with pity, and Nan cold with scorn, and Rosalind happy with lazy malice, and Pamela bright and cool and firm, like a woman doctor. Only Grandmamma took them unmoved, for she had always known them.

►•◄

VI

Grandmamma, settled in her special chair, remarked on the unusual (for July) fineness of the day, and requested Neville to read them the chief items of news in the *Observer*, which she had brought out with her. So Neville read about the unfortunate doings of the Supreme Council at Spa, and Grandmamma said, "Poor creatures," tolerantly, as she had said when they were at Paris, and again at San Remo; and about General Dyer and the Amritsar debate, and Grandmamma said, "Poor man. But one mustn't treat one's fellow creatures as he did, even the poor Indian, who, I quite believe, is intolerably provoking. I see the *Morning Post* is getting up a subscription for him, contributed to by Those who Remember Cawnpore, Haters of Trotsky, Montague, and Lansbury, Furious Englishwoman, and many other generous and emotional people. That is kind and right. We should not let even our more impulsive generals starve."

Then Neville read about Ireland, which was just then in a disturbed state, and Grandmamma said it certainly seemed restless, and mentioned that her friends the Dormers were there, with what looked like a gleam of hope that they would never return. Mrs. Hilary shot out, with still averted face, that the whole of Ireland ought to be sunk to the bottom of the sea, it was more bother than it was worth, which was her usual and only contribution towards a solution of the Irish question.

Then Mr. Churchill and Russia had their turn (it was the time of the Golovin trouble), and Grandmamma said people seemed always to get so very sly, as well as so very much annoyed and excited, whenever Russia was mentioned, and that seemed like a sign that God did not mean us, in this country, to mention it much, perhaps not even to think of it. She personally seldom did. Then Neville read a paragraph about the

Anglo-Catholic Congress, and about that Grandmamma was for the first time a little severe, for Grandpapa had not been an Anglo-Catholic, and indeed in his day there were none of these, you were either High Church, Broad Church or Evangelical. (Unless, of course, you had been led astray by Huxley and Darwin, and were nothing of the sort.) Grandpapa had been Broad, with a dash of Evangelical; or perhaps it was the other way round; but anyhow Grandpapa had not been High Church, or, as they called it in his time, Tractarian. So Grandmamma inquired, snippily, "Who *are* these Anglo-Catholics, my dear? One seems to hear so much of them in these days. I can't help thinking they are rather *noisy* ..." as she might have spoken of Bolshevists, or the Labour Party, or the National Party, or Sinn Fein, or any other of the organisations of which Grandpapa had been innocent. "There are so many of these new things," said Grandmamma. "I dare say modern young people like Gerda and Kay are quite in with it all."

"I'm afraid," said Neville, "that Gerda and Kay are secularists at present."

"Poor children," Grandmamma said gently. Secularism made her think of the violent and vulgar Mr. Bradlaugh. It was, in her view, a noisier thing even than Anglo-Catholicism. "Well, they have plenty of time to get over it and settle down to something quieter." Broad-Evangelical, she meant, or Evangelical-Broad; and Neville smiled at the idea of Gerda, in particular, as either of these, believing that if Gerda were to turn from secularism it would either be to Anglo-Catholicism or to Rome. Or Gerda might become a Quaker, or a lone mystic contemplating in woods, but a Broad-Evangelical, no. There was a delicate, reckless extravagance about Gerda which would prohibit that. If you came to that, what girl or boy did, in these days, fall into any of the categories which Grandmamma and Grandpapa had known, whether religiously or politically? You might as well suggest that Gerda and Kay should be Tories or Whigs.

And by this time they had given Mrs. Hilary so much time to recover her poise that she could join in, and say that Anglo-Catholics were very ostentatious people, and only gave all that money which they had, undoubtedly, given at the recent Congress in order to make a splash and show off.

"Tearing off their jewellery in public like that," said Mrs. Hilary, in disgust, as she might have said "tearing off their chemises," "and gold watches lying in piles on the collection table, still ticking ..." It was indecent, she felt, that the watches should have been still ticking; it made the thing an orgy, like a revival meeting, or some cannibal rite at which victims were offered up still breathing. ...

So much for the Anglo-Catholic Congress. The Church Congress was better, being more decent and in order, though Mrs. Hilary knew that the whole Established Church was wrong.

And so they came to literature, to a review of Mr. Conrad's new novel and a paragraph about a famous annual literary prize. Grandmamma thought it very nice that young writers should be encouraged by cash prizes. "Not," as she added, "that there seems any danger of any of them being discouraged even without that. ... But Nan and Kay and Gerda ought to go in for it. It would be a nice thing for them to work for."

Then Grandmamma, settling down with her pleased old smile to something which mattered more than the news in the papers, said, "And now, dear, I want to hear all about this friendship of Nan's and this nice young Mr. Briscoe."

So Neville again had to answer questions about that.

VII

Mrs. Hilary, abruptly leaving them, trailed away by herself to the house. Since she mightn't have Neville to herself for the afternoon she wouldn't stay and share her. But when she reached the house and looked out at them through the drawing-room windows, their intimacy stabbed her with a pang so sharp that she wished she had stayed.

Besides, what was there to do indoors? No novels lay about that looked readable, only *The Rescue* (and she couldn't read Conrad, he was so nautical), and a few others which looked deficient in plot and as if they were trying to be clever. She turned them over restlessly, and put them down again. She wasn't sleepy, and hated writing letters. She wanted some one to talk to, and there was no one, unless she rang for the housemaid. Oh, this dreadful ennui. ... Did any one in the world know it but her? The others all seemed busy and bright. That was because they were young. And Grandmamma seemed serene and bright. That was because she was old, close to the edge of life, and sat looking over the gulf into space, not caring. But for Mrs. Hilary there was ennui, and the dim, empty room in the cold grey July afternoon. The empty stage: no audience, no actors. Only a lonely, disillusioned actress trailing about it, hungry for the past. ... A book Gerda had been reading lay on the table. *The Breath of Life* it was called, which was surely just what Mrs. Hilary wanted. She picked it up, opened it, turned the pages, then, tucking it away out of sight under her arm, left the room and went upstairs.

"Many wonderful cures," Neville had said. And had mentioned depression as one of the diseases cured. What, after all, if there was something in this stuff which she had never tried to understand, had always dismissed, according to her habit, with a single label? "Labels don't help. Labels get you nowhere." How often the children had told her that, finding her terse terminology that of a shallow mind, endowed with inadequate machinery for acquiring and retaining knowledge, as indeed it was.

►•◄

VIII

Gerda, going up to Mrs. Hilary's room to tell her about tea, found her asleep on the sofa, with *The Breath of Life* fallen open from her hand. A smile flickered on Gerda's delicate mouth, for she had heard her grandmother on the subject of psycho-analysis, and here she was, having taken to herself the book which Gerda was reading for her Freud circle. Gerda read a paragraph on the open page.

"It will often be found that what we believe to be unhappiness is really, in the secret and unconscious self, a joy, which the familiar process of inversion sends up into our consciousness in the form of grief. If, for instance, a mother bewails the illness of her child, it is because her unconscious is experiencing the pleasure of importance, of being condoled and sympathised with, as also that of having her child (if it is a male) entirely for the time dependent on her ministrations. If, on the other hand, the sick child is her daughter, her grief is in reality a hope that this, her young rival, may die, and leave her supreme in the affections of her husband. If, in either of these cases, she can be brought to face and understand this truth, her grief will invert itself again and become a conscious joy. ..."

"I wonder if Grandmother believes all that," speculated Gerda, who did.

Then she said aloud, "Grandmother" (that was what Gerda and Kay called her, distinguishing her thus from Great-Grandmamma), "tea's ready."

Mrs. Hilary woke with a start. *The Breath of Life* fell on the floor with a bang. Mrs. Hilary looked up and saw Gerda, and blushed.

"I've been asleep. ... I took up this ridiculous book of yours to look at. The most absurd stuff. ... How can you children muddle your minds with

– 54 –

it? Besides, it isn't at all a *nice* book for you, my child. I came on several very queer things. ..."

But the candid innocence of Gerda's wide blue eyes on hers transcended "nice" and "not nice." ... You might as well talk like that to a wood anemone, or a wild rabbit. ... If her grandmother had only known, Gerda at twenty had discussed things which Mrs. Hilary, in all her sixty-three years, had never heard mentioned. Gerda knew of things of which Mrs. Hilary would have indignantly and sincerely denied the existence. Gerda's young mind was a cesspool, a clear little dew-pond, according to how you looked at it. Gerda and Gerda's friends knew no inhibitions of speech or thought. They believed that the truth would make them free, and the truth about life is, from some points of view, a squalid and gross thing. But better look it in the face, thought Gerda and her contemporaries, than pretend it isn't there, as elderly people do.

"I don't want you to pretend anything isn't there, darling," Neville, between the two generations, had said to Gerda once. "Only it seems to me that some of you children have one particular kind of truth too heavily on your minds. It seems to block the world for you."

"You mean sex," Gerda had told her bluntly. "Well, it runs all through life, mother. What's the use of hiding from it? The only way to get even with it is to face it. And *use* it."

"Face it and use it by all means. All I meant was, it's a question of emphasis. There *are* other things. ..."

Of course Gerda knew that. There was drawing, and poetry, and beauty, and dancing, and swimming, and music, and politics, and economics. Of course there were other things; no doubt about that. They were like songs, like colour, like sunrise, like flowers, these other things. But the basis of life was the desire of the male for the female and of the female for the male. And this had been warped and smothered and talked down and made a furtive, shameful thing, and it must be brought out into the day. ...

Neville smiled to hear all this tripping sweetly off Gerda's lips.

"All right, darling, don't mind me. Go ahead and bring it out into the day, if you think the subject really needs more airing than it already gets. I should have thought myself it got lots, and always had."

And there they were; they talked at cross purposes these two, across the gulf of twenty years, and with the best will in the world could not hope to understand, either of them, what the other was really at. And now here was Gerda, in Mrs. Hilary's bedroom, looking across a gulf of forty years, and saying nothing at all, for she knew it would be of no manner of use, since words don't carry as far as that.

So all she said was, "Tea's ready, grandmother."

And Mrs. Hilary supposed that Gerda hadn't, probably, noticed or understood those very queer things she had come upon while reading *The Breath of Life*.

They went down to tea.

CHAPTER IV

ROOTS

▶•◀

I

It was a Monday evening, late in July. Pamela Hilary, returning from a Care Committee meeting, fitted her latch-key into the door of the rooms in Cow Lane which she shared with Frances Carr, and let herself into the hot dark passage hall.

A voice from a room on the right called, "Come along, my dear. Your pap's ready."

Pamela entered the room on the right. A pleasant, Oxfordish room, with the brown paper and plain green curtains of the college days of these women, and Dürer engravings, and sweet peas in a bowl, and Frances Carr stirring bread and milk over a gas ring. Frances Carr was small and thirty-eight, and had a nice brown face and a merry smile. Pamela was a year older, and tall and straight and pale, and her ash-brown hair swept smoothly back from a broad white forehead. Her grey eyes regarded the world shrewdly and pleasantly through pince-nez. Pamela was distinguished-looking, and so well-bred that you never got through her guard; she never hurt the feelings of others or betrayed her own. Competent she was, too, and the best organiser in Hoxton, which is to say a great deal, Hoxton needing and getting, one way and another, a good deal of organisation. Some people complained that they couldn't get to know Pamela, the guard was too complete. But Frances Carr knew her.

Frances Carr had piled cushions in a deep chair for her.

"Lie back and be comfy, old thing, and I'll give you your pap."

She handed Pamela the steaming bowl, and proceeded to take off her friend's shoes and substitute moccasin slippers. It was thus that she and Pamela had mothered one another at Somerville eighteen years ago, and ever since. They had the maternal instinct, like so many women.

"Well, how went it? How was Mrs. Cox?"

Mrs. Cox was the chairwoman of the committee. All committee members know that the chairman or woman is a ticklish problem, if not a sore burden.

"Oh, well ..." Pamela dismissed Mrs. Cox with half a smile. "Might have been worse. ... Oh, look here, Frank, about the library fund ..."

The front door bell tingled through the house.

Frances Carr said, "Oh, hang. All right, I'll see to it. If it's Care or Continuation or Library, I shall send it away. You're not going to do any more business to-night."

She went to the door, and there, her lithe, drooping slimness outlined against the gas-lit street, stood Nan Hilary.

"Oh, Nan. ... But what a late call. Yes, Pamela's just in from a committee. Tired to death; she's had neuralgia all this week. She mustn't sit up late, really. But come along in."

▶•◀

II

Nan came into the room, her dark eyes blinking against the gas light, her small round face pale and smutty. She bent to kiss Pamela, then curled herself up in a wicker chair and yawned.

"The night is damp and dirty. No, no food, thanks; I dined. After dinner I was bored, so I came along to pass the time. ... When are you taking your holidays, both of you? It's time."

"Pamela's going for hers next week," said Frances Carr, handing Nan a cigarette.

"On the contrary," said Pamela, "Frances is going for *hers* next week. Mine is to be September this year."

"Now we've had all this out before, Pam, you know we have. You faithfully promised to take August if your neuralgia came on again, and it has. Tell her she is to, Nan."

"She wouldn't do it the more if I did," Nan said lazily. These competitions in unselfishness between Pamela and Frances Carr always bored her. There was no end to them. Women are so terrifically self-abnegatory; they must give, give, give to someone all the time. Women, that is, of the mothering type, such as these. They must be for ever cherishing something, sending someone to bed with bread and milk, guarding someone from fatigue.

"It ought to be their children," thought Nan swiftly. "But they pour it out on one another instead."

Having put her hand on the clue, she ceased to be interested in the exhibition. It was, in fact, no more and no less interesting than if it *had* been their children. Most sorts of love were rather dull, to the spectator. Pamela and Frances were all right; decent people, not soppy, not gushing, but fine and direct and keen, though rather boring when they began to talk to each other about some silly old thing that had happened in their last year at Oxford, or their first year, or on some reading party. Some people re-live their lives like this; others pass on their way, leaving the past behind. They were all right, Pamela and Frances. But all this mothering. ...

Yet how happy they were, these two, in their useful, competent work and devoted friendship. They had achieved contacts with life, permanent contacts. Pamela, in spite of her neuralgia, expressed calm and entirely unbumptious attainment. Nan feverish seeking. For Nan's contacts with life were not permanent, but sudden and vivid and passing; the links broke and she flew off at a tangent. Nan had lately been taken with a desperate fear of becoming like her mother, when she was old and couldn't write any more, or love any more men. Horrible thought, to be like Mrs. Hilary, roaming, questing, feverishly devoured by her own impatience of life. ...

In here it was cool and calm, soft and blurred with the smoke of their cigarettes. Frances Carr left them to talk, telling them not to be late. When she had gone, Pamela said, "I thought you were still down at Windover, Nan."

"Left it on Saturday. ... Mother and Grandmamma had been there a week. I couldn't stick it any longer. Mother was outrageously jealous, of course."

"Neville and Grandmamma? Poor mother."

"Oh, yes, poor mother. But it gets on my nerves. Neville's an angel. I can't think how she sticks it. For that matter, I never know how she puts up with Rodney's spoilt fractiousness. ... And altogether life was a bit of a strain. ... No peace. And I wanted some peace and solitude, to make up my mind in."

"Are you making it up now?" Pamela, mildly interested, presumed it was a man.

"Trying to. It isn't made yet. That's why I roam about your horrible slums in the dark. I'm considering; getting things into focus. Seeing them all round."

"Well, that sounds all right."

"Pam." Nan leant forward abruptly, her cigarette between two brown fingers. "Are you happy? Do you enjoy your life?"

Pamela withdrew, lightly, inevitably, behind guards.

"Within reason, yes. When committees aren't too tiresome, and the accounts balance, and ..."

"Oh, give me a straight answer, Pam. You dependable, practical people are always frivolous about things that matter. Are you happy? Do you feel upsides with life?"

"In the main—yes." Pamela was more serious this time. "One's doing one's job, after all. And human beings are interesting."

"But I've got that too. My job, and human beings. ... Why do I feel all tossed about, like a boat on a choppy sea? Oh, I know life's furiously amusing and exciting—of course it is. But I want something solid. You've got it, somehow."

Nan broke off and thought, "It's Frances Carr she's got. That's permanent. That goes on. Pamela's anchored. All these people I have—these men and women—they're not anchors, they're stimulants, and how different that is!"

They looked at each other in silence. Pamela said then, "You don't look well, child."

"Oh—" Nan threw her cigarette end impatiently into the grate. "I'm all right. I'm tired, and I've been thinking too much. That never suits me. ... Thanks, Pam. You've helped me to make up my mind. I like you, Pam," she added dispassionately, "because you're so gentlewomanly. You don't ask questions, or pry. Most people do."

"Surely not. Not most decent people."

"Most people aren't decent. You think they are. You've not lived in my set—nor in Rosalind's. You're still fresh from Oxford—stuck all over with Oxford manners and Oxford codes. You don't know the raddled gossip who fishes for your secrets and then throws them about for fun, like tennis balls."

"I know Rosalind, thank you, Nan."

"Oh, Rosalind's not the only one, though she'll do. Anyhow, I've trapped you into saying an honest and unkind thing about her for once; that's something. Wish you weren't such a dear old fraud, Pammie."

Frances Carr came back, in her dressing-gown, looking about twenty-three, her brown hair in two plaits.

"Pamela, you *mustn't* sit up any more. I'm awfully sorry, Nan, but her head ..."

"Right-o. I'm off. Sorry I've kept you up, Pammie. Good night. Good night, Frances. Yes, I shall get the bus at the corner. Good night."

The door closed after Nan, shutting in the friends and their friendship and their anchored peace.

►•◄

III

Off went Nan on the bus at the corner, whistling softly into the night. Like a bird her heart rose up and sang, at the lit pageant of London swinging by. Queer, fantastic, most lovely life! Sordid, squalid, grotesque life, bitter as black tea, sour as stale wine! Gloriously funny, brilliant as a flowerbed, bright as a street in hell—

> (Down in Hell's gilded street
> Snow dances fleet and sweet,
> Bright as a parakeet. ...)

unsteady as a swing-boat, silly as a drunkard's dream, tragic as a poem by Masefield. ... To have one's corner in it, to run here and there about the city, grinning like a dog—what more did one want? Human adventures, intellectual adventures, success, even a little fame, men and women, jokes, laughter and love, dancing and a little drink, and the fields and mountains and seas beyond—what more did one want?

Roots. That was the metaphor that had eluded Nan. To be rooted and grounded in life, like a tree. Someone had written something about that—

> Let your manhood be
> Forgotten, your whole purpose seem
> The purpose of a simple tree
> Rooted in a quiet dream. ...

Roots. That was what Neville had, what Pamela had; Pamela, with her sensible wisdom that so often didn't apply because Pamela was so far removed from Nan's conditions of life and Nan's complicated, unstable temperament. Roots. Mrs. Hilary's had been torn up out of the ground. ...

"I'm like mother." That was Nan's nightmare thought. Not intellectually, for Nan's brain was sharp and subtle and strong and fine, and Mrs. Hilary's an amorphous, undeveloped muddle. But where, if not from Mrs. Hilary, did Nan get her black fits of melancholy, her erratic and irresponsible gaieties, her passionate angers, her sharp jealousies and egotisms? The clever young woman saw herself in the stupid elderly one; saw herself slipping down the years to that. That was why, where Neville and Pamela and their brothers pitied, Nan, understanding her mother's bad moods better than they, was vicious with hate and scorn. For she knew these things through and through. Not the sentimentality; she didn't know that, being cynical and cool except when stirred to passion. And not the posing, for Nan was direct and blunt. But the feverish angers and the black boredom—they were hers.

Nevertheless, Nan's heart sang into the night. For she had made up her mind, and was at peace.

She had held life at arm's length, pushed it away, for many months, hiding from it, running from it, because she didn't with the whole of her want it. Again and again she had changed a dangerous subject, headed for safety, raced for cover. The week-end before this last, down at Windover, it had been like a game of hide-and-seek. ... And then she had come away, without warning, and he, going down there this last week-end, had not found her, because she couldn't meet him again till she had decided. And now she had decided.

How unsuited a pair they were, in many ways, and what fun they would have! Unsuited ... what did it matter? His queer, soft, laughing voice was in her ears, his lean, clever, merry face swam on the rushing tides of the night. His untidy, careless clothes, the pockets bulging with books, papers, and tobacco, his glasses, that left a red mark on either side of the bridge of his nose, his easily ruffled brown hair—they all merged for her into the infinitely absurd, infinitely delightful, infinitely loved Barry, who was going to give her roots.

She was going away, down into Cornwall, in two days. She would stay in rooms by herself at Marazion, and finish her book, and bathe and climb and lie in the sun (if only it came out), and sleep and eat and drink. There was nothing in the world like your own company; you could be purely animal then. And in a month Gerda and Kay were coming down, and they were going to bicycle along the coast, and she would ask Barry to come too, and when Barry came she would let him say what he liked, with no more fencing, no more cover. Down by the green edge of the Cornish sea they would have it out—"grip hard, become a root. ..." become men and trees walking, rooted in a quiet dream. Dream? No, reality. This was the dream, this world of slipping shadows and hurrying gleams of heartbreaking loveliness, through which one roamed, a child chasing butterflies that ever escaped, or, if captured, crumbled to dust in one's clutching hands. Oh, for something strong and firm to hold! Oh, Barry, Barry, these few more weeks of dream, of slipping golden shadows and wavering lights, and then reality. Shall I write, thought Nan, "Dear Barry, you may ask me to marry you now"? Impossible. Besides, what hurry was there? Better to have these few more gay and lovely weeks of dream. They would be the last.

Has Barry squandered and spilt his love about as I mine? Likely enough. Likely enough not. Who cares? Perhaps we shall tell one another all these things sometime; perhaps, again, we shan't. What matter? One loves, and passes on, and loves again. One's heart cracks and mends; one cracks the hearts of others, and these mend too. That is—*inter alia*—what life is for. If one day you want the tale of my life, Barry, you shall have it; though that's not what life is for, to make a tale about. So thrilling in the living, so flat and stale in the telling—oh, let's get on and live some more of it, lots and lots more, and let the dread past bury its dead.

Between a laugh and a sleepy yawn Nan jumped from the bus at the corner of Oakley Street.

CHAPTER V

SEAWEED

▶•◀

I

"Complexes," read Mrs. Hilary, "are of all sorts and sizes." And there was a picture of four of them in a row, looking like netted cherry-trees whose nets have got entangled with each other. So that was what they were like. Mrs. Hilary had previously thought of them as being more of the nature of noxious insects, or fibrous growths with infinite ramifications. Slim young trees. Not so bad, then, after all.

"A complex is characterised, and its elements are bound together by a specific emotional tone, experienced as feeling when the complex is aroused. Apart from the mental processes and corresponding actions depending on purely rational mental systems, it is through complexes that the typical mental process (the specific response) works, the particular complex representing the particular set of mental elements involved in the process which begins with perception and cognition and ends with the corresponding conation."

Mrs. Hilary read it three times, and the third time she understood it, if possible, less than the first. Complexes seemed very difficult things, and she had never been clever. Any of her children, or even her grandchildren, would understand it all in a moment. If you have such things—and every one has, she had learnt—you ought to be able to understand them. Yet why? You didn't understand your bodily internal growths; you left them to your doctor. There were doctors who explained your complexes to you. …

What a revolting idea! It would surely make them worse, not better. (Mrs. Hilary still vaguely regarded these growths as something of the nature of cancer.)

Sometimes she imagined herself a patient, interviewing one of these odd doctors. A man doctor, not a woman; she didn't trust women doctors of any kind; she had always been thankful that Neville had given it up and married instead.

"Insomnia," she would say, in these imaginary interviews, because that was so easy to start off with.

"You have something on your mind," the doctor would say. "You suffer from depression."

"Yes, I know that. I was coming to that. That is what you must cure for me."

"You must think back. … What is the earliest thing you can remember? Perhaps your baptism? Possibly even your first bath? It has been done …"

"You may be right. I remember some early baths. One of them may have been the first of all, who knows? What of it, doctor?"

But the doctor, in her imaginings, would at this point only make notes in a big book and keep silence, as if he had thought as much … Perhaps he knew no more than she of it.

Mrs. Hilary could hear herself protesting.

"I am *not* unhappy because of my baptism, which, so far as I know, went off without a hitch. I am *not* troubled by my first bath, nor by any later bath. Indeed, indeed, you must believe me, it is not that at all."

"The more they protest," the psycho-analyst would murmur, "the more it is so." For that was what Dr. Freud and Dr. Jung always said, so that there was no escape from their aspersions.

"Why do *you* think you are so often unhappy?" he would ask her, to draw her out, and she would reply, "Because my life is over. Because I am an old, discarded woman, thrown away on to the dust-heap like a broken eggshell. Because my husband is gone and my children are gone, and they do not love me as I love them. Because I have only my mother to live with, and she is calm and cares for nothing but only waits for the end. Because I have nothing to do from morning till night. Because I am sixty-three, and that is too old and too young. Because life is empty and disappointing, and I am tired, and drift like seaweed tossed to and fro by the waves."

It sounded indeed enough, and tears would fill her eyes as she said it. The psycho-analyst would listen, passive and sceptical but intelligent.

"Not one of your reasons is the correct one. But I will find the true reason for you and expose it, and after that it will trouble you no more. Now you shall relate to me the whole history of your life."

What a comfortable moment! Mrs. Hilary, when she came to it in her imagined interview, would draw a deep breath and settle down and begin. The story of her life! How absorbing a thing to relate to someone who really wanted to hear it! How far better than the confessional, for priests, besides requiring only those portions and parcels of the dreadful past upon which you had least desire to dwell, had almost certainly no interest at all in hearing even these, but only did it because they had to, and you would be boring them. They might even say, as one had said to Rosalind during the first confession which had inaugurated her brief ecclesiastical career, and to which she had looked forward with some interest as a luxurious re-living of a stimulating past—"No details, please." Rosalind, who had had many details ready, had come away disappointed, feeling that the Church was not all she had hoped. But the psycho-analyst doctor would really want to hear details. Of course he would prefer the kind of detail which Rosalind would have been able to furnish out of her experience, for that was what psycho-analysts recognised as true life. Mrs. Hilary's experiences were pale in comparison; but psycho-analysts could and did make much out of little, bricks without clay. She would tell him all about the children—how sweet they had been as babies, how Jim had nearly died of croup, Neville of bronchitis, and Nan of convulsions, whereas Pamela had always been so well, and Gilbert had only suffered from infant debility. She would relate how early and how unusually they had all given signs of intelligence; how Jim had always loved her more than anything in the world, until his marriage, and she him (this was a firm article in Mrs. Hilary's creed); how Neville had always cherished and cared for her, and how she loved Neville beyond anything in the world but Jim; how Gilbert had disappointed her by taking to writing instead of a man's job, and then by marrying Rosalind; how Nan had always been tiresome and perverse. And before the children came—all about Richard, and their courtship, and their young married life, and how he had loved and cared for her beyond anything, incredibly tenderly and well, so that all those who saw it had wondered, and some had said he spoilt her. And back before Richard, to girlhood and childhood, to parents and nursery, to her brother and sister, now dead. How she had fought with her sister, because they had both always wanted the same things and got in one another's way! The jealousies, the bitter, angry tears!

To pour it all out—what comfort! To feel that someone was interested, even though it might be only as in a case. The trouble about most people was that they weren't interested. They didn't, mostly, even pretend they were.

II

She tried Barry Briscoe, the week-end he came down and found Nan gone. Barry Briscoe was by way of being interested in people and things in general; he had that kind of alert mind and face.

He came up from the tennis lawn, where he had been playing a single with Rodney, and sat down by her Grandmamma in the shade of the cedar, hot and friendly and laughing and out of breath. Now Neville and Rodney were playing Gerda and Kay. Grandmamma's old eyes, pleased behind their glasses, watched the balls fly and thought every one clever who got one over the net. She hadn't played tennis in her youth. Mrs. Hilary's more eager, excited eyes watched Neville driving, smashing volleying, returning, and thought how slim and young a thing she looked, to have all that power stored in her. She was fleeter than Gerda, she struck harder than Kay, she was trickier than all of them, the beloved girl. That was the way Mrs. Hilary watched tennis, thinking of the players, not of the play. It is the way some people talk, thinking of the talkers, not of what they are saying. It is the personal touch, and a way some women have.

But Barry Briscoe, watching cleverly through his bright glasses, was thinking of the strokes. He was an unconscious person. He lived in moments.

"Well done, Gerda," Grandmamma would call when Gerda, cool and nonchalant, dropped a sitter at Rodney's feet, and when Rodney smashed it back she said, "But father's too much for you."

"Gerda's a scandal," Barry said. "She doesn't care. She can hit all right when she likes. She thinks about something else half the time."

His smile followed the small white figure with its bare golden head that gleamed in the grey afternoon. An absurd, lovable, teaseable child, he found her.

Grandmamma's maid came to wheel her down to the farm. Grandmamma had promised to go and see the farmer's wife and new baby. Grandmamma always saw wives and new babies when there were any. They never palled. You would think that by eighty-four she had seen enough new babies, more than enough, that she had seen through that strange business and could now take it for granted, the stream of funny new life cascading into the already so full world. But Grandmamma would always go and see it, handle it, admire it, peer at it with her smiling eyes that had seen so many lives come and go, and that must know, by now, that babies are born to trouble as the sparks fly upward.

So off Grandmamma rode in her wheeled chair, and Mrs. Hilary and Barry Briscoe were left alone; Mrs. Hilary and this pleasant, brown, friendly young man, who cared for Workers' Education, and Continuation Schools, and Penal Reform, and Garden Cities, and Getting Things Done by Acts of Parliament, about all which things Mrs. Hilary knew and cared nothing, but vaguely she felt that they sprang out of and must include a care for human beings as such, and that therefore Barry Briscoe would listen if she told him things.

So (it came out of lying on grass, which Barry was doing) she told him about the pneumonia of Neville as a child; how they had been staying in Cornwall, miles from a doctor and without Mr. Hilary, and Mrs. Hilary had been in despair; how Jim, a little chap of twelve, had ridden off on his pony in the night to fetch the doctor (the pluck of the child on those rough hill roads in the dark! But Jim had never been afraid of anything, he was like Nelson, he never saw fear); and how the doctor had been out, and how Jim had been told at the inn of another doctor, staying for his holidays five miles off on the moors, and had ridden off and found him. … A long story; stories about illnesses always are. Mrs. Hilary got worked up and excited as she told it; it came back to her so vividly, the dreadful night.

"He was a Dr. Chalmers, and so kind. He put a horse into the wagonette himself, and drove straight over across the moors; eight miles, it was. When he saw Neville he was horrified; by that time she was delirious. He said if Jim hadn't gone straight to him but had waited till the morning, it might have been too late. …"

"Too late; quite." … Barry Briscoe had an understanding, sympathetic grip of one's last few words. So much of the conversation of others eludes one, but one should hold fast the last few words.

"Oh, played, Gerda; did you that time, Bendish. …"

Gerda had put on, probably by accident, a sudden absurd twist that had made a fool of Rodney.

That was what Barry Briscoe was really attending to, the silly game. Just as if Neville had never had pneumonia, and Jim had never ridden his pony over the moors at night to fetch Dr. Chalmers. This alert, seemingly interested, attentive young man who was Nan's friend and cared for Workers' Education and Penal Reform—he had a nice manner, that led you on, but he didn't really care. He lived in the moment: he cared for prisoners and workers, and probably for people who were ill *now*, but he didn't care that someone had been ill all those years ago and had nearly died through not getting a doctor. He pretended to care; he was polite. He turned his keen, pleasant face up to her when he had done shouting about the game, and said, "How splendid that he got to you in time!" but he didn't really care. Mrs. Hilary, who had often told the story of Neville's pneumonia before (and it changed a little each time, gathering body, like a rolling snowball, but even now no one but herself thought it a really good story), found that women were better listeners than men. Women are perhaps better trained; they think it ill-mannered not to show interest. They will listen while you tell them idiotic stories about servants, how the housemaid has taken too much butter and the cook too little trouble. They will listen to your reports of the inane sayings of infants. They will hear you through, without the flicker of a yawn, but with ejaculations and noddings, while you tell them about your children's diseases. They are well-bred; they drive themselves on a tight rein, and endure. They are the world's martyrs.

But men, less restrained, will fidget and wander and sigh and yawn, and change the subject.

To trap and hold the sympathy of a man—how wonderful! Who wanted a pack of women? What you really wanted was some man whose trade it was to listen and to give heed. Some man to whom your daughter's pneumonia, of however long ago, was not irrelevant, but had its own significance, as having helped to build you up as you were, you, the problem, with your wonderful, puzzling temperament, so full of complexes, inconsistencies, and needs. Some man who didn't lose interest in you just because you were grey-haired and sixty-three.

"I'm afraid I've been disturbing you with my talk—taking your attention from the game," said Mrs. Hilary to Barry Briscoe.

His courtesy stabbed him with compunction. Had he been rude to this elderly lady, who had been telling him a long tale without a point while he watched the tennis and made polite, attentive sounds?

"Not a bit, Mrs. Hilary." He sat up, and looked friendlier than ever. "I've been thrilled." A charming, easy liar Barry was, when he deemed it necessary. His Quaker parents would have been shocked. But there was truth in it, after all. For people were so interesting, one was so much interested in themselves, that one was, in a sense, interested in the stories they told one, even stories about illness. Besides, this was the mother of Nan; Nan, who was so abruptly and inexplicably not here to-day, whose absence was hurting him, when he stopped to think, like an aching tooth; for he was not sure, yet feared, what she meant by it.

"Tell me," he said, half to please Nan's mother and half on his own account, "some stories of Nan when she was small. I should think she was a fearful child. ..."

He was interested, thought Mrs. Hilary, in Nan, but not in her. That was natural, of course. No man would ever again want to hear stories of *her* childhood. The familiar bitterness rose and beat in her like a wave. Nan was thirty-three and she was sixty-three. Nan had men all about her, all being interested; she had only the women of St. Mary's Bay. Nan could talk about Workers' Education, even though, being selfish, she mightn't want it, and Mrs. Hilary could only talk about old, unhappy, far-off things and fevers long ago, and the servants, and silly gossip about people, and general theories about conduct and life which sounded all right at first, but were exposed after two minutes as not having behind them the background of any knowledge or any brain. That hadn't mattered when she was a girl; who wanted girls to have knowledge or brain? Men would often rather they hadn't. But at sixty-three you have nothing. ... The bitter emptiness of sixty-three turned her sick with frustration. Over, over, over, for her—and she was to tell stories of Nan, who had everything.

Then the mother in her rose up, to claim and grasp for her child, even for the child she loved least.

"Nan? Nan was always a most dreadfully sensitive child, and temperamental. She took after me, I'm afraid; the others were more like their father. I remember when she was quite a little thing. ..."

Barry had asked for it. But he hadn't known that, out of the brilliant, uncertain Nan, exciting as a Punch and Judy show, anything so tedious could be spun. ...

▶•◀

III

Mrs. Hilary was up in town by herself for a day's shopping. The sales were on at Barker's and Derry and Tom's. Mrs. Hilary wandered about these shops, and even Ponting's, and bought little bags, and presents for every one, and remnants, and oddments, and underwear, and some green silk for a frock for Gerda, and a shady hat for herself, and a wonderful cushion for Grandmamma with a picture of the sea on it, and a silk knitted jumper for Neville, the purplish blue of her eyes. She was happy, going about like a bee from flower to flower, gathering this honey for them all. She had come up alone; she hadn't let Neville come with her. She had said she was going to be an independent old woman. But what she really meant was that she had proposed herself for tea with Rosalind in Campden Hill Square, and wanted to be alone for that.

Rosalind had been surprised, for Mrs. Hilary seldom favoured her with a visit. She had found the letter on the hall table when she and Gilbert had come in from a dinner party two evenings ago.

"Your mother's coming to tea on Thursday, Gilbert. Tea with me. She says she wants a talk. I feel flattered. She says nothing about wanting to see you, so you'd better leave us alone, anyhow for a bit."

Rosalind's beautiful, bistred brown eyes smiled. She enjoyed her talks with her mother-in-law; they furnished her with excellent material, to be worked up later by the raconteuse's art into something too delicious and absurd. She enjoyed, too, telling Mrs. Hilary the latest scandals; she was so shocked and disgusted; and it was fun dropping little accidental hints about Nan, and even about Gilbert. Anyhow, what a treasure of a relic of the Victorian age! And how comic in her jealousy, her ingenuous, futile boasting, her so readily exposed deceits! And how she hated Rosalind herself, the painted, corrupt woman who was dragging Gilbert down!

"Whatever does she want a talk about?" Rosalind wondered. "It must be something pretty urgent, to make her put up with an hour of my company."

▶•◀

IV

At four o'clock on Thursday afternoon Rosalind went upstairs and put on an extra coating of powder and rouge. She also blackened her eyelashes and put on her lips salve the colour of strawberries rather than of the human mouth. She wore an afternoon dress with transparent black sleeves through which her big arms gleamed, pale and smooth. She looked a superb and altogether improper creature, like Lucrezia Borgia or a Titian madonna. She came down and lay among great black and gold satin cushions, and lit a scented cigarette and opened a new French novel. Black and gold was her new scheme for her drawing-room; she had had it done this spring. It had a sort of opulent and rakish violence which suited her ripe magnificence, her splendid flesh tints, her brown eyes and corn-gold hair. Against it she looked like Messalina, and Gilbert rather like a decadent and cynical Pope. The note of the room was really too pronounced for Gilbert's fastidious and scholarly elegance; he lost vitality in it, and dwindled to the pale thin casket of a brain.

And Mrs. Hilary, when she entered it, trailing in, tall and thin, in her sagging grey coat and skirt, her wispy greyish hair escaping from under her floppy black hat, and with the air of having till a moment ago been hung about with parcels (she had left them in the hall) looked altogether unsuited to her environment, like a dowdy lady from the provinces, which she was.

Rosalind came forward and took her by the hands.

"Well, mother dear, this is an unusual honour. … *How* long is it since we last had you here?"

Rosalind, enveloping her mother-in-law in extravagant fragrance, kissed her on each cheek. The kiss of Messalina! Mrs. Hilary glanced at the great mirror over the fire-place to see whether it had come off on her cheeks, as well it might.

Rosalind placed her in a swelling, billowy, black and gold chair, piled cushions behind her shoulders, made her lie back at an obtuse angle, a grey, lank, elderly figure, strange in that opulent setting, her long, dusty, black feet stretched out before her on the golden carpet.

Desperately uncomfortable and angular Rosalind made you feel, petting you and purring over you and calling you "mother dear," with that glint always behind her golden-brown eyes which showed that she was up to no good, that she knew you hated her and was only leading you on that she might strike her claws into you the deeper. The great, beautiful cat: that was what Rosalind was. You didn't trust her for a moment.

She was pouring out tea.

"Lemon? But how dreadfully stupid of me! I'd forgotten you take milk … oh, yes; and sugar. …"

She rang, and ordered sugar. Mothers take it; not the mothers of Rosalind's world, but mothers' meetings, and school treats, and mothers-in-law up from the seaside.

"Are you up for shopping? How thrilling! Where have you been? … Oh, High Street. Did you *find* anything there?"

Mrs. Hilary knew that Rosalind would see her off, hung over with dozens of parcels, and despise them, knowing that if they were so many they must also be cheap.

"Oh, there's not much to be got there, of course," she said. "I got a few little things—chiefly for my mother to give away in the parish. She likes to have things …"

"But how noble of you both! I'm afraid I never rise to that. It's all I can manage to give presents to myself and nearest rellies. And you came up to town just to get presents for the parish! You're wonderful, mother!"

"Oh, I take a day in town now and then. Why not? Everyone does."

Extraordinary how defiant Rosalind made one feel, prying and questioning and trying to make one look absurd.

"Why, of course! It freshens you up, I expect; makes a change. ... But you've come up from Windover, haven't you, not the seaside?"

Rosalind always called St. Mary's Bay the seaside. To her our island coasts were all one; the seaside was where you went to bathe, and she hardly distinguished between north, south, east and west.

"How are they down at Windover? I heard that Nan was there, with that young man of hers who performs good works. So unlike Nan herself! I hope she isn't going to be so silly as to let it come to anything; they'd both be miserable. But I should think Nan knows better than to marry a square-toes. I dare say *he* knows better, too, really. ... And how's poor old Neville? I think this doctoring game of hers is simply a scream, the poor old dear."

To hear Rosalind discussing Neville ... Messalina coarsely patronising a wood-nymph ... the cat striking her claws into a singing-bird. ... And poor—and old! Neville was, indeed, six years ahead of Rosalind, but she looked the younger of the two, in her slim activity, and didn't need to paint her face either. Mrs. Hilary all but said so.

"It is a great interest to Neville, taking up her medical studies again," was all she could really say. (What a hampering thing it is to be a lady!) "She thoroughly enjoys it, and looks younger than ever. She is playing a lot of tennis, and beats them all."

How absurdly her voice rang when she spoke of Neville or Jim! It always made Rosalind's lip curl mockingly.

"Wonderful creature! I do admire her. When I'm her age I shall be too fat to take any exercise at all. I think it's splendid of women who keep it up through the forties. ... *She* won't be bored, even when she's sixty, will she?"

That was a direct hit, which Mrs. Hilary could bear better than hits at Neville.

"I see no reason," said Mrs. Hilary, "why Neville should ever be bored. She has a husband and children. Long before she is sixty she will have Kay's, and Gerda's children to be interested in."

"No, I suppose one can't well be bored if one has grandchildren, can one?" Rosalind said reflectively.

There was a silence, during which Mrs. Hilary's eyes, coldly meeting Rosalind's with their satirical comment, said, "I know you are too selfish a woman ever to bear children, and I thank God for it. Little Hilarys who should be half yours would be more than I could endure."

Rosalind, quite understanding, smiled her slow, full-mouthed, curling smile, and held out to her mother-in-law the gold case with scented cigarettes.

"Oh, no, you don't, do you. I never can remember that. It's—so unusual."

Her eyes travelled over Mrs. Hilary, from her dusty black shoes to her pale, lined face. They put her, with deliberation, into the class with companions, housekeepers, poor relations. Having successfully done that (she knew it was successful, by Mrs. Hilary's faint flush), she said, "You don't look up to much, mother dear. Not as if Neville had been looking after you very well."

Mrs. Hilary, seeing her chance, swallowed her natural feelings and took it.

"The fact is, I sleep very badly. Not particularly just now, but always. ... I thought ... that is, someone told me ... that there have been wonderful cures for insomnia lately ... through that new thing ..."

"Which new thing? Sedobrol? Paraldehyd? Gilbert keeps getting absurd powders and tablets of all sorts. Thank God, I always sleep like a top."

"No, not those. The thing *you* practise. Psycho-analysis, I mean."

"Oh, psycho. But you wouldn't touch that, surely? I thought it was anathema."

"But if it really does cure people. ..."

Rosalind's eyes glittered and gleamed. Her strawberry-red mouth curled joyfully.

"Of course it does. ... Not that insomnia is always a case for psycho, you know. It's sometimes incipient mania."

"Not in my case." Mrs. Hilary spoke sharply.

"Why, no, of course not. ... Well, I think you'd be awfully wise to get analysed. Who do you want to go to?"

"I thought you could tell me. I know no names … a *man*," Mrs. Hilary added quickly.

"Oh, it must be a man? I was going to say, I've a vacancy myself for a patient. But women usually want men doctors. They nearly all do. It's supposed to be part of the complaint. … Well, I could fix you up a preliminary interview with Dr. Claude Evans. He's very good. He turns you right inside out and shows you everything about yourself, from your first infant passion to the thoughts you think you're keeping dark from him as you sit in the consulting room. He's great."

Mrs. Hilary was flushed. Hope and shame tingled in her together.

"I shan't want to keep anything dark. I've no reason."

Rosalind's mocking eyes said, "That's what they all say." Her lips said, "The foreconscious self always has its reasons for hiding up the thing the unconscious self knows and feels."

"Oh, all that stuff. …" Mrs. Hilary was sick of it, having read too much about it in *The Breath of Life*. "I hope this Dr. Evans will talk to me in plain English, not in that affected jargon."

"He'll use language suited to you, I suppose," said Rosalind, "as far as he can. But these things can't always be put so that just anyone can grasp them. They're too complicated. You should read it up beforehand, and try if you can understand it a little."

Rosalind, who had no brains herself, insulting Mrs. Hilary's, was rather more than Mrs. Hilary could bear. Rosalind she knew for a fool, so far as intellectual matters went, for Nan had said so. Clever enough at clothes, and talking scandal, and winning money at games, and skating over thin ice without going through—but when it came to a book, or an idea, or a political question, Rosalind was no whit more intelligent than she was, in fact much less. She was a rotten psycho-analyst, all her in-laws were sure.

Mrs. Hilary said, "I've been reading a good deal about it lately. It doesn't seem to me very difficult, though exceedingly foolish in parts."

Rosalind was touchy about psycho-analysis; she always got angry if people said it was foolish in any way. She was like that; she could see no weak points in anything she took up; it came from being vain, and not having a brain. She said one of the things angry people say, instead of discussing the subject rationally.

"I don't suppose the amount of it you've been able to read *would* seem difficult. If you came to anything difficult you'd probably stop, you see. Anyhow, if it seems to you so foolish, why do you want to be analysed?"

"Oh, one may as well try things. I've no doubt there's something in it besides the nonsense."

Mrs. Hilary spoke jauntily, with hungry, unquiet, seeking eyes that would not meet Rosalind's. She was afraid that Rosalind would find out that she wanted to be cured of being miserable, of being jealous, of having inordinate passions about so little. Rosalind, in some ways a great stupid cow, was uncannily clever when it came to being spiteful and knowing about you the things you didn't want known. It must be horrible to be psycho-analysed by Rosalind, who had no pity and no reticence. The things about you would not only be known by her but spread abroad among all those whom she met. A vile, dreadful tongue.

"You wouldn't, I expect, like *me* to analyse you," said Rosalind. "Not a course, I mean, but just once, to advise you better who to go to. I'd have the advantage, anyhow, that I'd do it free. Anyone else will charge you three guineas at the least."

"I don't think," said Mrs. Hilary, "that relations—or connections— ought to do one another. No, I'd better go to some one I don't know, if you'll give me the name and address."

"I thought you'd probably rather," Rosalind said, in her slow, soft, cruel voice, like a cat's purr. "Well, I'll write down the address for you. It's Dr. Evans: he'll probably pass you on to some one down at the seaside, if he considers you a suitable case for treatment."

He would; of course he would. Mrs. Hilary felt no doubt as to that.

Gilbert came in from the British Museum. He looked thin and nervy and sallow amid all the splendour. He kissed his mother, thinking how queer and untidy she looked, a stranger and pilgrim in Rosalind's drawing-room. He, too, might look there at times a stranger and pilgrim, but at least, if not voluptuous, he was neat. He glanced proudly and yet ironically from his mother to his magnificent wife, taking in and understanding the supra-normal redundancies of her make-up.

"Rosalind," said Mrs. Hilary, knowing that it would be less than no use to ask Rosalind to keep her secret, "has been recommending me a psycho-analyst doctor. I think it is worth while trying if I can get my insomnia cured that way."

"My dear mother! After all your fulminations against the tribe! Well, I think you're quite right to give it a trial. Why don't you get Rosalind to take you on?"

The fond pride in his voice! Yet there was in his eyes, as they rested for a moment on Rosalind, something other than fond pride; something more like mockery.

Mrs. Hilary got up to go, and fired across the rich room the one shot in her armoury.

"I believe," she said, "that Rosalind prefers chiefly to take men patients. She wouldn't want to be bored with an old woman."

The shot drove straight into Gilbert's light-strung sensitiveness. Shell-shocked officers; any other officers; anything male, presentable and passably young; these were Rosalind's patients; he knew it, and everyone else knew it. For a moment his smile was fixed into the deliberate grin of pain. Mrs. Hilary saw it, saw Gilbert far back down the years, a small boy standing up to punishment with just that brave, nervous grin. Sensitive, defiant, vulnerable, fastidiously proud—so Gilbert had always been and always would be.

Remorsefully she clung to him.

"Come and see me out, dearest boy"—(so she called him, though Jim was really that)—and she ignored Rosalind's slow, unconcerned protest against her last remark, "Why, mother, you know I *asked* to do you." ... but she couldn't prevent Rosalind from seeing her out too, hanging her about with all the ridiculous parcels, kissing her on both cheeks.

Gilbert was cool and dry, pretending she hadn't hurt him. He would always take hurts like that, with that deadly, steely lightness. By its deadliness, its steeliness, she knew that it was all (and much more besides) true, what she had heard about Rosalind and her patients.

►•◄

V

She walked down to the bus with hot eyes. Rosalind had yawned, softly and largely, behind her as she went down the front steps. Wicked, monstrous creature! Lying about Gilbert's clever, nervous, eager life in great soft folds, and throttling it. If Gilbert had been a man, a real male man, instead of a writer and therefore effeminate, decadent, he would have beaten her into decent behaviour. As it was, she would ruin him, and he would go under, not able to bear it, but cynically grinning still. Perhaps the sooner the better. Anything was better than the way Rosalind went on now, disgracing him and getting talked about, and making him hate his mother for disliking her. He hadn't even come with her to the bus, to carry her parcels for her. … That wasn't like Gilbert, who, though not affectionate, like Jim, had as a rule excellent manners.

Jim, Jim, Jim. Should she go to Harley Street? What was the use? She would only find Margery there; Jim would be out. Margery had no serious faults except the one that she had taken the first place in Jim's affections. Before Margery, Neville had had this place, but Mrs. Hilary had been able, with Neville's never-failing and skilful help, to disguise this from herself. You can't disguise a wife's place in her husband's heart. And Jim's splendid children too, whom she adored—they looked at her with Margery's brown eyes instead of Jim's grey-blue ones. And they preferred really (she knew it) their maternal grandmother, a jolly lady who took them to theatres.

Mrs. Hilary passed a church. Religion. Some people found help there. But it required so much of you, was so exhausting in its demands. Besides, it seemed infinitely far away—an improbable, sad, remote thing, that gave you no human comfort; psycho-analysis was better; that opened gates into a new life. "Know thyself," Mrs. Hilary murmured, kindling at the prospect. Most knowledge was dull, but never that.

"I will ring up from Waterloo and make an appointment," she thought.

CHAPTER VI

JIM

►•◄

I

The psycho-analyst doctor was little and dark, and while he was talking he looked not at Mrs. Hilary but down at a paper whereon he drew or wrote something she tried to see and couldn't. She came to the conclusion after a time that he was merely scribbling for effect.

"Insomnia," he said. "Yes. You know what *that* means?"

She said, foolishly, "That I can't sleep," and he gave her a glance of contempt and returned to his scribbling.

"It means," he told her, "that you are afraid of dreaming. Your unconscious self won't *let* you sleep. ... Do you often recall your dreams when you wake?"

"Sometimes."

"Tell me some of them, please."

"Oh, the usual things, I suppose. Packing; missing trains; meeting people; and just nonsense that means nothing. All the usual things, that every one dreams about."

At each thing she said he nodded, and scribbled with his pencil. "Quite," he said, "quite. They're bad enough in meaning, the dreams you've mentioned. I don't suppose you'd care at present to hear what they symbolise. ... The dreams you haven't mentioned are doubtless worse. And those you don't even recall are worst of all. Your unconscious self is, very naturally and properly, frightened of them. ... Well, we must end all that, or you'll never sleep as you should. Psycho-analysis will cure these dreams; first it will make you remember them, then you'll talk them out and get rid of them."

"Dreams," said Mrs. Hilary. "Well, they may be important. But it's my whole life …"

"Precisely. I was coming to that. Of course, you can't cure sleeplessness until you have cured the fundamental things that are wrong with your life. Now, if you please, tell me all you can about yourself."

Here was the wonderful moment. Mrs. Hilary drew a long breath, and did so. A horrid (she felt that somehow he was rather horrid) little man with furtive eyes that wouldn't meet hers—and he wasn't quite a gentleman either—but still, he wanted to hear all about her, he was listening attentively, drinking it in. Not watching tennis while she talked, like Barry Briscoe in the garden. Ah, she could go on and on, never tired; it was like swimming in warm water.

He would interrupt her with questions. Which had she preferred, her father or her mother? Well, perhaps, on the whole, her father. He nodded; that was the right answer; the other he would have quietly put aside as one of the deliberate inaccuracies so frequently practised by his patients. "You can leave out the perhaps. There's no manner of doubt about it, you know." Lest he should say (instead of only looking it) that she had been in love with her good father and he with her, Mrs. Hilary hurried on. She had a chaste mind, and knew what these Freudians were. It would, she thought (not knowing her doctor and how it would have come to the same thing, only he would have thought her a more pronounced case, because of the deception) have been wiser to have said that she had preferred her mother, but less truthful, and what she was enjoying now was an orgy of truth-telling. She got on to her marriage, and how intensely Richard had loved her. He tried for a moment to be indecent about love and marriage, but in her deep excitement she hardly noticed him, but swept on to the births of the children, and Jim's croup.

"I see," he said presently, "that you prefer to avoid discussing certain aspects of life. You obviously have a sex complex."

"Of course, of course. Don't you find that in all your patients? Surely we may take that for granted. ..." She allowed him his sex complex, knowing that Freudians without it would be like children deprived of a precious toy; for her part she was impatient to get back to Jim, her life's chief passion. The Œdipus complex, of course, he would say it was; what matter, if he would let her talk about it? And Neville. It was strange to have a jealous passion for one's daughter. But that would, he said, be an extension of the ego complex—quite simple really.

She came to the present.

"I feel that life has used me up and flung me aside like a broken tool. I have no further relation to life, nor it to me. I have spent myself and been spent, and now I am bankrupt. Can you make me solvent again?"

She liked that as she said it.

He scribbled away, like a mouse scrabbling.

"Yes. Oh, yes. There is no manner of doubt about it. None whatever. If you are perfectly frank, you can be cured. You can be adjusted to life. Every age in human life has had its own adjustments to make, its own relation to its environment to establish. All that repressed libido must be released and diverted. ... You have some bad complexes, which must be sublimated. ..."

It sounded awful, the firm way he said it, like teeth or appendixes which must be extracted. But Mrs. Hilary knew it wouldn't be like that really, but delightful and luxurious, more like a Turkish bath.

"You must have a course," he told her. "You are an obvious case for a course of treatment. St. Mary's Bay? Excellent. There is a practising psycho-analyst doctor there now. You should have an hour's treatment twice a week, to be really effective. ... You would prefer a man, I take it?"

He shot his eyes at her for a moment, in statement, not in inquiry. Well he knew how much she would prefer a man. She murmured assent. He rose. The hour was over.

"How much will the course be?" she asked.

"A guinea an hour, Dr. Cradock charges. He is very cheap."

"Yes, I see. I must think it over. And you?"

He told her his fee, and she blenched, but paid it. She was not rich, but it had been worth while. It was a beginning. It had opened the door into a new and richer life. St. Mary's Bay was illumined in her thoughts, instead of drab and empty as before. Sublimated complexes twinkled over it like stars. Freed libido poured electrically about it. And Dr. Cradock, she felt, would be more satisfactory as a doctor than this man, who affected her with a faint nausea when he looked at her, which was seldom.

▶•◀

II

Windover, too, was illumined. She could watch almost calmly Neville talking to Grandmamma, wheeling her round the garden to look at the borders, for Grandmamma was a great gardener.

And then Jim came down for a week-end, and it was as if the sun had risen on Surrey. He sat with Mrs. Hilary in the arbour. She told him about Dr. Evans, and the other psycho-analyst doctor at St. Mary's Bay. He frowned over Dr. Evans, who lived in the same street as he did.

"Rosalind sent you to him; of course; she would. Why didn't you ask me, mother? He's a desperate Freudian, you know, and they're not nearly so much good as the others. Besides, this particular man is a shoddy scoundrel, I believe. ... Was he offensive?"

"I wouldn't let him be, Jim. I was prepared for that. I ... changed the conversation."

Jim laughed, and did his favourite trick with her hand, straightening the thin fingers one by one as they lay across his sensitive palm. How happy it always made her!

"Well," he said, "I dare say this man down at the Bay is all right. I'll find out if he's any good or not. ... They talk a lot of tosh, you know, mother; you'll have to sift the grain from the chaff."

But he saw that her eyes were interested, her face more alert than usual, her very poise more alive. She had found a new interest in life, like keeping a parrot, or learning bridge, or becoming a Roman Catholic. It was what they had all always tried to find for her in vain.

"So long," he said, "as you don't believe more than half what they tell you. ... Let me know how it goes on, won't you, and what this man is like. If I don't approve I shall come and stop it."

She loved that from Jim.

"Of course, dearest. Of course I shall tell you about it. And I know one must be careful."

It was something to have become an object for care; it put one more in the foreground. She would have gone on willingly with the subject, but Jim changed her abruptly for Neville.

"Neville's looking done up."

She felt the little sharp pang which Neville's name on Jim's lips had always given her. His very pronunciation of it hurt her—"Nivvle," he said it, as if he had been an Irishman. It brought all the past back; those two dear ones talking together, studying together, going off together, bound by a hundred common interests, telling each other things they never told her.

"Yes. It's this ridiculous work of hers. It's so absurd: a married woman of her age making her head ache working for examinations."

In old days Jim and Neville had worked together. Jim had been proud of Neville's success; she had been quicker than he. Mrs. Hilary, who had welcomed Neville's marriage as ending all that, foresaw a renewal of the hurtful business.

But Jim looked grave and disapproving over it.

"It is absurd," he agreed, and her heart rose. "And of course she can't do it, can't make up all that leeway. Besides, her brain has lost its grip. She's not kept it sharpened; she's spent her life on people. You can't have it both ways—a woman can't, I mean. Her work's been different. She doesn't seem to realise that what she's trying to learn up again now, in the spare moments of an already full life, demands a whole lifetime of hard work. She can't get back those twenty years; no one could. And she can't get back the clear, gripping brain she had before she had children. She's given some of it to them. That's nature's way, unfortunately. Hard luck, no doubt, but there it is; you can't get round it. Nature's a hybrid of fool and devil."

He was talking really to himself, but was recalled to his mother by the tears which, he suddenly perceived, were distorting her face.

"And so," she whispered, her voice choked, "we women get left. ..."

He looked away from her, a little exasperated. She cried so easily and so superfluously, and he knew that these tears were more for herself than for Neville. And she didn't really come into what he had been saying at all; he had been talking about brains.

"It's all right as far as most women are concerned," he said. "Most women have no brains to be spoilt. Neville had. Most women could do nothing at all with life if they didn't produce children; it's their only possible job. *They've* no call to feel ill-used."

"Of course," she said unsteadily, struggling to clear her voice of tears, "I know you children all think I'm a fool. But there was a time, when I read difficult books with your father ... he, a man with a first-class mind, cared to read with me and discuss with me ..."

"Oh, yes, yes, mother, I know."

Jim, and all of them knew all about those long-ago difficult books. They knew, too, about the clever friends who used to drop in and talk. ... If only Mrs. Hilary could have been one of the nice, jolly, refreshing people who own that they never read and never want to. All this fuss about reading and cleverness—how tedious it was? As if it mattered being stupid, as if it was worth bothering about.

"Of course we don't think you a fool, mother dear; how could we?"

Jim was kind and affectionate, never ironic, like Gilbert, or impatient like Nan. But he felt now the need for fresh air; the arbour was too small for him and Mrs. Hilary, who was as tiring to others as to herself.

"I think I shall go and interrupt Neville over her studies," said Jim, and left the arbour.

Mrs. Hilary looked after him, painfully loving his square, straight back, his fine dark head, just flecked with grey, the clean line of his profile, with the firm jaw clenched over the pipe. To have produced Jim—wasn't that enough to have lived for? Mrs. Hilary was one of those mothers who apply the Magnificat to their own cases. She always felt a bond of human sympathy between herself and that lady whom she thought over-estimated and called the Virgin Mary.

▶•◀

III

Neville raised heavy violet eyes, faintly ringed with shadows, to Jim as he came into the library. She looked at him for a moment absently, then smiled. He came over to her and looked at the book before her.

"Working? Where've you got to? Let's see how much you know."

He took the book from her and glanced at it to see what she had been reading.

"Now we'll have an examination; it'll be good practice for you."

He put a question, and she answered it, frowning a little.

"H'm. That's not very good, my dear."

He tried again; this time she could not answer at all. At the third question she shook her head.

"It's no use, Jimmy. My head's hopeless this afternoon. Another time."

He shut the book.

"Yes. So it seems. … You're overdoing it, Neville. You can't go on like this."

She lay back and spread out her hands hopelessly.

"But I must go on like this if I'm ever going to get through my exams."

"You're not going to, old thing. You're quite obviously unfitted to. It's not your job any more. It's absurd to try; really it is."

Neville shut her eyes.

"Doctors … doctors. They have the limitations of the feminine organism on the brain."

"Because they know something about it. But I'm not speaking of the feminine organism just now. I should say the same to Rodney if *he* thought of turning doctor now, after twenty years of politics.

"Rodney never could have been a doctor. He hates messing about with bodies."

"Well, you know what I think. I can't stop you, of course. It's only a question of time, in any case. You'll soon find out for yourself that it's no use."

"I think," she answered, in her small, unemotional voice, "that it's exceedingly probable that I shall."

She lay inertly in the deep chair, her eyes shut, her hands opened, palms downwards, as if they had failed to hold something.

"What, then Jim? If I can't be a doctor, what can I be? Besides Rodney's wife, I mean? I don't say besides the children's mother, because that's stopped being a job. They're charming to me, the darlings, but they don't need me any more; they go their own way."

Jim had noticed that.

"Well, after all, you do a certain amount of political work—public speaking, meetings, and so on. Isn't that enough?"

"That's all second-hand. I shouldn't do it but for Rodney. I'm not public-spirited enough. If Rodney dies before I do, I shan't go on with that. ... Shall I just be a silly, self-engrossed, moping old woman, no use to anyone and a plague to myself?"

The eyes of both of them strayed out to the garden.

"Who's the silly moping old woman?" asked Mrs. Hilary's voice in the doorway. And there she stood, leaning a little forward, a strained smile on her face.

"Me, mother, when I shall be old," Neville quickly answered her, smiling in return. "Come in, dear. Jim's telling me how I shall never be a doctor. He gave me a *viva voce* exam, and I came a mucker over it."

Her voice had an edge of bitterness; she hadn't liked coming a mucker, nor yet being told she couldn't get through exams. She had plenty of vanity; so far everyone and everything had combined to spoil her. She was determined, in the face of growing doubt, to prove Jim wrong yet.

"Well," Mrs. Hilary said, sitting down on the edge of a chair, not settling herself, but looking poised to go, so as not to seem to intrude on their conversation, "well, I don't see why you want to be a doctor, dear. Every one knows women doctors aren't much good. *I* wouldn't trust one."

"Very stupid of you, mother," Jim said, trying to pretend he wasn't irritated by being interrupted. "They're every bit as good as men."

"Fancy being operated on by a woman surgeon. I certainly shouldn't risk it."

"*You* wouldn't risk it ... *you* wouldn't trust them. ... You're so desperately personal, mother. You think that contributes to a discussion. All it does contribute to is your hearers' knowledge of your limitations. It's uneducated, the way you discuss."

He smiled at her pleasantly, taking the sting out of his words, turning them into a joke, and she smiled too, to show Neville she didn't mind, didn't take it seriously. Jim might hurt her, but if he did no-one should know but Jim himself. She knew that at times she irritated even his good temper by being uneducated and so on, so that he scolded her, but scolded her kindly, not venomously, as Nan did.

"Well, I've certainly no right to be that," she said, meaning uneducated. "And I can't say I'm ever called so, except by my children. ... Do you remember the discussions father and I used to have, half through the night?"

Jim and Neville, who did, thought, "Poor father," and were silent.

"I should think," said Mrs. Hilary, "there was very little we didn't discuss. Politics, books, trade unions, class divisions, moral questions, votes for women, divorce ... we thrashed everything out. We both thoroughly enjoyed it."

Neville said, "I remember," and indeed she did. Familiar echoes came back to her out of the agitated past.

"Those lazy men, all they want is to get a lot of money for doing no work."

"I like the poor well enough in their places, but I cannot abide them when they try to step into ours."

"Let women mind their proper business and leave men's alone."

- 91 -

"I'm certainly not going to be on calling terms with my grocer's wife."

"I hate these affected, posing, would-be clever books. Why can't people write in good plain English?"

And so on, and so on, and so on. Richard Hilary, a scholar and a patient man, blinded by conjugal love, had met futilities with argument, expressions of emotional taste with facts, trying to lift each absurd wrangle to the level of a discussion; and at last had died, leaving his wife with the conviction that she had been the equal mate of an able man. Her children had to face and conquer, with varying degrees of success, the temptation to undeceive her.

"But I'm interrupting," said Mrs. Hilary. "I know you two are having a private talk. I'll leave you alone …"

"No, no, mother." That was Neville, of course. "Stay and defend me from Jim's scorn."

How artificial one had to be in family life! What an absurd thing these emotions made of it!

Mrs. Hilary looked happier, and more settled in her chair.

"Where are Kay and Gerda?" Jim asked, not having seen them yet.

Neville told him, "In Guildford, helping Barry Briscoe with W.E.A. meetings. They're spending a lot of time over that just now; they're both as keen as mustard. Nearly as keen as he is. He sets people on fire. It's very good for the children. They're bringing him up here to spend Sunday. I think he hopes every time to find Nan back again from Cornwall, poor Barry. He was very down in the mouth when she suddenly took herself off."

"If Nan doesn't mean to have him, she shouldn't have encouraged him," said Mrs. Hilary. "He was quite obviously in love with her."

"Nan's always a dark horse," Neville said. "She alone knows what she means."

Jim said, "She's a flibberty-gibbet. She'd much better get married. She's not much use in the world at present. Now if *she* was a doctor … or doing something useful, like Pamela …"

"Don't be prejudiced, Jimmy. Because you don't read modern novels yourself, you think it's no use their being written."

"I read some modern novels. I read Conrad, in spite of the rather absurd attitude some people take up about him; and I read good detective stories, only they're so seldom good. I don't read Nan's kind. People tell me they're tremendously clever and modern and delightfully written and get very well reviewed. I dare say. I very seldom agree with reviewers, in any case. Even about Conrad they seem to me (when I read them—I don't often) to pick out the wrong points to admire and to miss the points I should criticise."

Mrs. Hilary said, "Well, I must say I can't read Nan's books myself. Simply, I don't think them good. I dislike all her people so much, and her style."

"You're a pair of old Victorians," Neville told them, pleasing Mrs. Hilary by coupling them together, and leaving Jim, who knew why she did it, undisturbed. Neville was full of graces and tact, which Jim had always appreciated in her.

"And there," said Neville, who was standing at the window, "are Barry Briscoe and the children coming in."

Jim looked over her shoulder and saw the three wheeling their bicycles up the drive.

"Gerda," he remarked, "is a prettier thing every time I see her."

CHAPTER VII

GERDA

▶•◀

I

It rained so hard, so much harder even than usual, that Sunday, that only Barry and Gerda went a walk: Barry walked in every kind of weather, even in the July of 1920, and Gerda was unreliable, you never knew when she would walk or when she would curl up in a chair and refuse to stir.

To-day after lunch Barry said, "I'm going to walk over the downs. Anyone coming?" and Gerda got up silently, as was her habit. Kay stretched himself and yawned, and said, "Me for the fireside. I shall have to walk every day for three weeks after to-day," for he was going to-morrow on a reading party. Rodney and Jim were playing a game of chess that had lasted since breakfast and showed every sign of lasting till bed-time, and Neville and Mrs. Hilary were talking, and Grandmamma was upstairs, having her afternoon nap.

▶•◀

||

They tramped along, waterproofed and bareheaded, down the sandy road. The rain swished in Gerda's golden locks, till they clung dank and limp about her cheeks and neck; it beat on Barry's glasses, so that he took them off and blinked instead. The trees stormed and whistled in the southerly wind that blew from across Merrow Downs. Barry tried to whistle down it, but it caught the sound from his puckered lips and whirled it away.

Through Merrow they strode, and up on to the road that led across the downs, and there the wind caught them full, and it was as if buckets of water were being flung into their faces. The downs sang and roared; the purple-grey sky shut down on the hill's shoulder like a tent.

"Lord, what fun!" said Barry, as they gasped for breath.

Gerda was upright and slim as a wand against the buffeting; her white little face was stung into shell-pink; her wet hair blew back like yellow seaweed.

Barry thought suddenly of Nan, who revelled in storms, and quickly shut his mind on the thought. He was schooling himself to think away from Nan, with her wild animal grace and her flashing mind, and her cruel, careless indifference.

Gerda could have walked like this for ever. Her wide blue eyes blinked away the rain; her face felt stung and lashed, yet happy and cold; her mouth was stiff and tight. She was part of the storm; as free, as fierce, as singing, though outwardly she was all held together and silent, only smiling a little with her shut mouth.

As they climbed the downs the wind blew more wildly in their faces. Gerda swayed against it, and Barry took her by the arm and half pushed her.

So they reached Newlands Corner, and all southern Surrey stormed below them, and beyond Surrey stormed Sussex, and beyond Sussex the angry, unseen sea.

They stood looking, and Barry's arm still steadied Gerda against the gale.

Gerda thought, "It will end. It will be over, and we shall be sitting at tea. Then Sunday will be over, and on Monday he will go back to town." The pain of that end of the world turned her cold beneath the glow of the storm. Then life settled itself, very simply. She must go too, and work with him. She would tell him so on the way home, when the wind would let them talk.

They turned their backs on the storm and ran down the hill towards Merrow. Gerda, light as a leaf on the wind, could have run all the way back; Barry, fit and light too, but fifteen years ahead of her, fell after five minutes into a walk.

Then they could talk a little.

"And to-morrow I shall be fugging in town," sighed Barry.

Gerda always went straight to her point.

"May I come into your office, please, and learn the work?"

He smiled down at her. Splendid child!

"Why, rather. Do you mean it? When do you want to come?"

"To-morrow."

He laughed. "Good. I thought you meant in the autumn. ... To-morrow by all means, if you will. As a matter of fact we're frightfully short-handed in the office just now. Our typist has crocked, and we haven't another yet, so people have to type their own letters."

"I can do the typing," said Gerda composedly. "I can type quite well."

"Oh, but that'll be dull for you. That's not what you want, is it? Though, if you want to learn about the work, it's not a bad way ... you get it all passing through your hands. ... Would you really take on that job for a bit?"

Gerda nodded.

They were rapid and decided people; they did not beat about the bush. If they wanted to do a thing and there seemed no reason why not, they did it forthwith.

"That's first-class," said Barry. "Give it a trial, anyhow. ... Of course, you'll be on trial too; we may find it doesn't work. If so, there are plenty of other jobs to be done in the office. But that's what we most want at the moment."

Barry had a way of assuming that people would want, naturally, to do the thing that most needed doing.

Gerda's soul sang and whistled down the whistling wind. It wasn't over, then: it was only beginning. The W.E.A. was splendid; work was splendid; Barry Briscoe was splendid; life was splendid. She was sorry for Kay at Cambridge, Kay who was just off on a reading party, not helping in the world's work, but merely getting education. Education was inspiring in connection with Democracy, but when applied to oneself it was dull.

The rain was lessening. It fell on their heads more lightly; the wind was like soft, wet kisses on their backs, as they tramped through Merrow and up the lane to Windover.

▶•◀

III

They all sat round the tea-table, and most of them were warm and sleepy from Sunday afternoon by the fire, but Barry and Gerda were warm and tingling from walking in the storm. Some people prefer one sensation, some the other.

Neville thought, "How pretty Gerda looks, pink like that." She was glad to know that she, too, looked pretty in her blue afternoon dress. It was good, in that charming room, that they should all look agreeable to the eye. Even Mrs. Hilary, with her nervous, faded grace, marred by self-consciousness and emotion. And Grandmamma, smiling and shrewd, with her old, indrawn lips; and Rodney, long and lounging and clever; and Jim, square set, sensible, clean-cut, beautiful to his mother and his women patients, good for everyone to look at; and Barry, brown and charming, with his quick smile; and the boy Kay, with his pale, rounded, oval face, and violet eyes like his mother's, only short-sighted, so that he had a trick of screwing them up and peering, and when he smiled his mouth widened into a happy sweetness.

They were all right; they all fitted in with the room and with each other.

Barry said, "I've not been idle while walking. I've secured a secretary. Gerda says she's coming to work at the office for us for a bit. Now at once."

He had not Gerda's knack of silence. Gerda would shut up tight over her plans and thoughts, like a little oyster. She was no babbler; she did things and never said. But Barry's plans brimmed up and over.

Neville said, "You sudden child! And in July and August too. ... But you'll only have a month before you join Nan in Cornwall, won't you?"

Gerda nodded, munching a buttered scone.

Grandmamma, like an old war-horse scenting the fray, thought, "Is it going to be an affair? Will they fall in love? And what of Nan?" then rebuked herself for forgetting what she really knew quite well, having been told it often, that men and girls in these days worked together and did everything together, with no thought of affairs or of falling in love. ... Only these two were very attractive, the young Briscoe and the pretty child Gerda.

Neville, who knew Gerda, and that she was certainly in love again (it happened so often with Gerda), thought, "Shall I stop it? Or shall I let things take their course? Oh, I'll let them alone. It's only one of Gerda's childish hero-worships, and he'll be kind without flirting. It'll do Gerda good to go on with this new work she's so keen on. And she knows he cares for Nan. I shall let her go."

Neville very nearly always let Gerda and Kay go their own way now that they were grown-up. To interfere would have been the part of the middle-aged, old-fashioned mother, and for that part Neville had no liking. To be her children's friend and good comrade, that was her role in life.

"It's good of you to have her," she said to Barry. "I hope you won't be sorry. … She's very stupid sometimes—regular Johnny Head-in-air."

"I should be a jolly sight more use," Kay remarked. "But I can't come, unfortunately. She can't spell, you know. And her punctuation is weird."

"She'll learn," said Barry cheerfully, and Gerda smiled serenely at them over her tea-cup.

▶•◀

IV

Barry in the office was quick and alert and cheerful and businesslike and very decided, and sometimes impatient. Efficient: that was the word. He would skim the correspondence and dictate answers out of his head, walking about the room, interrupted all the time by the telephone and by people coming in to see him. Gerda's hero-worship grew and grew; her soul swelled with it, and she shut it down tight and remained calm and cool. When he joked, when he smiled his charming smile, her heart turned over within her. When he had signed the typed letters, she would sometimes put her hand for a moment where his had rested on the paper. He was stern with her sometimes, spoke sharply and impatiently, and that, in a queer way, she liked. She had felt the same pleasure at school, when the head of the school, whom she had greatly and secretly venerated, had had her up to the sixth-form room and rowed her. Why? That was for psycho-analysts to discover. Gerda only knew the fact. And after Barry had spoken sharply to her, when he had got over his anger, he would smile and be even kinder than usual, and that was the best of all.

There were other people in the office, of course; men and women, busy, efficient, coming in and out, talking, working, organising. They were kind and pleasant people. Gerda liked them, but they were shadowy.

And behind them all, and behind Barry, there was the work. The work was enormously interesting. Gerda, child of her generation and of her parents, was really a democrat, really public-spirited, outside the little private cell of her withdrawn reserves. Beauty wasn't enough; making poetry and pictures wasn't enough; one had to give everyone his and her chance to have beauty and poetry and pictures too. In spite of having been brought up in this creed by parents, Gerda and Kay held to it, had not reacted from it to a selfish aristocracy, as you might think would be likely. Their democraticness went much farther than that of their parents. They had been used ardently to call themselves Bolshevists until such time as it was forced upon them that Bolshevism was not, in point of fact, a democratic system. They and some of their friends still occasionally used that label, in moments rather of after-dinner enthusiasm than of the precise thinking that is done in morning light. For, after all, even Mr. Bertrand Russell, even Mrs. Philip Snowden, might be wrong in their hurried jottings-down of the results of a cursory survey of so intricate a system. And, anyhow, Bolshevism had the advantage that it had not yet been tried in this country, and no-one, not even the most imaginative and clear-sighted political theorist, could forecast the precise form into which the curious British climate might mould it if it should ever adopt it. So that to believe in it was, anyhow, easier than believing in anything which *had* been tried (and, like all things which are tried, found wanting), such as Liberalism, Toryism, Socialism, and so forth.

But the W.E.A. was a practical body, which went in for practical adventure. Dowdy, schoolmarmish, extension-lecturish, it might be and doubtless was. But a real thing, with guts in it, really doing something; and, after all, you can't be incendiarising the political and economic constitution all your time. In your times off you can do something useful, something which shows results, and for which such an enormous amount of faith and hope is not required. Work for the Revolution—yes, of course, one did that; one studied the literature of the Internationals; one talked. … But did one help the Revolution on much, when all was said? Whereas in the W.E.A. office one really got things done; one typed a letter and something happened because of it; more adult classes occurred, more workers got educated. Gerda, too young and too serious to be cynical, believed that this must be right and good.

V

A clever, strange, charming child, old and young beyond her twenty years, Barry found her. Her wide-set blue eyes seemed to see horizons, and too often to be blind to foregrounds. She had a slow, deliberating habit of work, and was of some things astonishingly ignorant, with the ignorance of those who, when at school, have worked at what they preferred and quietly ignored the rest. If he let her compose a letter, its wording would be quaint. Her prose was, in fact, worse than her verse, and that was to say a good deal. But she was thorough, never slipshod. Her brain ground slowly, but it ground exceeding small; there were no blurred edges to her apprehension of facts; either she didn't know a thing or she did, and that sharp and clear distinction is none too common. She would file and index papers with precision, and find them again, slow and sure, when they were required. Added to these secretarial gifts, such as they were, she had vision; she saw always the dream through or in spite of the business; she was like Barry himself in that. She was a good companion, too, though she had no wit and not very much humour, and none of Nan's gifts of keen verbal brilliance, frequent ribaldry, and quick response; she would digest an idea slowly, and did not make jokes; her clear mind had the quality of a crystal rather than of a flashing diamond. The rising generation; the woman citizen of to-morrow: what did not rest on her, and what might she not do and be? Nan, on the other hand, was the woman citizen of to-day. And Nan did not bother to use her vote because she found all the parties and all the candidates about equally absurd. Barry had argued with Nan about that, but made no impression on her cynical indifference; she had met him with levity. To Gerda there was a wrong and a right in politics, instead of only a lot of wrongs; touching young faith. Nan called it, but Barry, who shared it, found it cheering.

This pretty little white pixyish person, with her yellow hair cut straight across her forehead and waving round her neck like the curled, shining petals of a celandine, with her straight-thinking mind, and her queer, secret, mystic thoughts—she was the woman of the future, a citizen and a mother of citizens. She and the other girls and boys were out to build the new heaven and the new earth, and their children would carry it on. This responsibility of Gerda's invested her with a special interest in the eyes of Barry, who lived and worked for the future, and who, when he saw an infant mewling and puking in a pram, was apt to think: "The hope for the world," and smile at it encouragingly, overlooking its present foolishness of aspect and habit. If ever he had children … if Nan would marry him … but Nan would always lightly slide away when he got near her. … He could see her now, with the cool, amused smile tilting her lips, always sliding away, eluding him. … Nan, like a wild animal for grace, brilliant like blown fire, cool like the wind, stabbing herself and him with her keen wit …

Gerda, looking up from her typewriter to say: "How do you spell comparatively?" saw his face in its momentary bitterness as he frowned, pen in hand, out of the window. He was waiting to sign the letters before he went out to a committee meeting, and she thought she was annoying him by her slowness. She spelt comparatively anyhow, and with the whole-hearted wrongness to which she and the typewriter, both bad spellers, often attained in conjunction, hastily finished, and laid the letters before him. Called back to work and actuality, Barry was cheerful again, and kind, and corrected comparatively with a smile.

"You might ask me," he suggested, "instead of experimenting, when I do happen to be at hand. Otherwise a dictionary, or Miss Pinner in the next room …?"

Gerda was happy, now that the shadow was off his face. Raillery and rebuke she did not mind; only the shadow, which fell coldly on her heart too.

He left the office then for the day, as he often did, but it was warm and alive with his presence, and she was doing his work, and she would see him again in the morning.

▶•◀

VI

Gerda only went home for week-ends now; it was too slow a journey to make every morning and evening. She stayed during the week at a hostel called the Red House, in an alley off Bouverie Street. It was a hostel kept by revolutionary souls exclusively for revolutionary souls. Gerda, who had every right there, had gained admittance through friends of hers who lodged there. Every evening at six o'clock she went back through the rain, as she did this evening, and changed her wet clothes and sat down to dinner, a meal which all the revolutionary souls ate together, so that it was sacramental, a breaking of common bread in token of a common faith.

They were a friendly party. At one end of the table Aunt Phyllis presided. Aunt Phyllis, who was really the aunt only of one young man, kept this Red House. She was a fiery little revolutionary in the late forties, small and thin and darting, full of ideals, faith and fire. She was on the staff of the *British Bolshevist*, and, for the rest, wrote leaflets, which showered from her as from trees in autumn gales. People are even as trees; it is in the autumn of life that they scatter leaflets in profusion, more leaflets and yet more, until at last in the winter they stand bare and bereft. But it would not for long years be winter with Aunt Phyllis, nor yet with the Reverend Anselm Digby, the only other person in the Red House who had attained his autumn and the leaflet habit. Mr. Digby had also the platform habit; he would go round the country talking and talking, denouncing and inciting to revolution in the name of Christ and of the Third International. Though grizzled, he belonged to the League of Youth, as well as to many other eager fraternities. He was unbeneficed, having no time for parish work. This ardent clergyman sat at the other end of Aunt Phyllis's table, as befitted his years.

The space between the two ends was filled by younger creatures. It was spring with them; their leaflets were yet green and unfallen; all that fell from them was poetry, pathetic in its sadness, bitter in its irony, free of metrical or indeed of any other restraints, and mainly either about how unpleasant had been the trenches in which they had spent the Great War, and those persons over military age who had not been called upon to enter them, or about freedom; free love, free thought, and a free world. (I am aware that both these subjects sound a little old-fashioned, but the Red House was concerned with these elemental things which do not change.) And some of them also wrote fiction, quiet and grey and a little tired, about unhappy persons to whom nothing was very glad or very sad, and certainly neither right nor wrong, but only rough or smooth of surface, bright or dark of hue, sweet or bitter of taste or smell. To sum up, most of those in the room belonged to a Freudian circle at their club, and all were anti-Christian, except an Irish Roman Catholic, who had taken an active part in the Easter Rising of 1916, and since then had been living in exile, Aunt Phyllis, who believed in no churches but in the Love of God, and, of course, Mr. Digby. All these people, though they did not always get on very well together, were linked by a common aim in life, and common hatreds. There are many bases on which rooms can be, and are, shared. There is love, which is all right while it lasts. There is financial convenience, which does not, on the whole, last quite so long, but leaves less bitterness behind it when it ceases to be. There is mere gregariousness, the dislike of solitude, which lasts for ever but does not necessarily make the selected alternative agreeable. There are other bonds, such as bridge, and lastly there are common distastes. When the members of the present

Government of Great Britain and Ireland come up for judgment (if indeed such as they survive this earthly life, and we may take it that if any of us do so they will, for they have brought survival to a fine art), it should be remembered in their favour that they were on this earth a link between many whom neither temperament nor circumstances would otherwise have joined.

But, in spite of hate, the Red House lodgers were a happy set of revolutionaries. The girls had the jolly spirits common to girls of every shade of political opinion or none; the young men had some wit, and Mr. Digby and Aunt Phyllis the merry jests natural to their years. When I say they were revolutionaries, the word must be understood in its extremest sense. They were not merely, as are most intelligent people, theoretical opposers of existing institutions, governments, and economic and social conditions, feeding their opinions on the radical and labour press, but taking no practical action on account of them. These were real revolutionaries; they had their leaflets printed by secret presses; they belonged to societies which exchanged confidential letters with the more eminent Russians, such as Litvinoff and Trotsky, collected for future publication secret circulars, private strike-breaking orders, and other *obiter dicta* of a rash government, and believed themselves to be working to establish the Soviet Government over Europe. They had been all this summer very angry because the Glasgow conference of the I.L.P. had broken with the Third International. They spoke with acerbity of Mr. Ramsay MacDonald and Mr. and Mrs. Philip Snowden. But now, in August, they had little acerbity to spare for anything but the Government's conduct of Irish affairs. Donnell O'Meagher, the Irishman, would sometimes stop eating and push back his chair, pale and frowning.

"Don't you like your pudding, Mr. O'Meagher?" Aunt Phyllis asked him, the first time he did this.

"I do not," said Mr. O'Meagher, but symbolically rather than literally, "and the Mayor dying in Brixton jail as we eat it." He unobtrusively crossed himself under the table; he was really devout.

But no one else left their pudding for that reason, though they sometimes had others. "After all," a practical young woman pointed out, "it isn't as if he would eat it, even if it was set before him. So *we* may as well."

Mr. Digby was roused.

"We ought none of us to eat—not a mouthful," he declaimed. "We ought all to go on hunger-strike until every Irish political prisoner is released and till every poor man has a living wage, every poor woman a maternity benefit, and every slum child a free meal."

"Slums! What about Central Europe?" interpolated Aunt Phyllis, who was something on the Save the Children Council.

"And," finished Mr. Digby, "till every starving child everywhere has its little stomach as tight as a drum. We should go on *strike*. It's the only way to bring a Government like this to its senses. Jesus Christ would have been the greatest strike organiser of the present century, had he lived in it."

One of the company, a fair young man, even more interested in art and letters than in strikes, sighed gently, as was his habit when Jesus Christ was mentioned, and said something about the forthcoming number of *Côterie*.

Aunt Phyllis thought Anselm Digby was a pathetic figure, beating his hand on the table and getting so earnest and excited among all the cynical young. Of them all, only the Sinn Feiner had religious associations with the name Jesus Christ, and his would be the incensey associations of the Catholic, mixed up with tabernacles and wafers and processions and the Blessed Virgin, rather than with the organisation of strikes. People's religions were so different, when they had any. Aunt Phyllis herself believed in God; a humanitarian, pacifist God of love, whose present chief aims were to Save the Children and abolish armaments, and without whom not one Conscientious Objector could fall to the ground. Not quite so fiery a God as Anselm Digby's, though affectionately encouraging to strikers. And no one else present believed in any God at all.

►•◄

VII

But, though these were Gerda's own people, the circle in which she felt at home, she looked forward every night to the morning, when there would be the office again, and Barry.

Sometimes Barry took her out to dinner and a theatre. They went to the *Beggar's Opera*, *The Grain of Mustard Seed*, *Mary Rose* (which they found sentimental), and the *Beggar's Opera* again. Gerda had her own ideas, very definite and critical, about dramatic merit. Barry enjoyed discussing the plays with her, listening to her clear little silver voice pronouncing judgment. Gerda might be for ever mediocre in any form of artistic expression, but she was an artist, with the artist's love of merit and scorn of the second-rate.

They went to *Mary Rose* with some girl cousins of Barry's, two jolly girls from Girton. Against their indiscriminating enthusiasm, Gerda and her fastidious distaste stood out sharp and clear, like some delicate etching among flamboyant pictures. That fastidiousness she had of both her parents, with something of her own added.

Barry went home with her. He wondered how her fastidiousness stood the grimy house in Magpie Alley and its ramshackle habit of life, after the distinctions and beauty of Windover, but he thought it was probably very good for her, part of the experience which should mould the citizen. Gerda shrank from no experience. At the corner of Bouverie Street they met a painted girl out for hire, strayed for some reason into this unpropitious locality. For the moment Gerda had fallen behind and Barry seemed alone. The girl stopped in his path, looked up in his face inquiringly, and he pushed his way, not ungently, past her. The next moment Gerda's hand caught his arm.

"Stop, Barry, stop."

"Stop? What for?"

"The woman. Didn't you see?"

"My dear child, I can't do anything for her."

Like the others of her generation, Gerda was interested in persons of that profession; he knew that already; only they saw them through a distorting mist.

"We can find out where she works, what wages she gets, why she's on the streets. She's probably working for sweated wages somewhere. We *ought* to find out."

"We can't find out about every woman of that kind we meet. The thing is to attack the general principle behind the thing, not each individual case. ... Besides, it would be so frightfully impertinent of us. How would you like it if someone stopped you in the street and asked you where you worked and whether you were sweated or not, and why you were out so late?"

"I shouldn't mind, if they wanted to know for a good reason. One *ought* to find out how things are, what people's conditions are."

It was what Barry, too, believed and practised, but he could only say, "It's the wrong way round. You've got to work from the centre to the circumference. ... And don't fall into the sentimental mistake of thinking that all prostitution comes from sweated labour. A great deal does, of course, but a great deal, too, because it seems to some women an easy and attractive way of earning a living. ... Oh, hammer away at sweated labour for all you're worth, of course. For that reason and every other; but you won't stop prostitution till you stop the demand for it. That's the poisonous root of the thing. So long as the demand goes on, you'll get the supply, whatever economic conditions may be."

Gerda fell silent, pondering on the strange tastes of those who desired for some reason the temporary company of these unfortunate females, so unpleasing to the eye, to the ear, to the mind, to the smell; desired it so much that they would pay money for it. *Why?* Against that riddle the non-comprehension of her sex beat itself, baffled. She might put it the other way round, try to imagine herself desiring, paying for, the temporary

– 108 –

attentions of some dirty, common, vapid and patchouli-scented man—and still she got no nearer. For she never could desire it. ... Well, anyhow, there the thing was. Stop the demand? Stop that desire of men for women? Stop the ready response of women to it? If that was the only way, then there was indeed nothing for it but education—and was even education any use for that?

"Is it love," she asked of Barry, "that the men who want these women feel?"

Barry laughed shortly. "Love? Good Lord, no."

"What then, Barry?"

"I don't know that it can be explained, exactly. ... It's a passing taste, I suppose, a desire for the company of another sex from one's own, just because it *is* another sex, though it may have no other attractions. ... It's no use trying to analyse it, one doesn't get anywhere. But it's not love."

"What's love, then? What's the difference?"

"Have I to define love, walking down Bouverie Street? You could do it as well as I could. Love has the imagination in it, and the mind. I suppose that's the difference. And, too, love wants to give. This is all platitude. No one can ever say anything new about love, it's all been said. Got your latchkey?"

Gerda let herself into the Red House and went up to bed and lay wakeful. Very certainly she loved Barry, with all her imagination and all her mind, and she would have given him more than all that was hers. Very surely and truly she loved him, even if after all he was to be her uncle by marriage, which would make their family life like that in one of Louis Couperus's books. But why unhappy like that? Was love unhappy? If she might see him sometimes, talk to him, if Nan wouldn't want all of him all the time—and it would be unlike Nan to do that—she could be happy. One could share, after all. Women must share, for there were a million more women in England than men.

But probably Nan didn't mean to marry him at all. Nan never married people. ...

▶●◀

VIII

Next morning at the office Barry said he had heard from Nan. She had asked him to come, too, and bicycle in Cornwall, with her and Gerda and Kay.

"You will, won't you?" said Gerda.

"Rather, of course."

A vaguely puzzled note sounded in his voice. But he would come.

Cornwall was illuminated to Gerda. The sharing process would begin there. But for a week more she had him to herself, and that was better.

CHAPTER VIII

NAN

►•◄

I

Nan at Marazion bathed and sailed and climbed and walked and finished her book. She had a room at St. Michael's Café, at the edge of the little town, just above the beach. Across a space of sea at high tide, and of wet sand and a paved causeway slimy with seaweed at the ebb, St. Michael's Mount loomed, dark against a sunset sky, pale and unearthly in the dawn, an embattled ship riding anchored on full waters, or stranded on drowned sands.

Nan stayed at the empty little town to be alone. But she was not alone all the time, for at Newlyn, five miles away, there was the artist colony and some of these were her friends. (In point of fact, it is impossible to be alone in Cornwall; the place to go to for that would be Hackney, or some other district of outer London, where inner Londoners do not go for holidays.) She could, if she had liked, have had friends to play with all day and talk and laughter and music all night, as in London. She did not like. She went out by herself, and worked by herself, and all the time, in company or alone, talking or working, she knew herself withdrawn really into a secret cove of her own which was warm and golden as no actual coves this chill summer were warm and golden; a cove on whose good brown sand she lay and made castles and played, while at her feet the great happy sea danced and beat, the great tumbling sea on which she would soon put out her boat.

She would count the days before Barry would be with her.

"Three weeks now. Twenty days; nineteen, eighteen ..." desiring neither to hurry nor to retard them, but watching them slip behind her in a deep content. When he came, he and Gerda and Kay, they would spend one night and day in Marazion, lounging about its beach, and in Newlyn, with its steep crooked streets between old grey walls hung with shrubs, and beyond Newlyn, in the tiny fishing hamlets that hung above the little coves from Penzance to Land's End. They were going to bicycle all along the south coast. But before that they would have had it out, she and Barry; probably here, in the little pale climbing fishing-town. No matter where, and no matter how; Nan cared nothing for scenic arrangements. All she had to do was to convey to Barry that she would say "yes" now to the question she had put off and off, let him ask it, give her answer, and the thing would be done.

▶•◀

II

Meanwhile she wrote the last chapters of her book, sitting on the beach among drying nets and boats, in some fishing cove up the coast. The Newlyn shore she did not like, because the artist-spoilt children crowded round her, interrupting.

"Lady, lady! Will you paint us?"

"No. I don't paint."

"Then what *are* you doing?"

"Writing. Go away."

"May we come with you to where you're staying?"

"No. Go away."

"Last year a lady took us to her studio and gave us pennies. And when she'd gone back to London she sent us each a doll."

Silence.

"Lady, if we come with you to your studio, will you give us pennies?"

"No. Why should I?"

"You might because you wanted to paint us. You might because you liked us."

"I don't do either. Go away now."

They withdrew a little and turned somersaults, supposing her to be watching. The artistic colony had a lot to answer for, Nan thought; they were making parasites and prostitutes of the infant populace. Children could at their worst be detestable in their vanity, their posing, their affectation, their unashamed greed.

"Barry's and mine," she thought ("I suppose we'll have some), shall at least not pose. They may break all the commandments, but if they turn somersaults to be looked at I shall drop them into a public *crèche* and abandon them."

The prettiest little girl looked sidelong at the unkind lady, and believed her half smile to denote admiration. Pretty little girls often make this error.

Stephen Lumley came along the beach. It was lunch-time, and after lunch they were going out sailing. Stephen Lumley was the most important artist just now in Newlyn. He had been in love with Nan since some months, and did not get on with his wife. Nan liked him; he painted brilliantly, and was an attractive, clever, sardonic person. Sailing with him was fun. They understood each other; they had rather the same cynical twist to them. They understood each other really better than Nan and Barry did. Neither of them needed to make any effort to apprehend one another's point of view. And each left the other where they were. Whereas Barry filled Nan, beneath her cynicism, beneath her levity, with something quite new—a queer desire, to put it simply, for goodness, for straight living and generous thinking, even, within reason, for usefulness. More and more he flooded her inmost being, drowning the old landmarks, like the sea at high tide. Nan was not a Christian, did not believe in God, but she came near at this time to believing in Christianity as a life, that it might be a fine and adventurous thing to live.

►•◄

III

Echoes of the great little world so far off came to the Cornish coasts, through the *Western Mercury,* and the stray, belated London papers one occasionally saw. Rumours of a projected coal strike, of fighting in Mesopotamia, of political prisoners on hunger-strike, of massacres in Ireland and murdered typists at watering-places; echoes of Fleet Street quarrels, of Bolshevik gold ("Not a bond! Not a franc! Not a rouble!"), and, from the religious world, of fallen man and New Faiths for Old. And on Sundays one bought a paper which had for its special star turn the reminiscences of the expansive wife of one of our more patient politicians. The world went on just the same, quarrelling and chattering and lying, sentimental, busy and richly absurd, its denizens tilting against each other's politics, murdering each other, trying and always failing to swim across the channel, and always talking, talking, talking. Marazion and Newlyn and every other place were the world in little, doing all the same things in their own miniature way. Each human soul was the world in little with all the same conflicts, hopes, emotions, excitements, and intrigues. But Nan, swimming and sailing, eating, writing, walking, and lounging, browning in salt winds and waters, was happy and remote, like a savage on an island who meditates exclusively on his own affairs.

►●◄

IV

Nan met them at Penzance station. The happy three; they would be good to make holiday with. Already they had holiday faces, though not yet browned like Nan's.

Barry's hand gripped Nan's. He was here, then, and it had come. Her head swam; she felt light, like thistledown on the wind.

They came up from the station into quiet, gay, warm Penzance, and had tea at a shop. They were going to stay at Marazion that night and the next, and spend the day bicycling to Land's End and back. They were all four full of vigour, brimming with life and energy that needed to be spent. But Gerda looked pale.

"She's been overworking in a stuffy office," Barry said. "And not, except when she dined with me, getting proper meals. What do you think she weighs, Nan?"

"About as much as that infant there," Nan said, indicating a stout person of five at the next table.

"Just about, I dare say. She's only six stone. What are we to do about it?"

His eyes caressed Gerda, as they might have caressed a child. He would be a delightful uncle by marriage, Nan thought.

They took the road to Marazion. The tide was going out. In front of them the Mount rode in a shallowing violet sea.

"My word!" said Barry, and Kay, screwing up his eyes, murmured, "Good old Mount." Gerda's lips parted in a deep breath; beauty always struck her dumb.

Into the pale-washed, straggling old village they rode, stabled their bicycles, and went down to the shining evening sands, where now the paved causeway to the Mount was all exposed, running slimy and seaweedy between rippled wet sands and dark, slippery rocks. Bare-footed they trod it, Gerda and Kay in front, Barry and Nan behind, and the gulls talking and wheeling round them.

Nan stopped, the west in her eyes. "Look."

Point beyond point they saw stretching westward to Land's End, dim and dark beyond a rose-flushed sea.

"Isn't it clear?" said Nan. "You can see the cliff villages ever so far along ... Newlyn, Mousehole, Clement's Island off it—and the point of Lamorna."

Barry said, "We'll go to Land's End by the coast road to-morrow, shan't we, not the high road?"

"Oh, the coast road, yes. It's about twice the distance, with the ups and downs, and you can't ride all the way. But we'll go by it."

For a moment they stood side by side, looking westward over the bay.

Nan said, "Aren't you glad you came?"

"I should say so!"

His answer came, quick and emphatic. There was a pause after it. Nan suddenly turned on him the edge of a smile.

Barry did not see it. He was not looking at her, nor over the bay, but in front of him, to where Gerda, a thin little upright form, moved bare-legged along the shining causeway to the moat.

Nan's smile flickered out. The sunset tides of rose flamed swiftly over her cheeks, her neck, her body, and receded as sharply, as if someone had hit her in the face. Her pause, her smile, had been equivalent, as she saw them, to a permission, even to an invitation. He had turned away unnoticing, a queer, absent tenderness in his eyes, as they followed Gerda ... Gerda ... walking light-footed up the wet causeway. ... Well, if he had got out of the habit of wanting to make love to her, she would not offer him chances again. When he got the habit back, he must make his own chances as best he could.

"Come on," said Nan. "We must hurry."

She left no more pauses, but talked all the time, about Newlyn, about the artists, about the horrid children, the fishing, the gulls, the weather.

"And how's the book?" he asked.

"Nearly done. I'm waiting for the end to make itself."

He smiled, and looking round at him she saw that he was not smiling at her or her book, but at Gerda, who had stepped off the causeway and was wading in a rock pool.

He must be obsessed with Gerda; he thought of her, apparently, all the time he was talking about other things. It was irritating for an aunt to bear.

They joined Kay and Gerda on the island. Kay was prowling about, looking for a way by which to enter the forbidden castle. Kay always trespassed when he could, and was so courteous and gentle when he was caught at it that he disarmed comment. But this time he could not manage to evade the polite but firm eye of the fisherman on guard. They crossed over to Marazion again all together, and went to the café for supper.

▶•◀

V

It was a merry, rowdy meal they had; ham and eggs and coffee in an upper room, with the soft sea air blowing in on them through open windows. Nan and Barry chattered, and Kay took his cheerful part; only Gerda was sparse of word, quiet and dreamy, with her blue eyes opened wide against sleep, for she had not slept until late last night.

"High time she had a holiday," Barry said of her. "Four weeks' grind in August—it's beginning to tell now."

Fussy Barry was about the child. As bad as Frances Carr with Pamela. Gerda was as strong as a little pony really, though she looked such a small, white, brittle thing.

They got out maps and schemed out roads and routes over their cigarettes. Then they strolled about the little town, exploring its alleys and narrow by-ways that gave on the sea. The moon had risen now, and Marazion was cut steeply in shadow and silver light, and all the bay lay in shadow and silver too, to where the lights of Penzance twinkled like a great lit church.

Barry thought once, as he had often thought in the past, "How brilliant Nan is, and how gay. No wonder she never needed me. She needs no-one," and this time it did not hurt him to think it. He loved to listen to her, to talk and laugh with her, to look at her, but he was free at last; he demanded nothing of her. Those restless, urging, disappeared hopes and longings lay dead in him, dead and at peace. He could not have put his finger on the moment of their death; there had been no moment; like good soldiers they had never died, but faded away, and till to-night he had not known that they had gone. He would show Nan now that she need fear no more pestering from him; she need not keep on talking without pause whenever they were alone together, which had been her old way of defence, and which she was beginning again now. They could drop now into undisturbed friendship. Nan was the most stimulating of friends. It was refreshing to talk things out with her again, to watch her quick mind flashing and turning and cutting its way, brilliant and clear and sharp, like a diamond.

They went to bed; Barry and Kay to the room they had got above a public-house. Nan and Gerda to Nan's room at the café, where they squeezed into one bed.

Gerda slept, lying very straight and still, as was her habit in sleep. Nan lay wakeful and restless, watching the moonlight steal across the floor, lie palely on the bed, and on Gerda's waxen face and yellow hair. The pretty, pale child, strange in sleep, like a little mermaiden lost on earth. Nan, sitting up in bed, one dark plait hanging over each shoulder, watched her with brooding, amber eyes. How young she was, how very, very young. It was touching to be so young. Yet why, when youth was, people said, the best time? It wasn't really touching to be young; it was touching not to be young, because you had less of life left. Touching to be thirty; more touching to be forty; tragic to be fifty, and heartbreaking to be sixty. As to seventy, as to eighty, one would feel as one did during the last dance of a ball, tired but fey in the paling dawn, desperately making the most of each bar of music before one went home to bed. That was touching; Mrs. Hilary and Grandmamma were touching. Not Gerda and Kay, with their dance just beginning.

A bore, this sharing one bed. You couldn't sleep, however small and quiet your companion lay. They must get a bed each when they could, during this tour. One must sleep. If one didn't one began to think. Every time Nan forced herself to the edge of sleep, a picture sprang sharply before her eyes—the flaming sky and sea, herself and Barry standing together on the causeway.

"Aren't you glad you came?" Her own voice, soft, encouraging.

"I should say so!" The quick, matter-of-fact answer.

Then a pause, and she turning on him the beginnings of a smile. An allowing, inviting ... seductive ... smile.

And he, smiling too, but not at her, looking away to where Gerda and Kay walked bare-legged to the Mount.

Flame scorched her again. The pause each time she saw it now became longer, more deliberate, more inviting, more emptily unfilled. Her smile became more luring, his more rejecting. As she saw it now, in the cruel, distorting night, he had seen her permission and refused it. By day she had known that simple Barry had seen nothing; by day she would know it again. Between days are set nights of white, searing flame, two in a bed so that one cannot sleep. Damn Gerda, lying there so calm and cool. It had been a mistake to ask Gerda to come; if it hadn't been for Gerda they wouldn't have been two in a bed.

"Barry's a good deal taken up with her just now," said Nan to herself, putting it into plain, deliberate words, as was her habit with life's situations. "He does get taken up with pretty girls, I suppose, when he's thrown with them. All men do, if you come to that. For the moment he's thinking about her, not about me. That's a bore. It will bore me to death if it goes on. ... I wonder how long it will go on? I wonder how soon he'll want to make love to me again?"

Having thus expressed the position in clear words, Nan turned her mind elsewhere. What do people think of when they are seeking sleep?

It is worse than no use to think of what one is writing; that wakes one up, goads every brain-cell into unwholesome activity. No use thinking of people; they are too interesting. Nor of sheep going through gates; they tumble over one another and make one's head ache. Nor of the coming day; that is too difficult; nor of the day which is past; that is too near. Wood paths, quiet seas, running streams—these are better. Or the wind in trees, or owls crying, or waves beating on warm shores. The waves beat now; ran up whisperingly with the incoming tide, broke, and sidled back, dragging at the wet sand. ... Nan, hearing them, drifted at last into sleep.

CHAPTER IX

THE PACE

▶•◀

I

The coast road to Land's End is like a switchback. You climb a mountain, and are flung down to sea-level like a shooting star, and climb a mountain again. Sometimes the road becomes a sandy cliff path, and you have to walk.

But at last, climbing up and being shot down and walking, Nan and Barry and Gerda and Kay reached Land's End. They went down to Sennan Cove to bathe, and the high sea was churning breakers on the beach. Nan dived through them with the arrowy straightness of a fish or a submarine, came up behind them, and struck out to sea. The others behind her, less skilful, floundered and were dashed about by the waves. Barry and Kay struggled through them somehow, bruised and choked; Gerda, giving it up—she was no great swimmer—tranquilly rolled and paddled in the surf by herself.

Kay called to her, mocking.

"Coward. Sensualist. Come over the top like a man."

Nan, turning to look at her from the high crest of a wave, thought, "Gerda's afraid in a high sea. She is afraid of things: I remember."

Nan herself was afraid of very little. She had that kind of buoyant physical gallantry which would take her into the jaws of danger with a laugh. When in London during the air raids she had walked about the streets to see what could be seen; in France with the Fannys she had driven cars over shelled roads with a cool composure which distinguished her even among that remarkably cool and composed set of young women; as a child she had ridden unbroken horses and teased and dodged savage bulls for the fun of it; she would go sailing in seas that fishermen refused to go out in, part angry dogs which no other onlooker would touch, sleep out alone in dark and lonely woods, and even on occasion brave pigs. The kind of gay courage she had was a physical gift which can never be acquired. What can be acquired, with blood and tears, is the courage of the will, stubborn and unyielding, but always nerve-racked, proudly and tensely strung up. Nan's form of fearlessness, combined as it was with the agility of a supple body excellently trained, would carry her lightly through all physical adventures, much as her arrowy strength and skill carried her through the breakers without blundering or mishap, and let her now ride buoyantly on each green mountain as it towered.

Barry, emerging spluttering from one of these, said, "All very jolly for you, Nan. You're a practised hand. We're being drowned. I'm going out of it," and dived through another wave for the shore. Kay, a clumsier swimmer, followed him, and Nan rode her tossing horses, laughing at them, till she was shot on to the beach and dug her fingers deep into the sucking sand.

"A very pretty landing," said Barry generously, rubbing his bruised limbs and coughing up water.

Gerda rose from the foam where she had been playing serenely impervious to the tauntings of Kay.

Barry said, "Happy child. She's not filled up with salt water and battered black and blue."

Nan remarked that neither was she, and they went to their rock crannies to dress. They dressed and undressed in a publicity, a mixed shamelessness, which would have appalled Councillor Clarke.

They rode back to Marazion after tea along the high road, more soberly than they had come.

"Tired, Gerda?" Barry said, at the tenth mile, as they pulled up a hill. "Hold on to me."

Gerda refused to do so mean a thing. She had her own sense of honour, and believed that every one should carry his or her own burden. But when they had to get off and walk up the hill, she let him help to push her bicycle.

"Give us a few days. Nan," said Barry, "and we'll all be as fit as you. At present we're fat and scant of breath from our sedentary and useful life."

"Our life"—as if they had only the one between them.

At Newlyn Nan stopped. She said she was going to supper with someone there and would come on later. She was, in fact, tired of them. She dropped into Stephen Lumley's studio, which was, as usual after painting hours, full of his friends, talking and smoking. That was the only way to spend the evening, thought Nan, talking and smoking and laughing and never pausing. That was, anyhow, the way she spent it.

She got back to Marazion at ten o'clock, and went to her room at the little café. Looking from its window, she saw the three on the shore by the moonlit sea. Kay was standing on the paved causeway, and Barry and Gerda, some way off, were wading among the rocks, bending over the pools, as if they were looking for crabs.

Nan went to bed. When Gerda came in presently, she lay very still and pretended to be asleep.

It was dreadful, another night of sharing a bed. Dreadful to he so close one to the other; dreadful to touch accidentally; touching people reminds you how alive they are, with their separate, conscious throbbing life so close against yours.

▶•◀

‖

Next morning they took the road eastward. They were going to ride along the coast to Talland Bay, where they were going to spend a week. They were giving themselves a week to get there, which would allow plenty of time for bathing by the way. It is no use hurrying in Cornwall, the hills are too steep and the sea too attractive, and lunch and tea, when ordered in shops, so long in coming. The first day they only got round the Lizard to Cadgwith, where they dived from steep rocks into deep blue water. Nan dived from a high rock with a swoop like a sea bird's, a pretty thing to watch. Barry was nearly as good; he too was physically proficient. The Bendishes were less competent; they were so much younger, as Barry said. But they, too, reached the water head first, which is, after all, the main thing in diving. And as often as Nan dived, with her arrowy swoop, Gerda tumbled in too, from the same rock, and when Nan climbed a yet higher rock and dived again, Gerda climbed too, and fell in sprawling after her. Gerda to-day was not to be outdone, anyhow in will to attempt, whatever her achievement might lack. Nan looked up from the sea with a kind of mocking admiration at the little figure poised on the high shelf of rock, slightly unsteady about the knees, slightly blue about the lips, thin white arms pointing forward for the plunge.

The child had pluck. ... It must have hurt, too, that slap on the nearly flat body as she struck the sea. She hadn't done it well. She came up with a dazed look, shaking the water out of her eyes, coughing.

"You're too ambitious," Barry told her. "That was much too high for you. You're also blue with cold. Come out."

Gerda looked up at Nan, who was scrambling nimbly on to the highest ledge of all, crying, "I must have one more."

Barry said to Gerda, "No, you're not going after her. You're coming out. It's no use you're thinking you can do all Nan does. None of us can."

Gerda gave up. The pace was too hard for her. She couldn't face that highest rock; the one below had made her feel cold and queer and shaky as she stood on it. Besides, why was she trying, for the first time in her life, to go Nan's pace, which had always been, and was now more than ever before, too hot and mettlesome for her? She didn't know why; only that Nan had been, somehow, all day setting the pace, daring her, as it were, to make it. It was becoming, oddly, a point of honour between them, and neither knew how or why.

▶●◀

III

On the road it was the same. Nan, with only the faintest, if any, application of brakes, would commit herself to lanes which leaped precipitously downwards like mountain streams, zigzagging like a dog's-tooth pattern, shingled with loose stones, whose unseen end might be a village round some sharp turn, or a cove by the sea, or a field path running to a farm, or merely the foot of one hill and the beginning of the steep pull up the next. Coast roads in Cornwall are like that—often uncertain in their ultimate goal (for map-makers, like bicyclists, are apt to get tired of them, and, tiring, break them off, so to speak, in mid air, leaving them suspended, like snapped ends of string). But, however uncertain their goal may be, their form is not uncertain at all; it can be relied on to be that of a snake in agony leaping down a hill or up; or, if one prefers it, that of a corkscrew plunging downwards into a cork.

Nan leaped and plunged with them. She was at the bottom while the others were still jolting, painfully brake-held, albeit rapidly, half-way down. And sometimes, when the slope was more than usually like the steep roof of a house, the zigzags more than usually acute, the end even less than usually known, the whole situation, in short, more dreadful and perilous, if possible, than usual, the others surrendered, got off and walked. They couldn't really rely on their brakes to hold them, supposing something should swing round on them from behind one of the corners; they couldn't be sure of turning with the road when it turned at its acutest, and such failure of harmony with one's road is apt to meet with a dreadful retribution. Barry was adventurous, and Kay and Gerda were calm, but to all of them life was sweet and limbs and bicycles precious; none of them desired an untimely end.

But Nan laughed at their prognostications of such an end. "It will be found impossible to ride down these hills," said their road-book, and Nan laughed at that too. You can, as she observed, ride down, anything; it is riding up that is the difficulty. Anyhow, she, who had ridden bucking horses and mountainous seas, could ride down anything that bore the semblance of a road. Only fools, Nan believed, met with disasters while bicycling. And jamming on the brakes was bad for the wheels and tiring to the hands. So, brakeless, she zigzagged like greased lightning to the bottom.

It was on the second day, on the long hill that runs from Manaccan down to Helford Ferry, that Gerda suddenly took her brakes off and shot after her. That hill is not a badly spiralling one, but it is long and steep, and usually ridden with brakes. And just above Helford village it has one very sharp turn to the left.

Nan, standing waiting for the others on the bridge, looked round and saw Gerda shooting with unrestrained wheels and composed face round the last bend. Nearly she had swerved over at the turn, but not quite. She got off at the bridge.

"Hallo," said Nan. "Quicker than usual, weren't you?" She had a half grudging, half ironic grin of appreciation for a fellow sportsman, the same grin with which she had looked up at her from the sea at Cadgwith. Nan liked daring. Though it was in her, and she knew that it was in her, to hate Gerda with a cold and deadly anger, the sportsman in her gave its tribute. For what was nothing and a matter of ordinary routine to her, might be, she suspected, rather alarming to the quiet, white-faced child.

Then the demon of mischief leapt in her. If Gerda meant to keep the pace, she should have a pace worth keeping. They would prove to one another which was the better woman, as knights in single combat of old proved it, or fighters in the ring to-day. As to Barry, he should look on at it, whether he liked it or not.

Barry and Kay rushed up to them, and they went through the little thatched, rose-sweet hamlet to the edge of the broad blue estuary and shouted for the ferry.

►•◄

IV

After that the game began in earnest. Nan, from being casually and unconsciously reckless, became deliberately dare-devil, and always with a backward ironic look for Gerda, as if she said, "How about it? Will this beat you?"

"A bicycling tour with Nan isn't nearly so safe as the front trenches of my youth used to be," Barry commented. "Those quiet, comfortable old days!"

There, indeed, one had been liable to be shot, or blown to pieces, or buried, or gassed, and that was about all. But life now was like the Apostle Paul's; they were in journeyings often, in weariness often, in perils of waters, in perils by their own countrymen, in perils on the road, in the wilderness, in the sea, in hunger and thirst, in cold and nakedness. In perils, too, so Gerda believed, of cattle; for these would stray in bellowing herds about narrow lanes, and they would all charge straight through them, missing the lowered horns by some incredible fluke of fortune. (If I seem to make out Gerda a coward, it should be remembered that she showed none of these inward blenchings of hers, but went on her way with the rest, composed as a little wax figure at Madame Tussaud's. She was, in fact, of the stuff of which martyrs are made, and would probably have gone to the stake for a conviction. But stampeding cattle, and high seas, and brakeless lightning descents, she did not like, however brave a face she was sustained by grace to meet them with. It should be remembered, too, that she was only twenty, an age when some people still look beneath their beds before retiring, to discover what is the worst that lies hid thereunder.)

Bulls, even, Gerda was called upon to face, in the wake of two unafraid males and a reckless aunt. What young female of twenty, always excepting those who have worked on the land, and whose chief reward is familiarity with its beasts, can face bulls with complete equanimity? One day a path they were taking down to the sea ran for a while along the top of a stone hedge, about five feet high and three feet wide. Most people would have walked along this, leading their bicycles. Nan, naturally, bicycled, and Barry and Kay, finding it an amusing experiment, bicycled after her. Gerda, in honour bound, bicycled too. She accepted stoically the probability that she would very soon bicycle off the hedge into the field and be hurt. In the fields on either side of them, cows stared at them in mild surprise and some disdain, coming up close to look. So, if one bicycled off, it would be into the very jaws, on to the very horns, of cattle. Female cattle, indeed, but still cattle.

Then Kay chanted, "Fat bulls of Basan came round about me on either side," and so indeed it was. One fat bull, anyhow, trotted up to the hedge, waving his tail and snorting, pawing with his feet and glaring with his eyes, evincing, in short, all the symptoms common to his unattractive kind.

So now if one bicycled off it would be into the very maw of an angry bull.

"You look out you don't fall, Gerda," Kay flung back at her over his shoulder. "It will be to a dreadful death, as you see. Nobody'll save you; nobody'll dare."

"Feeling unsteady?" Barry's gentler voice asked her from behind. "Get off and walk it. I will too."

But Gerda rode on, her eyes on Nan's swift, sure progress ahead. Barry should not see her mettle fail—Barry, who had been through the War and would despise cowards.

They reached the end of the hedge, and the path ran off it into a field. And between this field and the last there was an open gap, through which the bull of Basan lumbered with fierce eyes, and stood waiting for them to descend.

"I don't like that creature," Kay said. "I'm afraid of him. Aren't you, Barry?"

"Desperately," Barry admitted. "Any one would be, except Nan, of course."

Nan was bicycling straight along the field path, and the bull stood staring at her, his head well down, in act, as Gerda saw, to charge. But he did not charge Nan. Bulls and other ferocious beasts think it waste of time to charge the fearless; they get no fun out of an unfrightened victim. He waited instead for Gerda, as well she knew.

Kay followed Nan, still chanting his psalm. Gerda followed Kay. As she dropped from the hedge on to the path she turned round once and met Barry's eyes, her own wide and grave, and she was thinking, "I can bear anything if he is behind me and sees it happen. I couldn't bear it if I was the last and no one saw. To be gored all alone, none to care ... who could bear that?"

The next moment Barry was no longer behind her, but close at her side, bicycling on the grass by the path, between her and the bull. Did he know she was frightened? She hadn't shown it, surely.

"The wind," said Gerda, in her clear, small, crystalline voice, "has gone round more to the south. Don't you think so?" And reminded Barry of a French aristocrat demoiselle going with calm and polite conversation to the scaffold.

"I believe it has," he said, and smiled.

And after all the bull, perhaps, not liking the look of the bicycles, didn't charge at all, but only ran by their sides with snorting noises until they left him behind at the next gate.

"Did you," inquired Gerda casually, "notice that bull? He was an awfully fine one, wasn't he?"

"A remarkably noble face, I thought," Kay returned.

They scrambled down cliffs to the cove and bathed.

V

Nan, experienced in such things, as at the age of thirty-three and a half one is, if one has led a well-spent life, knew now beyond a peradventure what had happened to Barry and what would never happen again between him and her. So that was that, as she put it, definite and matter of fact to herself about it. He had stopped wanting her. Well, then, she must stop wanting him, as speedily as might be. It took a little time. You could not shoot down the hills of the emotions with the lightning rapidity with which you shot down the roads. Also, the process was excruciatingly painful. You had to unmake so many plans, unthink so many thoughts. ... Oh, but that was nothing. You had to hear his voice softened to someone else, see the smile in his eyes caressing someone else, feel his whole mind, his whole soul, reaching out in protecting, adoring care to someone else's charm and loveliness ... as once, as so lately, they had reached out to yours. ... That was torture for the bravest, far worse than any bulls or seas or precipices could be to Gerda. Yet it had to be gone through, as Gerda had to leap from towering cliffs into wild seas and ride calmly among fierce cattle. ... When Nan woke in the night it was like toothache, a sharp, gnawing, searing hell of pain. Memory choked her, bitter self-anger for joy once rejected and then for ever lost, took her by the throat, present desolation drowned her soul in hard, slow tears, jealousy scorched and seared.

But, new every morning, pride rose, mettlesome and gallant, making her laugh and talk, so that no one guessed. And with pride a more reckless physical daring than usual—a kind of scornful adventurousness, that courted danger for its own sake, and wordlessly taunted the weaker spirit with, "Follow if you like and can. If you don't like, if you can't, I am the better woman in that way, though you may be the beloved." And the more the mettle of the little beloved rose to meet the challenge, the hotter the pace grew. Perhaps they both felt, without knowing that they felt it, that there was something in Barry which leaped instinctively out to applaud reckless courage, some element in himself which responded to it even while he called it foolhardy. You could tell that Barry was of that type, by the quick glow of his eyes and smile. But the rivalry in daring was not really for Barry; Barry's choice was made. It was at bottom the last test of mettle, the ultimate challenge from the loser to the winner in the lists chosen by the loser as her own. It was also—for Nan was something of a bully—the heckling of Gerda. She might have won one game, and that the most important, but she should be forced to own herself beaten in another, after being dragged painfully along rough and dangerous ways. And over and above and beyond all this, beyond rivalry and beyond Gerda, was the eternal impatience for adventure as such, for quick, vehement living, which was the essence of Nan. She found things more fun that way: that summed it.

▶•◀

VI

The long, strange days slid by like many-coloured dreams. The steep, tumbling roads tilted behind them, with their pale old white and slate hamlets huddled between fields above a rock-bound sea. Sometimes they would stop early in the day at some fishing village, find rooms there for the night, and bathe and sail till evening. When they bathed, Nan would swim far out to sea, striking through cold green heaving waters, slipping cleverly between currents, numbing thought with bodily action, drowning emotion in the sea.

Once they were all caught in a current and a high sea and swept out, and had to battle for the shore. Even Nan, even Barry, could not get to the cove from which they had bathed; all they could try for was the jut of rocks to westward towards which the seas were sweeping, and to reach this meant a tough fight.

"Barry!"

Nan, looking over her shoulder, saw Gerda's blueing face and wide staring eyes, and quickening, flurried strokes. Saw, too, Barry at once at her side, heard his "All right, I'm here. Catch hold of my shoulder."

In a dozen strokes Nan reached them, and was at Gerda's other side.

"Put one hand on each of us and strike for all you're worth with your legs. That's the way ..."

Numbly Gerda's two hands gripped Barry's right shoulder and Nan's left. Between them they pulled her, her slight weight dragging at them heavily, helping the running sea against them. They were being swept westward towards the rocks, but swept also outwards, beyond them; they struck northward and northward, and were carried always south. It was a near thing between their swimming and the current, and it looked like the current winning.

"It'll have to be all we know now," said Nan, as they struggled ten yards from the point.

It would probably, she and Barry both rather thought, be all they knew and just the little more they didn't know. They would, it seemed likely, be swept round the point well to the south of the outermost rock, and then hey for open sea.

But their swimming proved, in this last fierce minute of the struggle, stronger than the sea. They were swept towards the jutting point, almost round it, when Nan, flinging forward to the right, caught a slippery ledge of rock with her two hands and held on. Barry didn't think she could hold on for more than a second against the swinging seas, or, if she did, could consolidate her position. But he did not know the full power of Nan's trained acrobatic body. Slipping her shoulder from Gerda's clutch, she grasped instead Gerda's right hand in her left, and with her other arm and with all her sinuous, wiry strength, heaved herself on to the rock and there flung her body flat, reaching out her free hand to Barry. Barry caught it just in time, as he was being swung on a wave outwards, and pulled himself within grip of the rock, and in another moment he lay beside her, and between them they hauled up Gerda.

Gerda gasped, "Kay," and they saw him struggling twenty yards behind.

"Can you do it?" Barry shouted to him, and Kay grinned back.

"Let you know presently. ... Oh, yes; I'm all right. Getting on fine."

Nan stood up on the rock, watching him, measuring with expert eye the ratio between distance and pace, the race between Kay's swimming and the sea. It seemed to her to be any one's race.

Barry didn't stand up. The strain of the swim had been rather too much for him, and in his violent lurch on to the rock he had strained his side. He lay flat, feeling battered and sick.

The sea, Nan judged after another minute of watching, was going to beat Kay in this race. For Kay's face had turned a curious colour, and he was blue round the lips. Kay's heart was not strong.

Nan's dive into the tossing waves was as pretty a thing as one would wish to see. The swoop of it carried her nearly to Kay's side. Coming up, she caught one of his now rather limp hands and put it on her left shoulder, saying, "Hold tight. A few strokes will do it."

Kay, who was no fool, and who had known that he was beaten, held tight, throwing all his exhausted strength into striking out with his other three limbs.

They were carried round the point, beyond reach of it had not Barry's outstretched hand been ready. Nan touched it, barely grasped it, just and no more, as they were swung seawards. It was enough. It pulled them to the rock's side. Again Nan wriggled and scrambled up, and then they dragged Kay heavily after them as he fainted.

"Neat," said Barry to Nan, his appreciation of a well-handled job, his love of spirit and skill, rising as it were to cheer, in spite of his exhaustion and his concern for Gerda's and Kay's. "My word, Nan, you're a sportsman."

"He does faint sometimes," said Gerda of Kay. "He'll be all right in a minute."

Kay came to.

"Oh, lord," he said, "that was a bit of a grind." And then, becoming garrulous with the weak and fatuous garrulity of those who have recently swooned, "Couldn't have done it without you, Nan. I'd given myself up for lost. All my past life went by me in a flash. ... I really did think it was U.P. with me, you know. And it jolly nearly was, for all of us, wasn't it. ... Whose idea was it, bathing just here? Yours, Nan? Of course. It would be. No wonder you felt our lives on your conscience and had to rescue us all. Oh, lord, the water I've drunk! I do feel rotten."

"We all look pretty rotten, I must say," Nan commented, looking from Kay's limp greenness to Gerda's shivering blueness, from Gerda to Barry, prostrate, bruised, and coughing, from Barry to her own cut and battered knees and elbows, which were bleeding with the immense and unaccountable profuseness of limbs cut by rocks in the sea. "I may die from loss of blood, and the rest of you from prostration, and all of us from cold. Are we well enough to scale the rocks now and get to our clothes?"

"We're not well enough for anything," Barry returned. "But we'd better do it. We don't want to die here, with the sea washing over us in this damp way."

They climbed weakly up to the top of the rock promontory, and along it till they dropped down into the little cove. They all felt beaten and limp, as if they had been playing a violent but not heating game of football. Even Nan's energy was drained.

Gerda said, with chattering teeth, as she and Nan dressed in their rocky corner, "I suppose, Nan, if it hadn't been for you and Barry, I'd have drowned."

"Well, I suppose you perhaps would. If you come to think of it, we'd most of us be dying suddenly half the time if it wasn't for something—some chance or other."

Gerda said, "Thanks, awfully, Nan," in her direct, childlike way, and Nan turned it off with, "You might have thanked me if you *had* drowned, seeing it was my fault we bathed there at all. I ought to have known it wasn't safe for you or Kay."

Looking at the little fragile figure shivering in its vest, Nan felt in that moment no malice, no triumph, no rivalry, no jealous anger; nothing but the protecting care for the smaller and weaker, for Neville's little pretty, precious child, that she had felt when Gerda's hand clutched her shoulder in the sea.

"Life-saving seems to soften the heart," she reflected grimly, conscious, as always, of her own reactions.

"Well," said Kay weakly, as they climbed up the cliff path to the little village, "I do call that a rotten bathe. Now let's make for the pub and drink whisky."

►•◄

VII

It was three days later. They had spent an afternoon and a night at Polperro, and the sun shone in the morning on that incredible place as they rode out of it after breakfast. Polperro shakes the soul and the aesthetic nerves like a glass of old wine; no one can survey it unmoved, or leave it as they entered it, any more than you can come out of a fairy ring as you went in. In the afternoon they had bathed in the rock pools along the coast. In the evening the moon had magically gleamed on the little town, and Barry and Gerda had sat together on the beach watching it, and then in the dawn they had risen (Barry and Gerda again) and rowed out in a boat to watch the pilchard haul, returning at breakfast-time sleepy, fishy, and bright-eyed.

As they climbed the steep hill path that leads to Talland, the sun danced on the little harbour, with its fishing-boats and its sad, crowding, crying gulls, and on the huddled white town with its narrow, crooked streets and overhanging houses, and Polperro had the eerie beauty of a dream or of a little foreign port. Such beauty, such charm, is on the edge of pain; you cannot disentangle them. They intoxicate, and pierce to tears.

The warm morning sun sparkled on a still blue sea, and burned the gorse and bracken by the steep path's edge to fragrance. So steep the path was that they had to push their bicycles up it with bent backs and labouring steps, so narrow that they had to go in single file. It was never meant for cyclists, only for walkers; the bicycling road ran far inland.

They reached the cliff's highest point, and looked down on Talland Bay. By the path's side, on a grass plateau, a stone war cross reared grey against a blue sky, with its roll of names, and its comment—"True love by life, true love by death is tried. ..."

The path, become narrower, rougher, and more winding, plunged sharply, steeply downwards, running perilously along the cliff's edge. Nan got on her bicycle.

Barry called from the rear, "Nan! It can't be done! It's not rideable. ... Don't be absurd."

Nan, remarking casually, "It'll be rideable if I ride it," began to do so.

"Man woman," Barry said, and Kay assured him, "Nan'll be all right. No one else would, but she's got nine lives, you know."

Gerda came next behind Nan. For a moment she paused, dubiously, watching Nan's flying, brakeless progress down the wild ribbon of a footpath, between the hill and the sea. A false swerve, a failure to turn with the path, and one would fly off the cliff's edge into space, fall down perhaps to the blue rock pools far below.

To refuse Nan's lead now would be to fail again in pluck and skill before Barry. "My word, Nan, you're a sportsman!" Barry had said, coughing weakly on the rock on to which Nan had dragged them all out of the sea. That phrase, and the ring in his hoarse voice as he said it, had stayed with Gerda.

She got on to her bicycle, and shot off down the precipitous path.

"My God!" It was Barry's voice again, from the rear. "Stop, Gerda ... oh, you little fool. ... *Stop* ..."

But it was too late for Gerda to stop then if she had tried. She was in full career, rushing, leaping, jolting over the gorse roots under the path, past thought and past hope and oddly past fear, past anything but the knowledge that what Nan did she too must do. Strangely, inaptly, the line of verse she had just read sung itself in her mind as she rushed.

"True love by life, true love by death is tried ..."

She took the first sharp turn, and the second. The third, a right angle bending inward from the cliff's very edge, she did not take. She dashed on instead, straight into space, like a young Phoebus riding a horse of the morning through the blue air.

►•◄

VIII

Nan, far ahead, nearly on the level, heard the crash and heard voices crying out. Jamming on her brakes she jumped off; looked back up the precipitous path; saw nothing but its windings. She left her bicycle at the path's side and turned and ran up, fleet of foot. Rounding a sharp bend, she saw them at last above her; Barry and Kay scrambling furiously down the side of the cliff, and below them, on a ledge half-way down to the sea, a tangled heap that was Gerda and her bicycle.

The next turn of the path hid them from sight again. But in two minutes she had reached the place where their two bicycles lay flung across the path, and was scrambling after them down the cliff.

When she reached them they had disentangled Gerda and the bicycle, and Barry held Gerda in his arms. She was unconscious, and a cut in her head was bleeding, darkening her yellow hair, trickling over her colourless face. Her right leg and her left arm lay stiff and oddly twisted.

Barry, his face drawn and tense, said, "We must get her up to the path before she comes to, if possible. It'll hurt like hell if she's conscious."

They had all learnt how to help their fellow creatures in distress, and how you must bind broken limbs to splints before you move their owner so much as a yard. The only splint available for Gerda's right leg was her left, and they bound it tightly to this with three handkerchiefs, then tied her left arm to her side with Nan's stockings, and used the fourth handkerchief (which was Gerda's, and the cleanest) for her head. She came to before the arm was finished, roused to pained consciousness by the splinting process, and lay with clenched teeth and wet forehead, breathing sharply but making no other sound.

Then Barry lifted her in his arms and the others supported her on either side, and they climbed slowly and gently up to the path, not by the sheer way of their descent, but by a diagonal track that joined the path farther down.

"I'm sorry, darling," Barry said through his teeth, when he jolted her. "I'm frightfully sorry. … Only a little more now."

They reached the path, and Barry laid her down on the grass by its side, her head supported on Nan's knee.

"Very bad, isn't it?" said Barry gently, bending over her.

She smiled up at him, with twisted lips.

"Not so bad, really."

"You little sportsman," said Barry softly, and, stooping, he kissed her pale cheek.

Then he stood up and spoke to Nan.

"I'm going to fetch a doctor if there's one in Talland. Kay must ride back and fetch the Polperro doctor, in case there isn't. In any case I shall bring up help and a stretcher from Talland and have her taken down."

He picked up his bicycle and stood for a moment looking down at the face on Nan's knee.

"You'll look after her," he said quickly, and got on the bicycle and dashed down the path, showing that he too could do that fool's trick if it served any good purpose.

Gerda, watching him, caught her breath and forgot pain in fear until, swerving round the next bend, he was out of sight.

►•◄

IX

Nan sat very still by the path, staring over the sea, shading Gerda's head from the sun. There was nothing more to be done than that; there was no water, even, to bathe the cut with.

"Nan."

"Yes?"

"Am I much hurt? How much hurt, do you think?"

"I don't know how much. I think the arm is broken. The leg may be only sprained. Then there's the cut—I dare say that isn't very much—but one can't tell yet."

"I must have come an awful mucker," Gerda murmured, after a pause. "It must have looked silly, charging over the edge like that. ... You didn't."

"No. I didn't."

"It was stupid," Gerda breathed, and shut her eyes.

"No, not stupid. Any one might have. It was a risky game to try."

"You tried it."

"Oh, I ... I do try things. That's no reason why you should. ... You'd better not talk. Lie quite quiet. It won't be very long now before they come. ... The pain's bad, I know."

Gerda's head was hot, and felt giddy. She moved it restlessly. Urgent thoughts pestered her; her normal reticences lay like broken fences about her.

"Nan."

"Yes. Shall I raise your head a little?"

"No, it's all right. ... About Barry, Nan."

Nan grew rigid, strung up to endure.

"And what about Barry?"

"Just that I love him. I love him very much; beyond anything in the world."

"Yes. You'd better not talk, all the same."

"Nan, do you love him too?"

Nan laughed, a queer little curt laugh in her throat.

"Rather a personal question, don't you think? Suppose, by any chance, that I did? But of course I don't."

"But doesn't he love you, Nan? He did, didn't he?"

"My dear, I think you're rather delirious. This isn't the way one talks. … You'd better ask Barry the state of his affections, since you're interested in them. I'm not, particularly."

Gerda drew a long breath, of pain or fatigue or relief.

"I'm rather glad you don't care for him. I thought we might have shared him if you had, and if he'd cared for us both. But it might have been difficult."

"It might; you never know. … Well, you're welcome to my share, if you want it."

Then Gerda lay quiet, with closed eyes and wet forehead, and concentrated wholly on her right leg, which was hurting badly.

Nan too sat quiet, and she was concentrated too.

Irrevocably it was over now; done, finished with. Barry's eyes, Barry's kiss, had told her that. Gerda, the lovely, the selfish child, had taken Barry from her, to keep for always. Walked into Barry's office, into Barry's life, and deliberately stolen him. Thinking, she said, that they might share him. … The little fool. The little thief. (She waved the flies away from Gerda's head.)

And even this other game, this contest of physical prowess, had ended in a hollow, mocking victory for the winner, since defeat had laid the loser more utterly in her lover's arms, more unshakably in his heart. Gerda, defeated and broken, had won everything. Won even that tribute which had been Nan's own. "You little sportsman," Barry had called her, with a break of tenderness in his voice. Even that, even the palm for valour, he had placed in her hands. The little victor. The greedy little grabber of other people's things. …

Gerda moaned at last.

"Only a little longer," said Nan, and laid her hand lightly and coolly on the hot, wet forehead.

The little winner ... damn her. ...

The edge of a smile, half ironic, wholly bitter, twisted at Nan's lips.

▶•◀

X

Voices and steps. Barry and a doctor, Barry and a stretcher, Barry and all kinds of help. Barry's anxious eyes and smile. "Well? How's she been?"

He was on his knees beside her.

"Here's the doctor, darling. ... I'm sorry I've been so long."

CHAPTER X

PRINCIPLES

▶•◀

I

Through the late September and October days Gerda would lie on a wicker couch in the conservatory at Windover, her sprained leg up, her broken wrist on a splint, her mending head on a soft pillow and eat pears. Grapes too, and apples, and figs, and naturally chocolates, but particularly pears. She also wrote verse, and letters to Barry, and drew in pen and ink, and read Sir Leo Chiozza Money's *Triumph of Nationalisation* and Mrs. Snowden on Bolshevik Russia, and *Côterie*, and listened while Neville read Mr. W. H. Mallock's Memoirs and Disraeli's Life. Her grandmother (Rodney's mother) sent her *The Diary of Opal Whiteley*, but so terrible did she find it that it caused a relapse, and Neville had to remove it. She occasionally struggled in vain with a modern novel, which she usually renounced in perplexity after three chapters or so. Her taste did not lie in this direction.

"I can't understand what they're all about," she said to Neville. "Poetry *means* something. It's about something real, something that really is so. So are books like this"—she indicated *The Triumph of Nationalisation*. "But most novels are so queer. They're about people, but not people as they are. They're not *interesting*."

"Not as a rule, certainly. Occasionally one gets an idea out of one of them, or a laugh, or a thrill. Now and then they express life, or reality, or beauty, in some terms or other—but not as a rule."

Gerda was different from Kay, who devoured thrillers, shockers and ingenious crime and mystery stories with avidity. She did not believe that life was really much like that, and Kay's assertion that if it wasn't it ought to be, she rightly regarded as pragmatical. Neither did she share Kay's more fundamental taste for the Elizabethans, Carolines, and Augustans; she and Kay only met (as regards literature) on economics, politics and modern verse. Gerda's mind was artistic rather than literary, and she felt no wide or acute interest in human beings, their actions, passions, foibles and desires.

So, surrounded by books from the *Times* library, and by nearly all the weekly and monthly reviews (the Bendishes, like many others, felt, with whatever regret, that they had to see all of these) Gerda for the most part, when alone, lay and dreamed dreams and ate pears.

▶•◀

II

Barry came down for week-ends. He and Gerda had declared their affections towards one another even at the Looe Infirmary, where Gerda had been conveyed from the scene of accident. It had been no moment then for anything more definite than statements of reciprocal emotion, which are always cheering in sickness. But when Gerda was better, well enough, in fact, to lie in the Windover conservatory, Barry came down from town and said, "When shall we get married?"

Then Gerda, who had had as yet no time or mind-energy to reflect on the probable, or rather certain, width of the gulf between the sociological theories of herself and Barry, opened her blue eyes wide and said, "Married?"

"Well, isn't that the idea? You can't jilt me now, you know; matters have gone too far."

"But, Barry, I thought you knew. I don't hold with marriage."

Barry threw back his head and laughed, because she looked so innocent and serious and young as she lay there among the pears and bandages.

"All right, darling. You've not needed to hold with it up till now. But now you'd better catch on to it as quickly as you can, and hold it tight, because it's what's going to happen."

Gerda moved her bandaged head in denial.

"Oh, no, Barry. I can't. … I thought you knew. Haven't we ever talked about marriage before?"

"Oh, probably. Yes, I think I've heard you and Kay both on the subject. You don't hold with legal ties in what should be purely a matter of emotional impulse, I know. But crowds of people talk like that and then get married. I've no doubt Kay will too, when his time comes."

"Kay won't. He thinks marriage quite wrong. And so do I."

Barry, who had stopped laughing, settled himself to talk it out.

"Why wrong, Gerda? Superfluous, if you like; irrelevant, if you like: but why wrong?"

"Because it's a fetter on what shouldn't be fettered. Love might stop. Then it would be ugly."

"Oh, very. One has to take that risk, like other risks. But love is really more likely to stop, as I see it, if there's no contract in the eyes of the world, if the two people know one can walk away from the other, and is expected to, directly they quarrel or feel a little bored. The contract, the legalisation—absurd and irrelevant to anything that matters as all legal things are—does, because we're such tradition-bound creatures, give a sort of illusion of inevitability which is settling, so that it doesn't occur to the people to fly apart at the first strain. They go through with it instead, and in nine cases out of ten come out on the other side. In the tenth case they just have either to make the best of it or to make a break. … Of course, people always *can* throw up the sponge, even if married, if things are insupportable. The door isn't locked. But there's no point, I think, in having it swinging wide open."

"I think it *should* be open," Gerda said. "I think people should be absolutely free. … Take you and me. Suppose you got tired of me, or

– 145 –

liked someone else better, I think you ought to be able to leave me without any fuss."

That was characteristic of both of them, that they could take their own case theoretically without becoming personal, without lovers' protestations to confuse the general issue."

"Well," Barry said, "I don't think I ought. I think it should be made as difficult for me as possible. Because of the children. There are usually children, of course. If I left you, I should have to leave them too. Then they'd have no father. Or, if it was you that went, they'd have no mother. Either is a pity, normally. Also, even if we stayed together always and weren't married, they'd have no legal name. Children often miss that, later on. Children of the school age are the most conventional, hide-bound of creatures. They'd feel ashamed before their schoolfellows."

"I suppose they'd have my name legally, wouldn't they?"

"I suppose so. But they might prefer mine. The other boys and girls would have their father's, you see."

"Not all of them. I know several people who don't hold with marriage either; there'd be all their children. And anyhow, it's not a question of what the children would prefer while they were at school. It's what's best for them. And anything would be better than to see their parents hating each other and still having to live together."

"Yes. Anything would be better than that. Except that it would be a useful and awful warning to them. But the point is, most married people don't hate each other. They develop a kind of tolerating, companionable affection, after the first excitement called being in love is past—so far as it does pass. That's mostly good enough to live on; that and common interests and so forth. It's the stuff of ordinary life; the emotional excitement is the *hors d'oeuvre*. It would be greedy to want to keep passing on from one *hors d'oeuvre* to another—leaving the meal directly the joint comes in."

"I like dessert best," Gerda said irrelevantly, biting into an apple.

"Well, you'd never get any at that rate. Nor much of the rest of the meal either."

"But people do, Barry. Free unions often last for years and

years—sometimes for ever. Only you wouldn't feel tied. You'd be sure you were only living together because you both liked to, not because you had to."

"I should feel I had to, however free it was. So you wouldn't have that consolation about me. I might be sick of you, and pining for some one else, but still I should stay."

"Why, Barry?"

"Because I believe in permanent unions, as a general principle. They're more civilised. It's unsocial, uncivic, dotting about from one mate to another, leaving your young and forgetting all about them and having new ones. Irresponsible, I call it. Living only for a good time. It's not the way to be good citizens, as I see it, nor to bring up good citizens. ... Oh, I know that the whole question of sex relationships is horribly complicated, and can't be settled with a phrase or a dogma. It's been for centuries so wrapped in cant and humbug and expediences and camouflage; I don't profess to be able to pierce through all that, or to so much as begin to think it out clearly. The only thing I can fall back on as a certainty is the children question. A confused and impermanent family life *must* be a bad background for the young. They want all they can get of both their parents, in the way of education and training and love."

"Family life is such a hopeless muddle, anyhow."

"A muddle, yes. Hopeless, no. Look at your own. Your father and mother have always been friends with one another and with you. They brought you up with definite ideas about what they wanted you to become—fairly well thought-out and consistent ideas, I suppose. I don't say they could do much—parents never can—but something soaks in."

"Usually something silly and bad."

"Often, yes. Anyhow, a queer kind of mixed brew. But at least the parents have their chance. It's what they're there for; they've got to do all they know, while the children are young, to influence them towards what they personally believe, however mistakenly, to be the finest points of view. Of course, lots of it is, as you say, silly and bad, because people *are* largely silly and bad. But no parent can be absolved from doing his or her best."

Barry was walking round the conservatory, eager and full of faith and hope and fire, talking rapidly, the educational enthusiast, the ardent citizen, the social being, the institutionalist all over. He was all these things; he was rooted and grounded in citizenship, in social ethics. He stopped by the couch and stood looking down at Gerda among her fruit, his hands in his pockets, his eyes bright and lit.

"All the same, darling, I shall never want to fetter you. If you ever want to leave me, I shan't come after you. The legal tie shan't stand in your way. And to me it would make no difference; I shouldn't leave you in any case, married or not. So I don't see how or why you score in doing without the contract."

"It's the idea of the thing, partly. I don't want to wear a wedding ring and be Mrs. Briscoe. I want to be Gerda Bendish, living with Barry Briscoe because we like to. ... I expect, Barry, in my case it *would* be for always, because, at present, I can't imagine stopping caring for you more than for anything else. But that doesn't affect the principle of the thing. It would be *wrong* for me to marry you. One oughtn't to give up one's principles just because it seems all right in a particular case. It would be cheap and shoddy and cowardly."

"Exactly," said Barry, "what I feel. I can't give up my principle either, you know. I've had mine longer than you've had yours."

"I've had mine since I was about fifteen."

"Five years. Well, I've had mine for twenty. Ever since I first began to think anything out, that is."

"People of your age," said Gerda, "people over thirty, I mean, often think like that about marriage. I've noticed that. So has Kay."

"Observant infants. Well, there we stand, then. One of us has got either to change his principles—her principles, I mean—or to be false to them. Or else, apparently, there can be nothing doing between you and me. That's the position, isn't it?"

Gerda nodded, her mouth full of apple.

"It's very awkward," Barry continued, "my having fallen in love with you. I hadn't taken your probable views on sociology into account. I knew that, though we differed in spelling and punctuation, we were agreed (approximately) on politics, economics and taste in amusements, and I thought that was enough. I forgot that divergent views on matrimony were of practical importance. It would have mattered less if I had discovered that you were a militarist and imperialist and quoted Maxse at me."

"I did tell you, Barry. I really did. I never hid it. And I never supposed that you'd want to *marry* me."

"That was rather stupid of you. I'm so obviously a marrying man. ... Now, darling, will you think the whole thing out from the beginning, after I've gone? Be first-hand; don't take over theories from other people, and don't be sentimental about it. Thrash the whole subject out with yourself and with other people—with your own friends, and with your family too. They're a modern, broad-minded set, your people, after all; they won't look at the thing conventionally; they'll talk sense; they won't fob you off with stock phrases, or talk about the sanctity of the home. They're not institutionalists. Only be fair about it; weigh all the pros and cons, and judge honestly, and for Heaven's sake don't look at the thing romantically, or go off on theories because they sound fine and large and subversive. Think of practical points, as well as of ultimate principles. Both, to my mind, are on the same side. I'm not asking you to sacrifice right for expediency, or expediency for right. I don't say, 'Be sensible,' or 'Be idealistic.' We've got to be both."

"Barry, I've thought and talked about it so often and so long. You don't know how much we do talk about that sort of thing, at the club and everywhere and Kay and I. I could never change my mind."

"What a hopeless admission! We ought to be ready to change our minds at any moment; they should be as changeable as pound notes."

"What about yours, then, darling?"

"I'm always ready to change mine. I shall think the subject out too, and if I do change I shall tell you at once."

"Barry." Gerda's face was grave; her forehead was corrugated. "Suppose we neither of us ever change? Suppose we both go on thinking as we do now for always? What then?"

He smoothed the knitted forehead with his fingers.

"Then one of us will have to be a traitor to his or her principles.

A pity, but sometimes necessary in this complicated world. Or, if we can neither of us bring ourselves down to that, I suppose eventually we shall each perpetrate with someone else the kind of union we personally prefer."

They parted on that. The thing had not grown serious yet; they could still joke about it.

▶•◀

III

Though Gerda said, "What's the use of my talking about it to people when I've made up my mind?" and though she had not the habit of talking for conversation's sake, she did obediently open the subject with her parents, in order to assure herself beyond a doubt what they felt about it. But she knew already that their opinions were what you might expect of parents, even of broad-minded, advanced parents, who rightly believed themselves not addicted to an indiscriminating acceptance of the standards and decisions of a usually mistaken world. But Barry was wrong in saying they weren't institutionalists: they were. Parents are.

Rodney was more opinionated than Neville on this subject as on most others. He said crossly, "It's a beastly habit, unlegitimised union. When I say beastly, I mean beastly; nothing derogatory, but merely like the beasts—the other beasts, that is."

Gerda said, "Well, that's not really an argument against it. In that sense it's beastly when we sleep out instead of in bed, or do lots of other quite nice things. The way men and women do things isn't necessarily the best way," and there Rodney had to agree with her. He fell back on, "It's unbusinesslike. Suppose you have children?" and Gerda, who had supposed all that with Barry, sighed. Rodney said a lot more, but it made little impression on her, beyond corroborating her views on the matrimonial theories of middle-aged people.

Neville made rather more. To Neville Gerda said, "How can I go back on everything I've always said and thought about it, and go and get married? It would be so *reactionary*."

Neville, who had a headache and was irritable, said, "It's the other thing that's reactionary. It existed long before the marriage tie did. That's what I don't understand about all you children who pride yourselves on being advanced. If you frankly take your stand on going back to nature, on *being* reactionary—well, it is, anyhow, a point of view, and has its own merits. But your minds seem to me to be in a hopeless muddle. You think you're going forward while you're really going back."

"Marriage," said Gerda, "is so Victorian. It's like antimacassars."

"Now, my dear, do you mean *anything* by either of those statements? Marriage wasn't invented in Victoria's reign. Nor did it occur more frequently in that reign than it did before or does now. Why Victorian, then? And why antimacassars? Think it out. How *can* a legal contract be like a doily on the back of a chair? Where is the resemblance? It sounds like a riddle, only there's no answer. No, you know you've got no answer. That kind of remark is sheer sentimentality and muddle-headedness. Why are people in their twenties so often sentimental? That's another riddle."

"That's what Nan says. She told me once that she used to be sentimental when she was twenty. Was she?"

"More than she is now, anyhow."

Neville's voice was a little curt. She was not happy about Nan, who had just gone to Rome for the winter.

"Well," Gerda said, "anyhow, I'm not sentimental about not meaning to marry. I've thought about it for years, and I know."

"Thought about it! Much you know about it." Neville, tired and cross from overwork, was, unlike herself, playing the traditional conventional mother. "Have you thought how it will affect your children, for instance?"

Those perpetual, tiresome children. Gerda was sick of them.

"Oh, yes, I've thought a lot about that. And I can't see it will hurt them. Barry and I talked for ever so long about the children. So did father."

- 151 -

So did Neville.

"Of course I know," she said, "that you and Kay would be only too pleased if father and I had never been married, but you've no right to judge the ones you and Barry may have by yourself. They may not be nearly so odd. ... And then there's your own personal position. The world's full of people who think they can insult a man's mistress."

"I don't meet people like that. The people I know don't insult other people for not being married. They think it's quite natural, and only the people's own business."

"You've moved in a small and rarefied clique so far, my dear. You'll meet the other kind of people presently; one can't avoid them, the world's so full of them."

"Do they matter?"

"Of course they matter. As mosquitoes matter, and wasps, and cars that splash mud at you in the road. You'd be constantly annoyed. Your own scullery-maid would turn up her nose at you. The man that left the milk would sneer."

"I don't think," Gerda said, after reflection, "that I'm very easily annoyed. I don't notice things very often. I think about other things rather a lot, you see. That's why I'm slow at answering."

"Well, Barry would be annoyed, anyhow."

"Barry does lots of unpopular things. He doesn't mind what people say."

"He'd mind for you. ... But Barry isn't going to do it. Barry won't have you on your terms. If you won't have him on his, he'll leave you and go and find some nicer girl."

"I can't help it, mother. I can't do what I don't approve of for that. How could I?"

"No, darling, of course you couldn't; I apologise. But do try and see if you can't get to approve of it, or anyhow to be indifferent about it. Such a little thing! It isn't as if Barry wanted you to become a Mormon or something. ... And after all you can't accuse him of being retrograde, or Victorian, if you like to use that silly word, or lacking in ideals for social progress—can you? He belongs to nearly all your illegal political societies, doesn't he? Why, his house gets raided for leaflets from time to time. I don't think they ever find any, but they look, and that's something. You can't call Barry hide-bound or conventionally orthodox."

"No. Oh, no. Not that. Or I shouldn't be caring for him. But he doesn't understand about this. And you don't, mother, nor father, nor anyone of your ages. I don't know how it is, but it is so."

"You might try your Aunt Rosalind," Neville suggested, with malice.

Gerda shuddered. "Aunt Rosalind … she wouldn't understand at all. …"

But the dreadful thought was, as Neville had intended, implanted in her that, of all her elder relatives, it was only Aunt Rosalind who, though she mightn't understand, might nevertheless agree. Aunt Rosalind on free unions … that would be terrible to have to hear. For Aunt Rosalind would hold with them not because she thought them right, but because she enjoyed them—the worst of reasons. Gerda somehow felt degraded by the introducing of Aunt Rosalind, whom she hated, and knew without having been told so that her mother and all of them hated, into the discussion. It dragged it down, made it vulgar.

Gerda lay back in silence, the springs of argument and talk dried in her. She wanted Kay.

It was no use; they couldn't meet. Neville could not get away from her traditions, nor Gerda from hers.

Neville, to change the subject (though scarcely for the better), read her the autobiography of Mrs. Asquith till tea-time.

►•◄

IV

They all talked about it again, and said the same things, and different things, and more things, and got no nearer one another with it all. Barry and Gerda, each apprehending soon the full measure of the serious intent of the other, stood helpless before it, the one in half-amused exasperation, the other in obstinate determination.

"She means business, then," thought Barry, and Gerda, "He won't come round," and their love pierced and stabbed them, making Barry hasty of speech and Gerda sullen.

"The *waste* of it," said Barry one Sunday evening, "when I've only got one day in the week, to spend it quarrelling about marriage. I've hundreds of things to talk about and tell you—interesting things, funny things— but I never get to them, with all this arguing we have to have first."

"I don't want to argue, Barry. Let's not. We've said everything now, lots of times. There can't be any more. Tell me your things instead."

He told her, and they were happy talking, and forgot how they thought differently on marriage. But always the difference lay there in the background, coiled up like a snake, ready to uncoil and seize them and make them quarrel and hurt one another. Always one was expecting the other at any moment to throw up the sponge and cry, "Oh, have it your own way, since you won't have it mine and I love you." But neither did. Their wills stood as stiff as two rocks over against one another.

Gerda grew thinner under the strain, and healed more slowly than before. Her fragile, injured body was a battle-ground between her will and her love, and suffered in the conflict. Barry saw that it could not go on. They would, he said, stop talking about it; they would put it in the background and go on as if it was not there, until such time as they could agree. So they became friends again, lovers who lived in the present and looked to no future, and, since better might not be, that had for the time to do.

CHAPTER XI

MIDDLE AGE

►•◄

I

Through September Neville had nursed Gerda by day and worked by night. In the middle of October, just when they usually moved into town for the winter, she collapsed, had what the doctor called a nervous breakdown.

"You've been overworking," he told her. "You're not strong enough in these days to stand hard brain-work. You must give it up."

For a fortnight she lay tired and passive, surrendered and inert, caring for nothing but to give up and lie still and drink hot milk. Then she struggled up and mooned about the house and garden, and cried weakly from time to time, and felt depressed and bored, and as if life were over and she were at the bottom of the sea.

"This must be what mother feels," she thought. "Poor mother ... I'm like her; I've had my life, and I'm too stupid to work, and I can only cry. ... Men must work and women must weep ... I never knew before that that was true. ... I mustn't see mother just now, it would be the last straw ... like the skeletons people used to look at to warn themselves what they would come to. ... Poor mother ... and poor me. ... But mother's getting better now she's being analysed. That wouldn't help me at all. I analyse myself too much already. ... And I was so happy a few months ago. What a dreadful end to a good ambition. I shall never work again, I suppose, in any way that counts. So that's that. ... Why do I want to work and to do something? Other wives and mothers don't. ... Or do they, only they don't know it because they don't analyse? I believe they do, lots of them. Or is it only my horrible egotism and vanity that can't take a back seat quietly? I was always like that, I know. Nan and I and Gilbert. Not Jim so much, and not Pamela at all. But Rodney's worse than I am; he wouldn't want to be counted out, put on the shelf, in the forties; he'd be frightfully sick if he had to stand by and see other people working and getting on and in the thick of things when he wasn't. He couldn't bear it; he'd take to drink, I think. ... I hope Rodney won't ever have a nervous breakdown and feel like this, poor darling, he'd be dreadfully tiresome. ... Not to work after all. Not to be a doctor. ... What then? Just go about among people, grinning like a dog. Winter in town, talking, dining, being the political wife. Summer in the country, walking, riding, reading, playing tennis. Fun, of course. But what's it all for? When I've got Gerda off my hands I shall have done being a mother, in any sense that matters. Is being a wife enough to live for? Rodney's wife? Oh, I want to be some use, I want to do things, to count. ... And Rodney will die some time—I know he'll die first—and then I shan't even be a wife. And in twenty years I shan't be able to do things with my body much more, and what then? What will be left? ... I think I'm getting hysterical, like poor mother. ... How ugly I look in these days."

She stopped before the looking-glass. Her face looked back at her, white and thin, almost haggard, traced in the last few weeks for the first time with definite lines round brow and mouth.

"Middle age," said Neville, and a cold hand was laid round her heart. "It had to come some time, and this illness has opened the door to it. Or shall I look young again when I'm quite well? No, never young again."

She shivered.

"I look like mother to-day. ... I *am* like mother ..."

So youth and beauty were to leave her, too. She would recover from this illness and this extinguishing of charm, but not completely, and not for long. Middle age had begun. She would have off-days in future, when she looked old and worn, instead of always, as hitherto, looking charming. She wouldn't, in future, be sure of herself; people wouldn't be

- 157 -

sure to think, "A lovely woman, Mrs. Rodney Bendish." Soon they would be saying, "How old Mrs. Bendish is getting to look," and then, "She was a pretty woman once."

Well, looks didn't matter much really, after all. ...

"They do, they do," cried Neville to the glass, passionately truthful. "If you're vain they do—and I am vain. Vain of mind and of my body. ... Vanity, vanity, all is vanity ... and now the silver cord is going to be loosed and the golden bowl is going to be broken, and I shall be hurt."

Looks did matter. It was no use canting, and minimising them. They affected the thing that mattered most—one's relations with people. Men, for instance, cared more to talk to a woman whose looks pleased them. They liked pretty girls, and pretty women. Interesting men cared to talk to them; they told them things they would never tell a plain woman. Rodney did. He liked attractive women. Sometimes he made love to them, prettily and harmlessly.

The thought of Rodney stabbed her. If Rodney were to get to care less ... to stop making love to her ... worse, to stop needing her. ... For he did need her; through all their relationship, disappointing in some of its aspects, his need had persisted, a simple, demanding thing.

Humour suddenly came back.

"This, I suppose, is what Gerda is anticipating, and why she won't have Barry tied to her. If Rodney wasn't tied to me he could flee from my wrinkles. ...

"Oh, what an absurd fuss one makes. What does any of it matter? It's all in the course of nature. And the sooner 'tis over the sooner to sleep. Middle age will be very nice and comfortable and entertaining, once one's fairly in it. ... I go babbling about my wasted brain and my fading looks as if I'd been a mixture of Sappho and Helen of Troy. ... That's the worst of being a vain creature. ... What will Rosalind do when *her* time comes? Oh, paint, of course, and dye—more thickly than she does now, I mean. She'll be a ghastly sight. A raddled harridan. At least I shall always look respectable, I hope. I shall go down to Gerda. I want to look at something young. The young have their troubles, poor darlings, but they don't know how lucky they are."

►•◄

II

In November Neville and Gerda, now both convalescent, joined Rodney in their town flat. Rodney thought London would buck up Neville. London does buck you up, even if it is November and there is no gulf stream and not much coal. For there is always music and always people. Neville had a critical appreciation of both. Then, for comic relief, there are politics. You cannot be really bored with a world which contains the Mother of Parliaments, particularly if her news is communicated to you at first hand by one of her members. Disgusted you may be and are, if you are a right-minded person, but at least you not bored.

What variety, what excitement, what a moving picture show, is this tragic and comic planet? Why want to be useful, why indulge such tedious vanities as ambitions, why dream wistfully of doing one's bit, making one's mark, in a world already as full of bits, bright, coloured, absurd bits, as a kaleidoscope, as full of marks (mostly black marks) as a novel from a free library? A dark and bad and bitter world, of course, full of folly, wickedness and misery, sick with poverty and pain, so that at times the only thing Neville could bear to do in it was to sit on some dreadful committee thinking of ameliorations for the lot of the very poor, or to go and visit Pamela in Hoxton and help her with some job or other— that kind of direct, immediate, human thing, which was a sedative to uneasiness and pity such as the political work she dabbled in, however similar its ultimate aim, could never be.

►•◄

III

To Pamela Neville said, "Are you afraid of getting old, Pamela?"

Pamela replied. "Not a bit. Are you?" and she confessed it.

"Often it's like a cold douche of water down my spine, the thought of it. I reason and mock at myself, but I *don't* like it. ... You're different; finer, more real, more unselfish. Besides, you'll have done something worth doing when you have to give up. I shan't."

Pamela's brows went up.

"Kay? Gerda? The pretty dears: I've done nothing so nice as them. You've done what's called a woman's work in the world—isn't that the phrase?"

"Done it—just so, but so long ago. What now? I still feel young, Pamela, even now that I know I'm not. ... Oh, lord, it's a queer thing, being a woman. A well-off woman of forty-three with everything made comfortable for her and her brain gone to pot and her work in the world done. I want something to bite my teeth into—some solid, permanent job—and I get nothing but sweetmeats, and people point at Kay and Gerda and say, 'That's your work, and it's over. Now you can rest, seeing that it's good, like God on the seventh day.'"

"*I* don't say, 'Now you can rest.' Except just now, while you're run down."

"Run down, yes; run down like a disordered clock because I tried to tackle an honest job of work again. Isn't it sickening, Pamela? Isn't it ludicrous?"

"Ludicrous—no. Every one comes up against their own limitations. You've got to work within them, that's all. After all, there are plenty of jobs you can do that want doing—simply shouting to be done."

"Pammie, dear, it's worse than I've said. I'm a low creature. I don't only want to do jobs that want doing: I want to count, to make a name. I'm damnably ambitious. You'll despise that, of course—and you're quite right, it is despicable. But there it is. Most men and many women are tormented by it—the itch for recognition."

"Of course. One is."

"You too, Pammie?"

"I have been. Less now. Life gets to look short, when you're thirty-nine."

"Ah, but you have it—recognition, even fame, in the world you work in. You count for something. If you value it, there it is. I wouldn't grumble if I'd played your part in the piece. It's a good part—a useful part, and a speaking part."

"I suppose we all feel we should rather like to play some one else's part for a change. There's nothing exciting about mine. Most people would far prefer yours."

They would, of course; Neville knew it. The happy political wife rather than the unmarried woman worker; Rodney, Gerda, and Kay for company rather than Frances Carr. There was no question which was the happier lot, the fuller, the richer, the easier, the more entertaining.

"Ah, well. ... You see, Rosalind spent the afternoon with me yesterday, and I felt suddenly that it wasn't for me to be stuck up about her—what am I too but the pampered female idler, taking good things without earning them? It made me shudder. Hence this fit of blues. The pampered, lazy, brainless animal—it is such a terrific sight when in human form. ... Rosalind talked about Nan, Pamela. In her horrible way—you know. Hinting that she isn't alone in Rome, but with Stephen Lumley."

Pamela took off her glasses and polished them.

"Rosalind would, of course. What did you say?"

"I lost my temper. I let out at her. It's not a thing I often do with Rosalind—it doesn't seem worth while. But this time I saw red. I told her what I thought of her eternal gossip and scandal. I said, what if Nan and Stephen Lumley, or Nan and any one else, did arrange to be in Rome at the same time and to see a lot of each other; where was the harm? No use. You can't pin Rosalind down. She just shrugged her shoulders and smiled, and said, 'My dear, we all know our Nan. We all know too that Stephen

Lumley has been in love with her for a year, and doesn't live with his wife. Then they go off to Rome at the same moment, and one hears that they are seen everywhere together. Why shut one's eyes to obvious deductions? You're so like an ostrich, Neville.' I said I'd rather be an ostrich than a ferret, eternally digging into other people's concerns—and by the time we had got to that I thought it was far enough, so I had an engagement with my dressmaker."

"It's no use tackling Rosalind," Pamela agreed. "She'll never change her spots. ... Do you suppose it's true about Nan?"

"I dare say it is. Yes, I'm afraid I do think it's quite likely true. ... Nan was so queer the few times I saw her after Gerda's accident. I was unhappy about her. She was so hard, and so more than usual cynical and unget-at-able. She told me it had been all her fault, leading Gerda into mischief, doing circus tricks that the child tried to emulate and couldn't. ... I couldn't read her, quite. Her tone about Gerda had a queer edge to it. And she rather elaborately arranged, I thought, so that she shouldn't meet Barry. Pamela, do you think she had finally and absolutely turned Barry down before he took up so suddenly with Gerda, or ..."

Pamela said, "I know nothing. She told me nothing. But I rather thought, when she came to see me just before she went down to Cornwall, that she had made up her mind to have him. I may have been wrong."

Neville leant her forehead on her hands and sighed.

"Or you may have been right. And if you were right, it's the ghastliest tragedy—for her. ... Oh, I shouldn't have let Gerda go and work with him; I should have known better. ... Nan had rebuffed him, and he flew off at a tangent, and there was Gerda sitting in his office, as pretty as flowers and with her funny little silent charm. ... And if Nan was all the time waiting for him, meaning to say yes when he asked her. ... Poor darling Nan, robbed by my horrid little girl, who doesn't even want to marry. ... If that's the truth, it would account for the Stephen Lumley business. Nan wouldn't stay on in London, to see them together. If Lumley caught her at that psychological moment, she'd very likely go off with him, out of mere desperation and bravado. That would be so terribly like Nan. ... What a desperate, wiry, cursed business life is. ... On the other hand, she may just be going about with Lumley on her own terms, not his. It's her own affair which it is; what we've got to do is to contradict the stories Rosalind is spreading whenever we get the chance. Not that one can scotch scandal once it starts—particularly Rosalind's scandal."

"Ignore it. Nan can ignore it when she comes back. It won't hurt her. Nan's had plenty of things said about her before, true and untrue, and never cared."

"You're splendid at the ignoring touch, Pam. I believe there's nothing you can't and don't ignore."

"Well, why not? Ignoring's easy."

"Not for most of us. I believe it is, for you. In a sense you ignore life itself; anyhow, you don't let it hold and bully you. When your time comes you'll ignore age, and later, death."

"They don't matter much, do they? Does anything? I suppose it's my stolid temperament, but I can't feel it does."

Neville thought, as she had often thought before, that Pamela, like Nan, only more calmly, less recklessly and disdainfully, had the aristocratic touch. Pamela, with her delicate detachments and her light, even touch on things great and small, made her feel fussy and petty and excitable.

"I expect you're right, my dear. … 'All is laughter, all is dust, all is nothingness, for the things that are arise out of the unreasonable. …' I must get back. Give my love to Frances … and when next you see Gerda do try to persuade her that marriage is one of the things that don't matter, and that she might just as well put up with it to please us all. The child is a little nuisance—as obstinate as a mule."

►•◄

IV

Neville, walking away from Pamela's grimy street in the November fog, felt that London was terrible, as indeed it is. An ugly clamour of strident noises and hard, shrill voices, jabbering of vulgar, trivial things. A wry, desperate, cursed world, as she had called it, a pot seething with bitterness and all dreadfulness, with its Rosalinds floating on the top like scum.

And Nan, her Nan, her little vehement sister, whom she had mothered of old, had pulled out of countless scrapes—Nan had now taken her life into her reckless hands and done what with it? Given it, perhaps, to a man she didn't love, throwing cynical defiance thereby at love, which had hurt her, escaping from the intolerable to the shoddy. Even if not, even supposing the best, Nan was hurt and in trouble; Neville was somehow sure of that. Men were blind fools; men were fickle children. Neville almost wished now that Barry would give up Gerda and go out to Rome and fetch Nan back. But, to do that, Barry would have to fall out of love with Gerda and into love again with Nan; and even Barry, Neville imagined, was not such a weathercock as that. And Barry would really be happier with Gerda. With all their differences, they were both earnest citizens, both keen on social progress. Nan was a cynical flibberty-gibbet; it might not have been a happy union. Perhaps happy unions were not for such as Nan. But at the thought of Nan playing that desperate game with Stephen Lumley in Rome, Neville's face twitched. ...

She would go to Rome. She would see Nan; find out how things were. Nan always liked to see her, would put up with her even when she wanted no one else.

That was, at least, a job one could do. These family jobs—they still go on, they never cease, even when one is getting middle-aged and one's brain has gone to pot. They remain, always, the jobs of the affections.

She would write to Nan to-night, and tell her she was starting for Rome in a few days, to have a respite from the London fogs.

V

But she did not start for Rome, or even write to Nan, for when she got home she went to bed with influenza.

CHAPTER XII

THE MOTHER

▶•◀

I

The happiness Mrs. Hilary now enjoyed was of the religious type—a deep, warm glow, which did not lack excitement. She felt as those may be presumed to feel who have just been converted to some church—newly alive, and sunk in spiritual peace, and in profound harmony with life. Where were the old rubs, frets, jars, and ennuis? Vanished, melted like yesterday's snows in the sun of this new peace. It was as if she had cast her burden upon the Lord. That, said her psycho-analyst doctor, was quite in order; that was what it ought to be like. That was, in effect, what she had, in point of fact, done; only the place of the Lord was filled by himself. To put the matter briefly, transference of burden had been effected; Mrs. Hilary had laid all her cares, all her perplexities, all her grief, upon this quiet, acute-looking man, who sat with her twice a week for an hour, drawing her out, arranging her symptoms for her, penetrating the hidden places of her soul, looking like a cross between Sherlock Holmes and Mr. Henry Ainley. Her confidence in him was, he told her, the expression of the father-imago, which surprised Mrs. Hilary a little, because he was twenty years her junior.

Mrs. Hilary felt that she was getting to know herself very well indeed. Seeing herself through Mr. Cradock's mind, she felt that she was indeed a curious jumble of complexes, of strange, mysterious impulses, desires, and fears. Alarming, even horrible in some ways; so that often she thought,

"Can he be right about me? Am I really like that? Do I really hope that Margery" (Jim's wife) "will die so that Jim and I may be all in all to each other again? Am I really so wicked?" But Mr. Cradock said that it was not at all wicked, perfectly natural and normal—the Unconscious *was* like that. And worse than that; how much worse he had to break to Mrs. Hilary, who was refined and easily shocked, by gentle hints and slow degrees, lest she should be shocked to death. Her dreams, which she had to recount to him at every sitting, bore such terrible significance—they grew worse and worse, as Mrs. Hilary could stand more.

"Ah, well," Mrs. Hilary sighed uneasily, after an interpretation into strange terms of a dream she had had about bathing. "It's very odd, when I've never even thought about things like that."

"Your Unconscious," said Mr. Cradock firmly, "has thought the more. The more your Unconscious is obsessed by a thing, the less your conscious self thinks of it. It is shy of the subject, for that very reason."

Mrs. Hilary was certainly shy of the subject, for that reason or others. When she felt too shy of it, Mr. Cradock let her change it. "It may be true." she would say, "but it's very terrible, and I would rather not dwell on it."

So he would let her dwell instead on the early days of her married life, or on the children's childhood, or on her love for Neville and Jim, or on her impatience with her mother.

II

They were happy little times, stimulating, cosy little times. They spoke straight to the heart, easing it of its weight of tragedy. A splendid man, Mr. Cradock, with his shrewd, penetrating sympathy, his kind firmness.

He would listen with interest to everything; the sharp words she had had with Grandmamma, troubles with the maids, the little rubs of daily life (and what a rubbing business life is, to be sure!) as well as to profounder, more tragic accounts of desolation, jealousy, weariness, and despair. He would say, "Your case is a very usual one," so that she did not feel ashamed of being like that. He reduced it all, dispassionately and yet not unsympathetically, and with clear scientific precision, to terms of psychical and physical laws. He trained his patient to use her mind and her will, as well as to remember her dreams and to be shocked at nothing that they signified.

Mrs. Hilary would wake each morning, or during the night, and clutch at the dream which was flying from her, clutch and secure it, and make it stand and deliver its outlines to her. She was content with outlines; it was for Mr. Cradock to supply the interpretation thereof. Sometimes, if Mrs. Hilary couldn't remember any dreams, he would supply, according to a classic precedent, the dream as well as the interpretation. But on the whole, deeply as she revered and admired him, Mrs. Hilary preferred to remember her own dreams; what they meant was bad enough, but the meaning of the dreams that Mr. Cradock told her she had dreamt was beyond all words. … That terrible Unconscious! Mrs. Hilary disliked it excessively; she felt rather as if it were a sewer, sunk beneath an inadequate grating.

But from Mr. Cradock she put up with hearing about it. She would have put up with anything. He was so steadying and so wonderful. He enabled her to face life with a new poise, a fresh lease of strength and vitality. She told Grandmamma so. Grandmamma said, "Yes, my dear, I've observed it in you. It sounds to me an unpleasing business, but it is obviously doing you good, so far. I only wish it may last. The danger may be reaction, after you have finished the course and lost touch with this young man." (Mr. Cradock was forty-five, but Grandmamma, it must be remembered, was eighty-four.) "You will have to guard against that. In a way it was a pity you didn't take up church-going instead; religion lasts."

"And these quackeries do not," Grandmamma finished her sentence to herself, not wishing to be discouraging.

"Not always," Mrs. Hilary truly replied, meaning that religion did not always last.

"No," Grandmamma agreed. "Unfortunately, not always. Particularly when it is High Church. There was your Uncle Bruce, of course. ..."

Mrs. Hilary's Uncle Bruce, who had been High Church for a season, and had even taken Orders in the year 1860, but whose faith had wilted in the heat and toil of the day, so that by 1870 he was an agnostic barrister, took Grandmamma back through the last century, and she became reminiscent over the Tractarian movement, and, later, the Ritualists.

"The Queen could never abide them," said Grandmamma. "Nor could Lord Beaconsfield, nor your father, though he was always kind and tolerant. I remember when Dr. Jowett came to stay with us, how they talked about it. ... Ah, well, they've become very prominent since then, and done a great deal of good work, and there are many very able, excellent men and women among them. ... But they're not High Church any longer, they tell me. They're Catholics in these days. I don't know enough of them to judge them, but I don't think they can have the dignity of the old High Church party, for if they had I can't imagine that Gilbert's wife, for instance, would have joined them, even for so short a time as she did. ... Well, it suits some people, and psycho-analysis obviously suits others. Only I do hope you will try to keep moderate and balanced, my child, and not believe all this young man tells you. Parts of it do sound so very strange."

(But Mrs. Hilary would not have dreamt of repeating to Grandmamma the strangest parts of all.)

"I feel a new woman," she said, fervently, and Grandmamma smiled, well pleased, thinking that it certainly did seem rather like the old evangelical conversions of her youth. (Which, of course, did not always last, any more than the High Church equivalents did.)

All Grandmamma committed herself to, in her elderly caution, which came, however, less from age than from having known Mrs. Hilary for sixty-three years, was, "Well, well, we must see."

▶•◀

III

And then Rosalind's letter came. It came by the afternoon post—the big, mauve, scented, sprawled sheets, dashingly monographed across one corner.

"Gilbert's wife," pronounced Grandmamma non-committally from her easy-chair, and, said in that tone, it was quite sufficient comment. "Another cup of tea, please, Emily."

Mrs. Hilary gave it her, then began to read aloud the letter from Gilbert's wife. Gilbert's wife was one of the topics upon which she and Grandmamma were in perfect accord, only that Mrs. Hilary was irritated when Grandmamma pushed the responsibility for the relationship on to her by calling Rosalind "your daughter-in-law."

Mrs. Hilary began to read the letter in the tone used by well-bred women when they would, if in a slightly lower social stratum, say, "Fancy that, now! Did you ever, the brazen hussy!" Grandmamma listened, cynically disapproving, prepared to be disgusted yet entertained. On the whole she thoroughly enjoyed letters from Gilbert's wife. She settled down comfortably in her chair with her second cup of tea, while Mrs. Hilary read two pages of what Grandmamma called, "foolish chit-chat." Rosalind's letters were really like the gossiping imbecilities written by the incredibly gay and feminine ladies who enliven our shinier-papered weeklies with their bright personal babble. She did not often waste one of them on her mother-in-law; only when she had something to say which might annoy her.

"Do you hear from Nan?" the third page of the letter began. "I hear from the Bramertons, who are wintering in Rome—the Charlie Bramertons, you know, great friends of mine and Gilbert's: he won a pot of money on the Derby this year, and they've a dinky flat in some palace out there—and they meet Nan about, and she's always with Stephen Lumley, the painter (rotten painter, if you ask me, but he's somehow diddled London into admiring him, don't expect you've heard of him down at the seaside). Well, they're quite simply *always* together, and the Brams say that everyone out there says it isn't in the least an ambiguous case—no two ways about it. He doesn't live with his wife, you know. You'll excuse me passing this on to you, but it does seem you ought to know. I mentioned it to Neville the other day, just before the poor old dear went down with the plague, but you know what Neville is, she always sticks up for Nan and doesn't care *what* she does, or what people say. People are talking; beasts, aren't they! But that's the way of this wicked old world, we all do it. Gilbert's quite upset about it, says Nan ought to manage her affairs more quietly. But after all and between you and me, it's not the first time Nan's been a Town Topic, is it?

"How's the psycho going? Isn't Cradock rather a priceless pearl? You're over head and ears with him by now, of course, we all are. Psycho wouldn't do you any good if you weren't, that's the truth. Cradock told me himself once that transference can't be effected without the patient being a little bit smitten. Personally I should give up a man patient at once if he didn't rather like me. But isn't it soothing and comforting, and doesn't it make you feel good all over, like a hot bath when you're fagged out. ..."

But Mrs. Hilary didn't get as far as this. She stopped at "not the first time Nan's been a Town Topic ..." and dropped the thin mauve sheets on to her lap, and looked at Grandmamma, her face queerly tight and flushed, as if she were about to cry.

Grandmamma had finished her tea, and had been listening quietly.

Mrs. Hilary said, "Oh, my God," and jerked her head back, quivering like a nervous horse who has had a shock and does not care to conceal it.

"Your daughter-in-law," said Grandmamma, without excitement, "is an exceedingly vulgar young woman."

"Vulgar? Rosalind? But of course. ... Only that doesn't affect Nan. ..."

"Your daughter-in-law," Grandmamma added, "is also a very notorious liar."

"A liar ... oh, yes, yes yes. ... But this time it's true. Oh, I feel, I know, it's true. Nan *would*. That Stephen Lumley—he's been hanging about her for ages. ... Oh, yes, it's true what they say. The very worst. ..."

Grandmamma glanced at her curiously. The very worst, in that direction, had become strangely easier of credence by Mrs. Hilary lately: Grandmamma had observed that. Mr. Cradock's teaching had not been without its effect. According to Mr. Cradock people were usually engaged either in practising the very worst, or in desiring to practise it, or in wishing and dreaming that they had practised it. It was the nature of mankind, and not in the least reprehensible, though curable. Thus Mr. Cradock. Mrs. Hilary had, against her own taste, absorbed part of his teaching, but nothing could ever persuade her that it was not reprehensible: it quite obviously was. Also disgusting. Mr. Cradock might say what he liked. It *was* disgusting. And when the man had a wife. ...

"It is awful," said Mrs. Hilary. "Awful. ... It must be stopped. I shall go to Rome. At once."

"That won't stop it, dear, if it is going on. It will only irritate the young people."

"Irritate! You can use a word like that! Mother, you don't realise this ghastly thing."

"I quite see, my dear, that Nan may be carrying on with this artist. And very wrong it is, if so. All I say is, that your going to Rome won't stop it. You know that you and Nan don't always get on very smoothly. You rub each other up. ... It would be far better if someone else went. Neville, say."

"Neville is ill." Mrs. Hilary shut her lips tightly on that. She was glad Neville was ill; she had always hated (she could not help it) the devotion between Neville and Nan. Nan, in her tempestuous childhood, flaring with rage against her mother, or sullen, spiteful, and perverse, long before she could have put into words the qualities in Mrs. Hilary which made her so, had always gone to Neville, ten years older, to be soothed and restored to good temper. Neville had reprimanded the little naughty sister, had told her she must be "decent to mother"—"feel decent if you can, behave decent in any case," was the way she had put it. It was Neville who had heard Nan's confidences and helped her out of scrapes in childhood, schoolgirlhood, and ever since. This was very bitter to Mrs. Hilary. She was jealous of both of them—jealous that so much of Neville's love should go elsewhere than to her, jealous that Nan, who gave her nothing except generous and extravagant gifts and occasional, spasmodic, remorseful efforts at affection and gentleness, should to Neville give all.

"Neville is ill," she said. "She certainly won't be fit to travel out of England this winter. Influenza coming on the top of that miserable breakdown she had is a thing to be treated with the greatest care. Even when she is recovered, post-influenza will keep her weak till the summer. I am really anxious about her. No; Neville is quite out of the question."

"Well, what about Pamela?"

"Pamela is up to her eyes in her work. ... Besides, why should Pamela go, or Neville, rather than I? A girl's mother is obviously the right person. I may not be much use to my children in these days, but at least I hope I can save them from themselves."

"It takes a clever parent to do that, Emily," said Grandmamma, who doubtless knew.

"But mother, what would you *have* me do? Sit with my hands before me while my daughter lives in sin? What's *your* plan?"

"I'm too old to make plans, dear. I can only look on at the world. I've looked at the world now for many, many years, and I've learnt that only great wisdom and great love can change people's decisions as to their way of life, or turn them from evil courses. Frankly, my child, I doubt if you have, where Nan is concerned, enough wisdom or enough love. Enough sympathy, I should rather say, for you have love. But do you feel you understand the child enough to interfere wisely and successfully?"

"Oh, you think I'm a fool, mother; of course I know you've always thought me a fool. Good God, if a mother can't interfere with her own daughter to save her from wickedness and disaster, who can, I should like to know?"

"One would indeed like to know that," Grandmamma said sadly.

"Perhaps you'd like to go yourself," Mrs. Hilary shot at her, quivering now with anger and feeling.

"No, my dear. Even if I were able to get to Rome I should know that

I was too old to interfere with the lives of the young. I don't understand them enough. You believe that you do. Well, I suppose you must go and try. I can't stop you."

"You certainly can't. Nothing can stop me. ... You're singularly unsympathetic, mother, about this awful business."

"I don't feel so, dear. I am very, very sorry for you, and very, very sorry for Nan (whom, you must remember, we may be slandering). I have always looked on unlawful love as a very great sin, though there may be great provocation to it."

"It is an awful sin." Mr. Cradock could say what he liked on that subject; he might tell Mrs. Hilary that it was not awful except in so far as any other yielding to nature's promptings in defiance of the law of man was awful, but he could not persuade her. Like many other people, she set that particular sin apart, in a special place by itself; she would talk of "a bad woman," "an immoral man," a girl who had "lost her character," and mean merely the one kind of badness, the one manifestation of immorality, the one element in character. Dishonesty and cruelty she could forgive, but never that.

"I shall start in three days," said Mrs. Hilary becoming tragically resolute. "I must tell Mr. Cradock to-morrow."

"That young man? Must he know about Nan's affairs, my dear?"

"I have to tell him everything, mother. It's part of the course. He is as secret as the grave."

Grandmamma knew that Emily, less secret than the grave, would have to ease herself of the sad tale to someone or other in the course of the next day, and supposed, that it had better be to Mr. Cradock, who seemed to be a kind of hybrid of doctor and clergyman, and so presumably was more discreet than an ordinary human being. Emily must tell. Emily always would. That was why she enjoyed this foolish psycho-analysis business so much.

At the very thought of it a gleam had brightened Mrs. Hilary's eyes, and her rigid, tense pose had relaxed. Oh, the comfort of telling Mr. Cradock. Even if he did tell her how it was all in the course of nature, at least he would sympathise with her trouble about it, and her annoyance with Grandmamma. And he would show her how best to deal with Nan when he got to her. Nan's was the sort of case that Mr. Cradock really did understand. Any situation between the sexes—he was all over it. Psycho-analysts adored sex; they made an idol of it. They communed with it, as devotees with their god. They couldn't really enjoy, with their whole minds, anything else, Mrs. Hilary sometimes vaguely felt. But as, like the gods of the other devotees, it was to them immanent, everywhere and in everything, they could be always happy. If they went up into heaven it was there; if they fled down into hell it was there also. Once, when Mrs. Hilary had tentatively suggested that Freud, for instance, overstated its importance, Mr. Cradock had said firmly, "It is impossible to do that," which settled it once and for all.

Mrs. Hilary stood up. Her exalted, tragic mood clothed her like a flowing garment.

"I shall write to Cook," she said. "Also to Nan, to tell her I am coming."

Grandmamma, after a moment's silence, seemed to gather herself together for a final effort.

"Emily, my child. Is your mind set to do this?"

"Absolutely, mother. Absolutely and entirely."

"Shall I tell you what I think? No, you don't want to hear it, but you drive me to it. … If you go to that foolish, reckless child and attempt to interfere with her, or even to question her, you will run the risk, if she is innocent, of driving her into what you are trying to prevent. If she is already committed to it, you run the risk of shutting the door against her return. In either case you will alienate her from yourself: that is the least of the risks you run, though the most certain. … That is all. I can say no more. But I ask you, my dear … I beg you, for the child's sake and your own … to write neither to Cook nor to Nan."

Grandmamma's breath came rather fast and heavily; her heart was troubling her; emotion and effort were not good for it.

Mrs. Hilary stood looking down at the old shrunk figure, shaking a little as she stood, knowing that she must be patient and calm.

"You will please allow me to judge. You will please let me take the steps I think necessary to help my child. I know that you have no confidence in my judgment or my tact; you've always shown that plainly enough, and done your best to teach my children the same view of me. ..."

Grandmamma put up her hand, meaning that she could not stand, neither she nor her heart could stand, a scene. Mrs. Hilary broke off. For once she did not want a scene either. In these days she found what vent was necessary for her emotional system in her interviews with Mr. Cradock.

"I dare say you mean well, mother. But in this matter I must be the judge. I am a mother first and foremost. It is the only thing that life has left for me to be." (Scarcely a daughter, she meant: that was made too difficult for her; you would almost imagine that the office was not wanted.)

She turned to the writing table.

"First of all I shall write to Rosalind, and tell her what I think of her and her abominable gossip."

She began to write.

Grandmamma sat shrunk and old and tired in her chair.

Mrs. Hilary's pen scratched over the paper, telling Rosalind what she thought.

"Dear Rosalind," she wrote, "I was very much surprised at your letter. I do not know why you should trouble to repeat to me these ridiculous stories about Nan. You cannot suppose that I am likely to care either what you or any of your friends are saying about one of my children. ..." And so on. One knows the style. It eases the mind of the writer and does not deceive the reader. When the reader is Rosalind Hilary it amuses her vastly.

IV

Next day, at 3 p.m., Mrs. Hilary told Mr. Cradock all about it. Mr. Cradock was not in the least surprised. Nor had he the slightest, nor the remotest doubt that Nan and Stephen Lumley were doing what Mrs. Hilary called living in sin, what he preferred to call obeying the natural ego. (After all, as any theologian would point out, the terms are synonymous in a fallen world.)

"I must have your advice," Mrs. Hilary said. "You must tell me what line to take with her."

"Shall you," Mr. Cradock inquired, thoughtful and intelligent, "find your daughter in a state of conflict?"

Mrs. Hilary spread her hands helplessly before her.

"I know nothing; nothing."

"A very great deal," said Mr. Cradock, "depends on that. If she is torn between the cravings of the primitive ego and the inhibitions put upon these cravings by the conventions of society—if, in fact, her censor, her endopsychic censor, is still functioning. ..."

"Oh, I doubt if Nan's got an endopsychic censor. She is so lawless always."

"Every psyche has a censor." Mr. Cradock was firm. "Regarded, of course, by the psyche with very varying degrees of respect. Well, what I mean to say is, if your daughter is in a state of conflict, with forces pulling both ways, her case will be very much easier to deal with than if she has let her primitive ego so take possession of the situation that she feels in a state of harmony. In the former case, you will only have to strengthen the forces which are opposing her sexual craving. ..."

Mrs. Hilary fidgeted uneasily. "Oh, I don't think Nan feels *that*, exactly. None of my children ..."

Mr. Cradock gave her an amused glance. It seemed sometimes that he would never get this foolish lady properly educated.

"Your children, I presume, are human, Mrs. Hilary. Sexual craving means a craving for intimacy with a member of another sex."

"Oh, well, I suppose it does. I don't care for the *name,* somehow. But please go on."

"I was going to say, if you find, on the other hand, that your daughter's nature has attained harmony in connection with this course she is pursuing, your task will be far more difficult. You will then have to *create* a discord, instead of merely strengthening it. … May I ask your daughter's age?"

"Nan is thirty-three."

"A dangerous age."

"All Nan's ages," said Mrs. Hilary, "have been dangerous. Nan is like that."

"As to that," said Mr. Cradock, "we may say that all ages are dangerous to all people, in this dangerous life we live. But the thirties are a specially dangerous time for women. They have outlived the shynesses and restraints of girlhood, and not attained to the caution and discretion of middle age. They are reckless, and consciously or unconsciously on the look-out for adventure. They see ahead of them the end of youth, and that quickens their pace. … Has passion always been a strong element in your daughter's life?"

"Oh, passion …" (another word not liked by Mrs. Hilary). "Not quite that, I should say. Nan has been reckless; she has got into scrapes, got herself talked about. She has played about with men a good deal always. But as to passion …"

"A common thing enough," Mr. Cradock told her, as it were reassuringly. "Nothing to fight shy of, or be afraid of. But something to be regulated, of course. … Now, the thing is to oppose to this irregular desire of your daughter's for this man a new and a stronger set of desires. Fight one group of complexes with another. You can't, I suppose, persuade her to be analysed? There are good analysts in Rome."

"Oh, no. Nan laughs at it. She laughs at everything of that sort."

"A great mistake. A mistake often made by shallow and foolish people.

They might as well laugh at surgery. ... Well, now, to go into this question of the battle between the complex-groups. ... "

He went into it, patiently and exhaustively. His phrases drifted over Mrs. Hilary's head.

"... a deterrent force residing in the ego and preventing us from stepping outside the bounds of propriety. ... Rebellious messages sent up from the Unconscious, which wishes to live, love, and act in archaic modes ... conflict with the progress of human society ... inhibitory and repressive power of the censor ..." (how wonderful, thought Mrs. Hilary, to be able to talk so like a book for so long together!) ... "give the censor all the help we can ... keep the Unconscious in order by turning its energies into some other channel ... give it a substitute. ... The energy involved in the intense desire for someone of another sex can be diverted ... employed on some useful work. Libido ... it should all be used. Find another channel for your daughter's libido. ... Her life is perhaps a rather vacant one?"

That Mrs. Hilary was able to reply to.

"Nan's? Vacant? Oh, no. She is quite full of energy. Too full. Always doing a thousand things. And she writes, you know."

"Ah. That should be an outlet. A great deal of libido is used up by that. Well, her present strong desire for this man should be sublimated into a desire for something else. ... I gather that her root trouble is lawlessness. That can be cured. You must make her remember her first lawless action." (Man's first disobedience and the fruit thereof, thought Mrs. Hilary.)

"Oh, dear me," she said, "I'm afraid that would be impossible. When she was a month old she used to attempt to dash her bottle on to the floor."

"People have even remembered their baptisms, when driven back to them by analysis."

"Our children were not baptized. My husband was something of a Unitarian. He said he would not tie them up with a rite against which they might react in later life. So they were merely registered."

"Ah. In a way that is a pity. Baptism is an impressive moment in the sensitive consciousness of the infant. It has sometimes been found to be a sort of lamp shining through the haze of the early memory. Registration, owing to the non-participation of the infant, is useless in that way."

"Nan might remember how she kicked me when I short-coated her," Mrs. Hilary mused hopefully.

Mr. Cradock flowed on. Mrs. Hilary listened, assented, was impressed. It all sounded so simple, so wonderful, even so beautiful. But she thought once or twice: "He doesn't know Nan."

"Thank you," she said, rising to go when her hour was over. "You have made me feel so much stronger, as usual. I can't thank you enough for all you do for me. I could face none of my troubles and problems but for your help."

"That merely means," said Mr. Cradock, who always got the last word, "that your ego is at present in what is called the state of infantile dependence or tutelage. A necessary but an impermanent stage in its struggle towards the adult level of the reality-principle."

"I expect so," Mrs. Hilary said. "Good-bye."

"He is too clever for me," she thought, as she went home. "He is often above my head." But she was used to that in the people she met.

CHAPTER XIII

THE DAUGHTER

▶•◀

I

Mrs. Hilary hated travelling, which is indeed detestable. The Channel was choppy and she a bad sailor; the train from Calais to Paris continued the motion, and she remained a bad sailor (bad sailors often do this). She lay back and smelt salts, and they were of no avail. At Paris she tried and failed to dine. She passed a wretched night, being of those who detest nights in trains without wagons-lit, but save money by not having wagons-lit, and wonder dismally all night if it was worth it. Modane in the chilly morning annoyed her as it annoys us all. The customs people were rude, and the other travellers in the way. Mrs. Hilary, who was not good in crowds, pushed them, getting excited and red in the face. Psycho-analysis had made her more patient and calm than she had been before, but even so neither patient nor calm when it came to jostling crowds.

"I am not strong enough for all this," she thought, in the Mont Cenis tunnel.

Rushing out of it into Italy, she thought: "Last time I was here was in '99, with Richard. If Richard were here now he would help me." He would face the customs at Modane, find the tickets and passports, deal with uncivil Germans—(Germans were often uncivil to Mrs. Hilary and she to them, and though she had not met any yet on this journey, owing doubtless to their state of collapse and depression consequent on the Great Peace, one might get in at any moment, Germans being naturally buoyant). Richard would have got hold of pillows, seen that she was comfortable at night, told her when there was time to get out for coffee and when there wasn't (Mrs. Hilary was no hand at this; she would try no runs and get run out, or all but run out) and helped to save Nan. Nan and her father had got on pretty well, for a naughty girl and an elderly parent. They had appreciated one another's brains, which is not a bad basis. They had not accepted or even liked one another's ideas on life, but this is not necessary or indeed usual in families. Mrs. Hilary certainly did not go so far as to suppose that Nan would have obeyed her father had he appeared before her in Rome and bidden her change her way of life, but she might have thought it over. And to make Nan think over anything which *she* bade her do would be a phenomenal task. What had Mr. Cradock said—make her remember her first disobedience, find the cause of it, talk it out with her, get it out into the open—and then she would be cured of her present lawlessness. Why? That was the connection that always puzzled Mrs. Hilary a little. Why should remembering that you had done, and why you had done, the same kind of thing thirty years ago cure you of doing it now? Similarly, why should remembering that a nurse had scared you as an infant cure you of your present fear of burglars? In point of fact, it didn't. Mr. Cradock had tried this particular cure on Mrs. Hilary. It must be her own fault, of course, but somehow she had not felt much less nervous about noises in the house at night since Mr. Cradock had brought up into the light, as he called it, that old fright in the nursery. After all, why should one? However, hers not to reason why; and perhaps the workings of Nan's mind might be more orthodox.

At Turin Germans got in. Of course. They were all over Italy. Italy was welcoming them with both hands, establishing again the economic *entente*. These were a mother and a *backfisch*, and they looked shyly and sullenly at Mrs. Hilary and the other Englishwoman in the compartment. They were thin, and quite right too; Mrs. Hilary noted it with satisfaction. She didn't believe for one moment in starving Germans, but these certainly did not look so prosperous and buxom as a pre-War German mother and *backfisch* would have looked. They were equally uncivil though. They pulled both windows up to the top. The two English ladies promptly pulled them down half-way. English ladies are the only beings in the world who like open windows in winter. English lower-class women do not, nor do English gentlemen. If you want to keep warm while travelling (to frowst, as the open-air school call it) do not get in with well-bred Englishwomen.

The German mother broke out in angry remonstrance, indicating that she had neuralgia and the *backfisch* a cold in the head. There followed one of those quarrels which occur on this topic in trains, and are so bitter and so devastating. It had now more than the pre-war bitterness; between the combatants flowed rivers of blood; behind them ranked male relatives killed or maimed by the male relatives of their foes on the opposite seat. The English ladies won. Germany was a conquered race, and knew it. In revenge, the *backfisch* coughed and sneezed "all over the carriage," as Mrs. Hilary put it, "in the disgusting German way," and her mother made noises as if she could be sick if she tried hard enough.

So it was a detestable journey. And the second night in the train was worse than the first. For the Germans, would you believe it, shut both windows while the English were asleep, and the English, true to their caste and race, woke with bad headaches.

II

When they got to Rome in the morning Mrs. Hilary felt thoroughly ill. She had to strive hard: for self-control; it would not do to meet Nan in an unnerved, collapsed state. All her psychical strength was necessary to deal with Nan. So when she stood on the platform with her luggage she looked and felt, not only like one who has slept (but not much) in a train for two nights and fought with Germans about windows (that is to say, weary, tousled and unkempt), but also like an elderly virgin martyr (that is to say, spiritually tense and strung up and distraught, and on the line between exultation and hysteria).

Nan was there. Nan, pale and pinched, and looking plain in the nipping morning air, though wrapped in a fur coat. (One of the points about Nan was that, though she sometimes looked plain, she never looked dowdy; there was always a distinction, a *chic*, about her.)

Nan kissed her mother and helped with the luggage and got a cab. Nan was good at railway stations and such places. Mrs. Hilary was not.

They drove out into the hideous new streets. Mrs. Hilary shivered.

"Oh, how ugly!"

"Rome is ugly, this part."

"It's worse since '99."

But she did not really remember clearly how it had looked in '99. The old desire to pose, to show that she knew something, took her. Yet she felt that Nan, who knew that she knew next to nothing, would not be deceived.

"Oh ... the Forum!"

"The Forum of Trajan," Nan said. "We don't pass the Roman Forum on the way to our street."

"The Forum of Trajan, of course, I meant that."

But she knew that Nan knew she had meant the Forum Romanum.

"Rome is always Rome," she said, which was safer than identifying particular buildings, or even Forums, in it. "Nothing like it anywhere. ..."

"How long can you stay, mother? I've got you a room in the house I'm lodging in. It's in a little street the other side of the Corso. Rather a medieval street, I'm afraid. That is, it smells. But the rooms are clean."

"Oh, I'm not staying long. ... We'll talk later; talk it all out. A thorough talk. When we get in. After a cup of tea."

Mrs. Hilary remembered that Nan did not yet know why she had come. After a cup of strong tea. ... A cup of tea first. ... Coffee wasn't the same. One needed tea, after those awful Germans. She told Nan about these. Nan knew that she would have had tiresome travelling companions she always did; if it wasn't Germans it would be inconsiderate English. She was unlucky.

"Go straight to bed and rest when we get in," Nan advised; but she shook her head. "We must talk first."

Nan, she thought, looked pinched about the lips, and thin, and her black brows were at times nervous and sullen. Nan did not look happy. Was it guilt, or merely the chill morning air?

They stopped at a shabby old house in a narrow medieval street in the Borgo, which had been a palace and was now let in apartments. Here Nan had two bare, gilded, faded rooms. Mrs. Hilary sat by a charcoal stove in one of them, and Nan made her some tea. After the tea Mrs. Hilary felt revived. She wouldn't go to bed; she felt that the time for the talk had come. She looked round the rooms for signs of Stephen Lumley, but all the signs she saw were of Nan: Nan's books, Nan's proofs strewing the table. Of course, that bad man wouldn't come while she was there. He was, no doubt, waiting eagerly for her to be gone. Probably they both were. ...

"Nan—" They were still sitting by the stove, and Nan was lighting a cigarette. "Nan—do you guess why I've come?"

Nan threw away the match.

"No, mother. How should I? ... One does come to Rome, I suppose, if one gets a chance."

"Oh, I've not come to see Rome. I know Rome. Long before you were born. ... I've come to see you. And to take you back with me."

Nan glanced at her quickly, a sidelong glance of suspicion and comprehension. Her lower lip projected stubbornly.

"Ah, I see you know what I mean. Yes, I've heard. Rumours reached us—it was through Rosalind, of course. And I'm afraid … I'm afraid that for once she spoke the truth."

"Oh, no, she didn't. I don't know what Rosalind's been saying this time, but it would be odd if it was the truth."

"Nan, it's no use denying things. I *know*."

It was true; she did know. A few months ago she would have doubted and questioned; but Mr. Cradock had taught her better. She had learnt from him the simple truth about life; that is that nearly everyone is nearly always involved up to the eyes in the closest relationship with someone of another sex. It is nature's way with mankind. Another thing she had learnt from him was that the more they denied it the more it was so; protests of innocence and admissions of guilt were alike proofs of the latter. So she was accurate when she said that it was no use for Nan to deny anything. It was no use whatever.

Nan had become cool and sarcastic—her nastiest, most dangerous manner.

"Do you think you would care to be a little more explicit, mother? I'm afraid I don't quite follow. What is it no use my denying? *What* do you know?"

Mrs. Hilary gathered herself together. Her head trembled and jerked with emotion; wisps of her hair, tousled by the night, escaped over her collar. She spoke tremulously, tensely, her hands wrung together.

"That you are going on with a married man. That you are his mistress," she said, putting it at its crudest, since Nan wanted plain speaking.

Nan sat quite still, smoking. The silence thrilled with Mrs. Hilary's passion.

"I see," Nan said at last. "And it's no use my denying it. In that case I won't." Her voice was smooth and clear and still, like cold water. "You know the man's name too, I presume?"

"Of course. Everyone knows it. I tell you, Nan, everyone's talking of you and him. A town topic, Rosalind calls it."

"Rosalind would. Town must be very dull just now, if that's all they have to talk of."

"But it's not the scandal I'm thinking of," Mrs. Hilary went on, "though, God knows, that's bad enough—I'm thankful father died when he did and was spared it—but the thing itself. The awful, awful thing itself. Have you no shame, Nan?"

"Not much."

"For all our sakes. Not for mine—I know you don't care a rap for that—but for Neville, whom you do profess to love …"

"I should think we might leave Neville out of it. She's shown no signs of believing any story about me."

"Well, she does believe it, you may depend upon it. No one could help it. People write from here saying it's an open fact."

"People here can't have much to put in their letters."

"Oh, they'll make room for gossip. People always will. Always. But I'm not going to dwell on that side of things, because I know you don't care what anyone says. It's the *wrongness* of it. … A married man. … Even if his wife divorces him! It would be in the papers. … And if she doesn't you can't ever marry him. … Do you care for the man?"

"What man?"

"Don't quibble. Stephen Lumley, of course."

"Stephen Lumley is a friend of mine. I'm fond of him."

"I don't believe you do love him. I believe it's all recklessness and perversity. Lawlessness. That's what Mr. Cradock said."

"Mr. Cradock?" Nan's eyebrows went up.

Mrs. Hilary flushed a brighter scarlet. The colour kept running over her face and going back again, all the time she was talking.

"Your psycho-analyst doctor," said Nan, and her voice was a little harder and cooler than before. "I expect you had an interesting conversation with him about me."

"I have to tell him everything," Mrs. Hilary stammered. "It's part of the course. I did consult him about you. I'm not ashamed of it. He understands about these things. He's not an ordinary man."

"This is very interesting." Nan lit another cigarette. "It seems that I've been a boon all round as a town topic—to London, to Rome, and to St. Mary's Bay. ... Well, what did he advise about me?"

Mrs. Hilary remembered vaguely and in part, but did not think it would be profitable just now to tell Nan.

"We have to be very wise about this," she said, collecting herself. "Very wise and firm. Lawlessness ... I wonder if you remember, Nan, throwing your shoes at my head when you were three?"

"No. But I can quite believe I did. It was the sort of thing I used to do."

"Think back, Nan. What is the first act of naughtiness and disobedience you remember, and what moved you to it?"

Nan, who knew a good deal more about psycho-analysis than Mrs. Hilary did, laughed curtly.

"No good, mother. That won't work on me. I'm not susceptible to the treatment. Too hard-headed. What was Mr. Cradock's next brain-wave?"

"Oh, well, if you take it like this, what's the use ..."

"None at all. I advise you not to bother yourself. It will only make your headache worse. ... Now, I think after all this excitement you had better go and lie down, don't you? I'm going out, anyhow."

Then Stephen Lumley knocked at the door and came in. A tall, slouching, hollow-chested man of forty, who looked unhappy and yet cynically amused at the world. He had a cough, and unusually bright eyes under overhanging brows.

Nan said: "This is Stephen Lumley, mother. My mother, Stephen," and left them to do the rest, watching, critical and aloof, to see how they would manage the situation.

Mrs. Hilary managed it by rising from her chair and standing rigidly in the middle of the room, breathing hard and staring. Stephen Lumley looked inquiringly at Nan.

"How do you do, Mrs. Hilary," he said. "I expect you're pretty well played out by that beastly journey, aren't you?"

Mrs. Hilary's voice came stifled, choked, between pants. She was working up; or rather worked up: Nan knew the symptoms.

"You dare to come into my presence. ... I must ask you to leave my daughter's sitting-room *immediately*. I have come to take her back to

– 188 –

England with me at once. Please go. There is nothing that can possibly be said between you and me—nothing."

Stephen Lumley, a cool and quiet person, raised his brows, looked inquiry once more at Nan, found no answer, said: "Well, then, I'll say good-bye," and departed.

Mrs. Hilary wrung her hands together.

"How dare he! How dare he! Into my very presence! He has no shame. …"

Nan watched her coolly. But a red spot had begun to burn in each cheek at her mother's opening words to Lumley, and still burned. Mrs. Hilary knew of old that still-burning, deadly anger of Nan's.

"Thank you, mother. You've helped me to make up my mind. I'm going to Capri with Stephen next week. I've refused up till now. He was going without me. You've made up my mind for me. You can tell Mr. Cradock that if he asks."

Nan was fiercely, savagely desirous to hurt. In the same spirit she had doubtless thrown her shoes at Mrs. Hilary thirty years ago. Rage and disgust, hot rebellion and sick distaste—what she had felt then she felt now. During her mother's breathless outbreak at Stephen Lumley, standing courteous and surprised before her, she had crossed her Rubicon. And now with flaming words she burned her boats.

Mrs. Hilary burst into tears. But her tears had never yet quenched Nan's flames. Nan made her lie down and gave her sal volatile. Sal volatile eases the head and nervous system and composes the manners, but no more than tears does it quench flames.

▶••◀

IV

The day that followed was strange, and does not sound likely, but life often does not. Nan took Mrs. Hilary out to lunch at a *trattoria* near the Forum, as it were to change the subject, and they spent the usual first afternoon of visitors in Rome, who hasten to view the Forum with a guide to the most recent excavations in their hands. Mrs. Hilary felt completely uninterested to-day in recent or any other excavations. But, obsessed even now with the old instinctive desire (the fond hope, rather) not to seem unintelligent before her children, more especially when she was not on good terms with them, she accompanied Nan, who firmly and deftly closed or changed the subjects of unlawful love, Stephen Lumley, Capri, returning to England, and her infant acts of wilfulness, whenever her mother opened them, which was frequently, as Mrs. Hilary found these things easier conversational topics than the buildings in the Forum. Nan was determined to keep the emotional pressure low for the rest of the day, and she was fairly competent at this when she tried. As Mrs. Hilary had equal gifts at keeping it high, it was a well-matched contest. When they left the Forum for a tea-shop, both were tired out. The Forum is tiring; emotion is tiring; tears are tiring; quarrelling is tiring; travelling through to Rome is tiring; all five together are annihilating.

However, they had tea.

Mrs. Hilary was cold and bitter now, not hysterical. Nan, who was living a bad life, and was also tiresomely exactly informed about the differences between the Forum in '99 and the Forum to-day (a subject on which Mrs. Hilary was hazy) was not fit, until she came to a better mind, to be spoken to. Mrs. Hilary shut her lips tight and averted her reddened eyes. She hated Nan just now. She could have loved her had she been won to repentance, but now—"Nan was never like the rest," she thought.

Nan persisted in making light, equable conversation, which Mrs. Hilary thought in bad taste. She talked of England and the family, asked after Grandmamma, Neville, and the rest.

"Neville is extremely ill," Mrs. Hilary said, quite untruly, but that was, to do her justice, the way in which she always saw illness, particularly Neville's. "And worried to death about Gerda, who seems to have gone off her head since that accident in Cornwall. She is still sticking to that insane, wicked notion about not getting married."

Nan had heard before of this.

"She'll give that up," she said coolly, "when she finds she really can't have Barry if she doesn't. Gerda gets what she wants."

"Oh, you all do that, the whole lot of you. ... And a nice example *you're* setting the child."

"She'll give it up," Nan repeated, keeping the conversation on Gerda. "Gerda hasn't the martyr touch. She won't perish for a principle. She wants Barry and she'll have him, though she may hold out for a time. Gerda doesn't lose things, in the end."

"She's a very silly child, and I suppose she's been mixing with dreadful friends and picked up these ideas. At twenty there's some excuse for ignorant foolishness." But none at thirty-three, Mrs. Hilary meant.

"Barry Briscoe," she added, "is being quite firm about it. Though he is desperately in love with her, Neville tells me; desperately."

He's soon got over you, even if he did care for you once, and even if you did send him away, her emphasis implied.

In Nan, casually flicking the ash off her cigarette, a queer impulse came and went. For a moment she wanted to cry; to drop hardness and lightness and pretence, and cry like a child and say: "Mother, comfort me. Don't go on hurting me. I love Barry. Be kind to me, oh, be kind to me!"

If she had done it, Mrs. Hilary would have taken her in her arms and been all mother, and the wound in their affection would have been temporarily healed.

Nan said nonchalantly: "I expect he is. They're sure to be all right. ... Now what next, mother? It's getting dark for seeing things."

"I am tired to death," said Mrs. Hilary. "I shall go back to those dreadful rooms and try to rest. ... It has been an awful day. ... I hate Rome. In '99 it was so different. Father and I went about together; he showed me everything. He *knew* about it all. Besides ..."

Besides, how could I enjoy sight-seeing after that scene this morning, and with this awful calamity that has happened?

They went back. Mrs. Hilary was desperately missing her afternoon hour with Mr. Cradock. She had come to rely on it on a Wednesday.

▶•◀

V

Nan sat up late, correcting proofs, after Mrs. Hilary had gone to bed. Galley slips lay all round her on the floor by the stove. She let them slip from her knee and lie there. She hated them. ...

She pressed her hands over her eyes, shutting them out, shutting out life. She was going off with Stephen Lumley. She had told him so this morning. Both their lives were broken: hers by Barry, whom she loved, his by his wife, whom he disliked. He loved her; he wanted her. She could with him find relief, find life a tolerable thing. They could have a good time together. They were good companions; their need, though dissimilar, was mutual. They saw the same beauty, spoke the same tongue, laughed at the same things. In the very thought of Stephen, with his cynical humour, his clear, keen mind, his lazy power of brain, Nan had found relief all that day, reacting desperately from a mind fuddled with sentiment and emotion as with drink, a soft, ignorant brain, which knew and cared about nothing except people, a hysterical passion of anger and malice. They had pushed her sharply and abruptly over the edge of decision, that mind and brain and passion. Stephen, against whom their fierce anger was concentrated, was so different. ...

To get away, to get right away from everything and everyone, with Stephen. Not to have to go back to London alone, to see what she could not, surely, bear to see—Barry and Gerda, Gerda and Barry, always, everywhere, radiant and in love. And Neville, Gerda's mother, who saw so much. And Rosalind, who saw everything, everything, and said so. And Mrs. Hilary. ...

To saunter round the queer, lovely corners of the earth with Stephen, light oneself by Stephen's clear, flashing mind, look after Stephen's weak, neglected body as he never could himself ... that was the only anodyne. Life would then sometime become an adventure again, a gay stroll through the fair, instead of a desperate sickness and nightmare.

Barry, oh, Barry. ... Nan, who had thought she was getting better, found that she was not. Tears stormed and shook her at last. She crumpled up on the floor among the galley-slips, her head upon the chair.

Those damned proofs—who wanted them? What were books? What was anything?

VI

Mrs. Hilary came in, in her dressing-gown, red-eyed. She had heard strangled sounds, and knew that her child was crying.

"My darling!"

Her arms were round Nan's shoulders; she was kneeling among the proofs.

"My little girl—Nan!"

"Mother …"

They held each other close. It was a queer moment, though not an unprecedented one in the stormy history of their relations together. A queer, strange, comforting, healing moment, the fleeting shadow of a great rock in a barren land—a strayed fragment of something which should have been between them always but was not. Certainly an odd moment.

"My own baby. … You're unhappy. …"

"Unhappy—yes. … Darling, mother, it can't be helped. Nothing can be helped. … Don't let's talk … darling."

Strange words from Nan. Strange for Mrs. Hilary to feel her hand held against Nan's wet cheek and kissed.

Strange moment: and it could not last. The crying child wants its mother; the mother wants to comfort the crying child. A good bridge, but one inadequate for the strain of daily traffic. The child, having dried its tears, watches the bridge break again, and thinks it a pity but inevitable. The mother, less philosophic, may cry in her turn, thinking perhaps that the bridge may be built this time, in that way; but, the child having the colder heart, it seldom is.

There remain the moments, impotent but in-destructible.

CHAPTER XIV

KAY SPEAKS

▶•◀

I

Kay was home for the Christmas vacation. He was full less of Cambridge than of schemes for establishing a co-operative press next year. He was learning printing and binding, and wanted Gerda to learn too.

"Because if you're really not going to marry Barry, and if Barry sticks to not having you without, you'll be rather at a loose end, won't you, and you may as well come and help us with the press. ... But of course, you know," Kay added absently, his thoughts still on the press, "I should advise you to give up on that point."

"Give up, Kay? Marry, do you mean?"

"Yes. ... It doesn't seem to me to be a point worth making a fuss about. Of course, I agree with you in theory—I always have. But I've come to think lately that it's not a point of much importance. And perfectly sensible people are doing it all the time. You know Jimmy Kenrick and Susan Mallow have done it? They used to say they wouldn't, but they have. The fact is, people *do* do it, whatever they say about it beforehand. And though in theory it's absurd, it seems often to work out pretty well in actual life. Personally I should make no bones about it, if I wanted a girl and she wanted marriage. Of course, a girl can always go on being called by her own name if she likes. That has points."

"Of course one could do that," Gerda pondered.

"It's a sound plan in some ways. It saves trouble and explanation to go on with the name you've published your things under before marriage. … By the way, what about your poems, Gerda? They'll be about ready by the time we get our press going, won't they? We can afford to have some slight stuff of that sort if we get hold of a few really good things to start with, to make our name."

Gerda's thoughts were not on her poems, nor on Kay's press, but on his advice about matrimony. For the first time she wavered. If Kay thought that. … It set the business in a new light. And of course, other people *were* doing it—sound people, the people who talked the same language and belonged to the same set as oneself.

Kay had spoken. It was the careless, authentic voice of youth speaking to youth. It was a trumpet-blast making a breach in the walls against which the batteries of middle-age had thundered in vain. Gerda told herself that she must look further into this, think it over again, talk it over with other people of the age to know what was right. If it could be managed with honour, she would find it a great relief to give up on this point. For Barry was so firm; he would never give up; and, after all, one of them must, if it could be done with a clear conscience.

►•◄

II

Ten days later Gerda said to Barry: "I've been thinking it over again, Barry, and I've decided that perhaps it will be all right for us to get married after all."

Barry took both her hands and kissed each in turn, to show that he was not triumphing but adoring.

"You mean it? You feel you can really do it without violating your conscience? Sure, darling?"

"Yes, I think I'm sure. Lots of quite sensible, good people have done it lately."

"Oh, any number, of course—if *that's* any reason."

"No, not those people. My sort of people, I mean. People who believe what I do, and wouldn't tie themselves up and lose their liberty for anything."

"I agree with Lenin. He says liberty is a bourgeois dream."

"Barry, I may keep my name, mayn't I? I may still be called Gerda Bendish by people in general?"

"Of course, if you like. Rather silly, isn't it? Because it won't *be* your name. But that's your concern."

"It's the name I've always written and drawn under, you see."

"Yes. I see your point. Of course, you shall be Gerda Bendish anywhere you like, only not on cheques, if you don't mind."

"And I don't much want to wear a wedding-ring, Barry."

"That's as you like, too, of course. You might keep it in your purse when travelling, to produce if censorious hotel-keepers look askance at us. Even the most abandoned ladies do that sometimes, I believe. Or your marriage lines will do as well ... Gerda, you blessed darling, it's most frightfully decent and sporting of you to have changed your mind and owned up. Next time we differ I'll try to be the one to do it, I honestly will. ... I say, let's come out by ourselves and dine and do a theatre to celebrate the occasion."

So they celebrated the triumph of institutionalism.

▶●◀

III

Their life together, thought Barry, would be a keen, jolly, adventuring business, an ardent thing, full of gallant dreams and endeavours. It should never grow tame or stale or placid, never lose its fine edge. There would be mountain peak beyond mountain peak to scale together. They would be co-workers, playmates, friends, and lovers all at once, and they would walk in liberty as in a bourgeois dream.

So planned Barry Briscoe, the romantic, about whose head the vision splendid always hovered, a realisable, capturable thing.

Gerda thought, "I'm happy. Poetry and drawing and Barry. I've everything I want, except a St. Bernard pup, and Kay's giving me that for Christmas. *I'm happy.*"

It was a tingling, intense, sensuous feeling, like stretching warm before a good fire, or lying in fragrant thymy woods in June, in the old Junes when suns were hot. Life was a song and a dream and a summer morning.

"You're happy, Gerda," Neville said to her once, gladly but half wistfully, and she nodded, with her small, gleaming smile.

"Go on being happy," Neville told her, and Gerda did not know that she had nearly added, "for it's cost rather a lot, your happiness." Gerda seldom cared how much things had cost; she did not waste thought on such matters. She was happy.

CHAPTER XV

THE DREAM

▶•◀

I

Barry and Gerda were married in January in a registry office, and, as all concerned disliked wedding parties, there was no wedding party.

After they had gone Neville, recovered now from the lilies and languors of illness, plunged into the roses and raptures of social life. One mightn't, she said to herself, be able to accomplish much in this world, or imprint one's personality on one's environment by deeds and achievements, but one could at least enjoy life, be a pleased participator in its spoils and pleasures, an enchanted spectator of its never-ending flux and pageant, its richly glowing moving pictures. One could watch the play out, even if one hadn't much of a part oneself. Music, art, drama, the company of eminent, pleasant, and entertaining persons, all the various forms of beauty, the carefully cultivated richness, graces, and elegances which go to build up the world of the fortunate, the cultivated, the prosperous and the well-bred—Neville walked among these like the souls in the lordly pleasure-house built for her by the poet Tennyson, or like Robert Browning glutting his sense upon the world—"Miser, there waits the gold for thee!"—or Frances Thompson swinging the earth a trinket at his wrist. In truth, she was at times self-consciously afraid that she resembled all these three, whom (in the moods they thus expressed) she disliked beyond reason, finding them morbid and hard to please.

She, too, knew herself morbid and hard to please. If she had not been so, to be Rodney's wife would surely have been enough; it would have satisfied all her nature. Why didn't it? Was it perhaps really because, though she loved him, it was not with the uncritical devotion of the early days? She had for so many years now seen clearly, through and behind his charm, his weakness, his vanities, his scorching ambitions and jealousies, his petulant angers, his dependence on praise and admiration. She had no jealousy now of his frequent confidential intimacies with other attractive women; they were harmless enough, and he never lost the need of and dependence on her; but they may have helped to clarify her vision of him.

Rodney had no failings beyond what are the common meed of human nature; he was certainly good enough for her. Their marriage was all right. It was only the foolish devil of egotism in her which goaded the other side of her nature, that need for self-expression which marriage didn't satisfy, to unwholesome activity.

▶•◀

II

In February she suddenly tired of London and the British climate, and was moved by a desire to travel. So she went to Italy, and stayed in Capri with Nan and Stephen Lumley, who were leading on that island lives by turns gaily indolent and fiercely industrious, finding the company stimulating and the climate agreeable and soothing to Stephen's defective lungs.

From Italy Neville went to Greece. Corinth, Athens, the islands, Tempe, Delphi, Crete—how good to have money and be able to see all these! Italy and Greece are Europe's pleasure grounds; there the cultivated and the prosperous traveller may satisfy his soul and forget carking cares and stabbing ambitions, and drug himself with loveliness.

If Neville abruptly tired of it, and set her face homewards in early April, it was partly because she felt the need of Rodney, and partly because she saw, fleetingly but day by day more lucidly, that one could not take one's stand, for satisfaction of desire, on the money which one happened to have but which the majority bitterly and emptily lacked. Some common way there had to be, some freedom all might grasp, a liberty not for the bourgeois only, but for the proletariat; the poor, the sad, the gay proletariat, who also grew old and lost their dreams, and had not the wherewithal to drug their souls, unless indeed they drank much liquor, and that is but a poor artificial way to peace.

Voyaging homewards through the spring seas, Neville saw life as an entangling thicket, the Woods of Westermain she had loved in her childhood, in which the scaly dragon squatted, the craving monster self that had to be subjugated before one could walk free in the enchanted woods.

> Him shall change, transforming late,
> Wonderously renovate ...

Dimly discerning through the thicket the steep path that climbed to such liberty as she sought, seeing far off the place towards which her stumbling feet were set, where life should be lived with alert readiness and response, oblivious of its personal achievements, its personal claims and spoils, Neville, the spoilt, vain, ambitious, disappointed egoist, strained her eyes into the distance and half smiled. It might be a dream, that liberty, but it was a dream worth a fight. ...

CHAPTER XVI

TIME

►•◄

I

February at St. Mary's Bay. The small fire wickered and fluttered in the grate with a sound like the windy beating of wings. The steady rain sloped against the closed windows of The Gulls, and dropped patteringly on the asphalt pavements of Marine Crescent outside, and the cold grey sea tumbled moaning.

Grandmamma sat in her arm-chair by the hearth, reading the autobiography of a Cabinet Minister's wife, and listening to the fire, the sea, and the rain, and sleeping a little now and again.

Mrs. Hilary sat in another arm-chair, surrounded by bad novels, as if she had been a reviewer. She was regarding them, too, with something of the reviewer's pained and inimical distaste, dipping now into one, shutting it with a sharp sigh, trying another, flinging it on the floor with an ejaculation of anger and fatigue.

Grandmamma woke with a start, and said, "What fell? Did something fall?" and adjusted her glasses and opened the autobiography again.

"A vulgar, untruthful, and ill-written book. The sort of autobiography Gilbert's wife will write when she has time. It reminds me very much of her letters, and is, I am sure, still more like the diary which she no doubt keeps. Poor Gilbert. …" Grandmamma seemed to be confusing Gilbert momentarily with the Cabinet Minister. "I remember," she went on, "meeting this young woman at Oxford, in the year of the first Jubilee. ... A very bright talker. They can so seldom write. ..." She dozed again.

"Will this intolerable day," Mrs. Hilary inquired of the housemaid who came in to make up the fire, "never be over? I suppose it will be bed-time *sometime*. ..."

"It's just gone a quarter-past six, ma'am," said the housemaid, offering little hope, and withdrew.

Mrs. Hilary went to the window and drew back the curtains and looked out at Marine Crescent in the gloomy, rainy twilight. The long evening stretched in front of her—the long evening which she had never learnt to use. Psycho-analysis, which had made her so much better while the course lasted, now that it was over (and it was too expensive to go on with for ever) had left her worse than before. She was like a drunkard deprived suddenly of stimulants; she had nothing to turn to, no one now who took an interest in her soul. She missed Mr. Cradock and that bi-weekly hour; she was like a creeper wrenched loose from its support and flung flat on the ground. He had given her mental exercises and told her to continue them; but she had always hated mental exercises; you might as well go in for the Pelman course and have done. What one needed was a *person*. She was left once more face to face with time, the enemy; time, which gave itself to her lavishly with both hands when she had no use for it. There was nothing she wanted to do with time, except kill it.

"What, dear," murmured Grandmamma as she rattled the blind tassel against the sill. "How about a game of piquet?"

But Mrs. Hilary hated piquet, and all card games, and halma, and dominoes, and everything. Grandmamma used to have friends in to play with her, or the little maid. This evening she rang for the little maid, May, who would rather have been writing to her young man, but liked to oblige the nice old lady, of whom the kitchen were fond.

It was all very well for Grandmamma, Mrs. Hilary thought, stormily revolting against that placidity by the hearth. All very well for Grandmamma to sit by the fire contented with books and papers and games and sleep, unbitten by the murderous hatred of time that consumed herself. Everyone always thought that about Grandmamma, that things were all very well for her, and perhaps they were. For time could do little more hurt to Grandmamma. She need not worry about killing time; time would kill her soon enough if she left it alone. Time, so long to Mrs. Hilary, was short now to Grandmamma, and would soon be gone. As to May, the little maid, to her time was fleeting, and flew before her face, like a bird she could never catch. …

Grandmamma and May were playing casino. A bitter game, for you build and others take, and your labour is but lost that builded; you sow and others reap. But Grandmamma and May were both good-tempered and ladylike. They played prettily together, age and youth.

Why did life play one these tricks? Mrs. Hilary cried within herself. What had she done to life that it should have deserted her and left her stranded on the shores of a watering-place, empty-handed and pitiful, alone with time the enemy, and with Grandmamma, for whom it was all very well?

▶•◀

II

In the Crescent music blared out—once more the Army, calling for strayed sheep in the rain.

"Glory for you, glory for me!" it shouted.

And then, presently:

> "Count—you—blessings! Count them one by one!
> And it will *surprise* you what the Lord has done!"

Grandmamma, as usual, was beating time with her hand on the arm of her chair.

"Detestable creatures," said Mrs. Hilary with acrimony, as usual.

"But a very racy tune, my dear," said Grandmamma placidly, as usual.

"Blood! Blood!" sang the Army exultantly, as usual.

May looked happy, and her attention strayed from the game. The Army was one of the joys, one of the comic turns, of this watering-place.

"Six and two are eight," said Grandmamma, and picked them up, recalling May's attention. But she herself still beat time to the merry music-hall tune and the ogreish words.

Grandmamma could afford to be tolerant, as she sat there, looking over the edge into eternity, with time, his fangs drawn, stretched sleepily behind her back. Time, who flew, bird-like, before May's pursuing feet, time, who stared balefully into Mrs. Hilary's face, returning hate for hate, rested behind Grandmamma's back like a faithful steed who had carried her thus far and whose service was nearly over.

The Army moved on; its music blared away into the distance. The rain beat steadily on wet asphalt roads; the edge of the cold sea tumbled and moaned; the noise of the fire flickering was like unsteady breathing, or the soft fluttering of wings.

"Time is so long," thought Mrs. Hilary. "I can't bear it."

"Time gets on that quick," thought May, "I can't keep up with it."

"Time is dead," thought Grandmamma. "What next?"

CHAPTER XVII

THE KEY

▶•◀

Not Grandmamma's and not Neville's should be, after all, the last word, but Pamela's. Pamela, who seemed lightly, and, as it were, casually, to swing a key to the door against which Neville, among many others, beat, Pamela, going about her work, keen, debonair and detached, ironic, cool and quiet, responsive to life and yet a thought disdainful of it, lightly holding and easily renouncing, the world's lover yet not its servant, her foot at times carelessly on its neck to prove her power over it—Pamela said blandly to Grandmamma, when the old lady commented one day on her admirable composure, "Life's so short, you see. Can anything which blasts such a little while be worth making a fuss about?"

"Ah," said Grandmamma, "that's been my philosophy for ten years ... only ten years. You've no business with it at your age, child."

"Age," returned Pamela, negligent and cool, "has extremely little to do with anything that matters. The difference between one age and another is, as a rule, enormously exaggerated. How many years we've lived on this ridiculous planet—how many more we're going to live on it—what a trifle! Age is a matter of exceedingly little importance."

"And so, you would imply, is everything else on the ridiculous planet," said Grandmamma shrewdly.

Pamela smiled, neither affirming nor denying. Lightly the key seemed to swing from her open hand.

"I certainly don't see quite what all the fuss is about. ..."

►•◄   ►•◄   ►•◄

AFTERWORD

►•◄

If you are looking for a novel showing a snapshot of what it was like to be a woman – or at least a middle-class, white woman – in the early 1920s, you could hardly do better than *Dangerous Ages*. In Rose Macaulay's 11th novel, published when she was 40, she shows the different 'dangers' faced by women of various ages: those in their twenties, forties, sixties, and eighties. Handily, they are also four generations of the same family. As Macaulay lets us know early in the book, the male relatives are of little significance and we won't be hearing much from them.

In a wide-ranging novel, Macaulay covers many issues of the day through the lens of this family – from debates about the point of marriage to a mother exploring the relatively new possibility of being a doctor, now that her children have grown up. As Neville thinks:

> Polygamy. Sex. Free Love. Love in chains. The children seemed so often to be discussing these. Just as, twenty years ago, she and her friends had seemed always to be discussing the Limitations of Personality, the Ethics of Friendship, and the Nature, if any, of God.

Macaulay is making the reader aware that she is deliberately writing a novel grounded very much in the 1920s, and intends to be ironic and satirical about it. (Incidentally, the masculine name 'Neville' for a female character follows a pattern Macaulay returned to frequently in her fiction – other heroines include Stanley, John and Julian, and the reader doesn't learn the gender of the main character in Macaulay's final novel, *The Towers of Trebizond*, until close to the end.)

■•◀   ■•◀   ■•◀

There are any number of subjects that could form the basis of an afterword, but I've chosen the one that seems most of its moment: Mrs Hilary's investigation of Freudianism. In the 1910s and 20s, Freudian psychoanalysis progressed with astonishing rapidity from a scientific curio to the topic of conversation in almost every home. As D.H. Lawrence wrote in 1923, 'the Oedipus complex was a household word, the incest motive a commonplace of tea-time chat'.

The first mention of Freud in *Dangerous Ages* refers to Gerda and the youngest generation in the quartet of ages: 'They would read and discuss Freud, whom Neville, unfairly prejudiced, found both an obscene maniac and a liar. [...They] took seriously things which seemed to Neville merely loathsome imbecilities.' But it is Mrs Hilary – in her sixties – who eventually takes up and embraces Freudian psychoanalysis. She is introduced to it by Rosalind, the daughter-in-law that neither she nor anybody else particularly likes, who has started practising psychoanalysis without any obvious qualifications:

> Rosalind, who was always taking up things – art, or religion, or spiritualism, or young men – and dropping them when they bored her, had lately taken up psycho-analysis. She was studying what she called her mother-in-law's 'case,' looking for and finding complexes in her past which should account for her somewhat unbalanced present.

As Mrs Hilary indignantly replies, she has never had complexes. And as far as she is concerned, psychoanalysts 'have only one idea, and that is a disgusting one' and, if challenged, she would claim that 'she had also looked into Freud, and been rightly disgusted'.

'Looking into Freud' was certainly an option available to readers, and that included readers who were unable to read the German original or unwilling to read the English translation. Freud's work first appeared in English in 1910, but the following decade saw a proliferation of books making Freud's ideas available to the layman, with titles like *Psycho-analysis for Normal People* (Geraldine Coster, 1926). As Coster's frequently reprinted book accurately describes it, psychoanalysis became 'the rather dangerous plaything of society' – applied, as by Rosalind, with only the vaguest knowledge. In 1920, the year that *Dangerous Ages* is set, Barbara Low's *Psycho-analysis: A Brief Account of Freudian Theory* was one of the more popular books through which the general public was getting to grip with what Freud was talking about. When the novelist Rebecca West reviewed Low's work, she said: 'This cool little book, if the current controversialist can be induced to stop talking for a minute and read it, ought to help considerably to curtail this period of braying.'

Low and others did their best to explain the complexity of psychoanalysis, and there was certainly a widespread awareness that it came complete with a complicated and often-satirised vocabulary (which Mrs Hilary calls 'affected jargon'), but the public fundamentally received and understood a highly edited version of Freudianism. It can be boiled down to 'sex' and 'dreams'.

In the year *Dangerous Ages* was published, the *Saturday Review* newspaper wrote that psychoanalysis 'wallows in sex; and a large number of people take to the mixture as to a new liqueur. Its chief ingredient, which is sex, tickles the palate, and the faint aroma of soul in the background sanctifies the smell'. This might be what makes it a commonplace of Gerda's conversation but, at the outset at least, Mrs Hilary certainly doesn't feel enthusiastic at the prospect. She is initially disgusted, and this is the connotation that Macaulay was to return to on several occasions. In her 1928 novel *Keeping Up Appearances*, for instance, the main character would still call Freud's work 'nasty', while that of 1930's *Staying With Relations* says, 'Repression is damned, but unrepression is more damned.'

Ernest Jones was one of the most high-profile disciples of Freud in England in the 1920s. While he described the 'salient characteristic' of most popular guides as 'muddleheadedness', he also wrote one himself. In it, he protests against the popular idea that psychoanalysis is either 'nothing but the translation into high-sounding jargon of platitudes that are well known to every writer about human nature' or 'a number of statements and conclusions that would be in the highest degree repellent were it not that the fantastic improbability of them prevents their being taken seriously'.

His protests were certainly not unfounded: these are precisely the attitudes taken by many popular novelists of the period, and many of the characters they created. They responded to this dominating cultural phenomenon with amusement rather than credulity. When the *Times Literary Supplement* reviewed *Dangerous Ages*, the reviewer asked, 'But what will the psycho-analysts say to the delicious fun she pokes at them? Her levity, we fear, will strike them as the sign of an abominable complex.' Taken so seriously by its proponents, the laughter with which psychoanalysis was often received was unwelcome and shocking to Freudians. And in researching *Dangerous Ages*, Macaulay apparently disguised herself as an older woman and visited a psychoanalyst, but her pretence was seen through and she was sent away.

But, though Mrs Hilary initially responds with a mixture of revulsion and disbelief, as the novel progresses she gradually becomes more interested. In a conversation with her daughter Neville, she says, "This psycho-analysis. I suppose it does make wonderful cures, doesn't it, when all is said?" Neville caustically replies that it can cure more or less anything, giving a list including 'shell-shock, insomnia, nervous depression, lumbago, suicidal mania, family life'. Shell shock was a recent addition to the nation's vocabulary, having been first mentioned in a medical journal in 1915.

Mrs Hilary begins to imagine what it would be like to be psychoanalysed. When the psychoanalyst of Mrs Hilary's imagination asks why *she* believes she is unhappy, she answers:

"Because my life is over. Because I am an old, discarded woman, thrown away on to the dust-heap like a broken eggshell. Because my husband is gone and my children are gone, and they do not love me as I love them. Because I have only my mother to live with, and she is calm and cares for nothing but only waits for the end. Because I have nothing to do from morning till night. Because I am sixty-three, and that is too old and too young. Because life is empty and disappointing, and I am tired, and drift like seaweed tossed to and fro by the waves."

It is perhaps at this point that the reader realises, if they have not done so already, that 'Mrs Hilary' is almost always called by her married name in the narrative – and not as 'Emily'. Her personality has been subsumed with motherhood and wifehood, and now she has little left. Macaulay's masterstroke in depicting psychoanalysis is the twist that, rather than a source of anxiety, disregarded women like Mrs Hilary could see it as an opportunity to be listened to. She is restored and invigorated at the prospect of having a captive audience for her reminiscences. It is the balm to the particular problems of her 'dangerous age':

What you really wanted was some man whose trade it was to listen and to give heed. Some man to whom your daughter's pneumonia, of however long ago, was not irrelevant, but had its own significance, as having helped to build you up as you were, you, the problem, with your wonderful, puzzling temperament, so full of complexes, inconsistencies, and needs. Some man who didn't lose interest in you just because you were grey-haired and sixty-three.

And when she does go to see a psychoanalyst, despite initial warnings that her dreams about 'packing; missing trains; missing people' are likely to portend dreadful things, it is every bit as blissful as Mrs Hilary had hoped: 'Ah, she could go on and on, never tired; it was like swimming in warm water'. Swimming appears in the novel (as in many of Macaulay's novels) as an activity that relaxes the young and exhausts the old. Mrs Hilary has found her equivalent.

As well as swimming, these sessions are compared to a religion: 'She had found a new interest in life, like keeping a parrot, or learning bridge, or becoming a Roman Catholic'. Macaulay had her own rather complex and varying relationship with God and the church, and enough familiarity to hide a reference to verses from Psalm 139 ('Whither shall I go from thy spirit? Or whither shall I flee from thy presence? / If I ascend upon into heaven, thou art there: if I make my bed in hell, behold, thou art there') in Mrs Hilary's thoughts about the links between religion and psychoanalysts' obsession with sex:

> Psycho-analysts adored sex; they made an idol of it. They communed with it, as devotees with their god. They couldn't really enjoy, with their whole minds, anything else, Mrs Hilary sometimes vaguely felt. But as, like the gods of the other devotees, it was to them immanent, everywhere and in everything, they could be always happy. If they went up into heaven it was there; if they fled down into hell it was there also.

As this quote shows, ultimately Mrs Hilary's opinion of Freudians hasn't drastically altered from the outset. She maintains that psychoanalysts 'have only one idea' and when Dr Cradock says she evidently has a sex complex, she replies:

> "Of course, of course. Don't you find that in all your patients? Surely we may take that for granted …" She allowed him his sex complex, knowing that Freudians without it would be like children deprived of a precious toy.

►•◄　►•◄　►•◄

Even if she – like her author – appears to identify sexual hypotheses as the deliberate choice and passionate obsession of psychoanalysts, she has stopped being disgusted and started being indulgent. Faced with a doctrine that unsettled many with the suggestion of uncontrollable urges, Mrs Hilary has taken control. And perhaps both she and Dr Cradock are being a little manipulative, as Macaulay suggests ironically: 'Her dreams, which she had to recount to him at every sitting, bore such terrible significance – they grew worse and worse, as Mrs Hilary could stand more'. But they are both getting what they want from the situation – though there is still no happy ending. Mrs Hilary can control everything about it other than the cost: 'Psycho-analysis, which had made her so much better while the course lasted, now that it was over (and it was too expensive to go on with for ever) had left her worse than before.'

So, while Macaulay maintains her ironic tone and was certainly tapping into a contemporary issue that many writers were finding a rich opportunity for irony, she is simultaneously exposing the real dangers of certain ages of women in the 1920s. These dangers for women like Mrs Hilary were likely not to be sublimated complexes or repressed libidos, but rather being ignored and sidelined once they had finished bearing children. And as for the title – the final word on the topic goes to the psychoanalyst Dr Cradock himself: "We may say that all ages are dangerous to all people, in this dangerous life we live."

Simon Thomas

Series consultant **Simon Thomas** created the middlebrow blog Stuck in a Book in 2007. He is also the co-host of the popular podcast Tea or Books? Simon has a PhD from Oxford University in Interwar Literature.